RED LINE

THE GAMES WE PLAY, BOOK 1

L.A. WITT

RED LINE

L.A. WITT

Copyright Information

This is a work of fiction. Names, characters, places, and incidents are either the product of the author's imagination or are used fictitiously. Any resemblance to actual persons living or dead, business establishments, events, or locales is entirely coincidental.

Red Line

First edition

Cover Art by L.C. Chase

Editor: Mackenzie Walton

eBook ISBN: 978-1-64230-191-5

Paperback ISBN: 979-8-32457-905-0

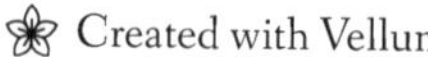
Created with Vellum

ARTIFICIAL INTELLIGENCE

No artificial intelligence was used in the making of this book or any of my books. This includes writing, co-writing, cover artwork, translation, and audiobook narration.

I do not consent to any Artificial Intelligence (AI), generative AI, large language model, machine learning, chatbot, or other automated analysis, generative process, or replication program to reproduce, mimic, remix, summarize, train from, or otherwise replicate any part of this creative work, via any means: print, graphic, sculpture, multimedia, audio, or other medium. This applies to all existing AI technology and any that comes into existence in the future.

I support the right of humans to control their artistic works.

THE GAMES WE PLAY HOCKEY LEAGUES

- **NAPH** (North American Professional Hockey) - Major league.
- **PHL** (Professional Hockey League) - Minor league.
- **HLENA** and **HLWNA** (Hockey League of Eastern North America and the Hockey League of Western North America) - Second tier minor league.

RED LINE

The Games We Play, Book 1

Theo Mathis doesn't regret defying the general manager during his brief stint on the Seattle Rainiers last season. The rainbow tape on his stick cost him dearly, but he'd do it again in a heartbeat... even though it means he'll never get called up from the minors again while that GM is at the helm.

Then a flood of injuries leaves Seattle desperate for players, and Theo gets called up after all. But he's warned: provoke the GM again, and he *will* regret it.

Except stick tape wasn't the only line Theo skated over, and the temptation to cross it again has nothing to do with spite.

Equipment manager Christian Hayes has had that hot minor league player living rent free in his head ever since they hooked up last year. It wasn't love, but it was fun, and he wishes they could do it again because they want to—not as an act of rebellion. If Christian's dad ever finds out, there will be hell to pay. But it's a non-issue, since his dad—the team's GM—has vowed to never call up that player again no matter how bad the team needs him... and he doesn't even know Theo and Christian hooked up.

Now Theo's back in the Rainiers' locker room. They don't dare risk a rematch—they both value their careers too much. All they have to do is ride this out for a few games until Theo's sent back down. Easy enough. Right?

But their mutual attraction refuses to be ignored.

And it looks like Theo's going to be staying a while.

The Games We Play is a multi-author minor league hockey romance series! All titles run concurrently through the same hockey season, and the books can be read in any order, so jump in anywhere!

CHAPTER 1
THEO

Last season

For the two long years I'd been playing in the minors, I'd dreamed of finally getting the call-up to our NAPH team, the Seattle Rainiers. Even if I didn't stay up—if I never actually made the roster for any length of time—I wanted to play at that level so bad I could taste it.

Last season, I'd finally been called up for one of the road trips. I'd almost lost my mind on the plane, but shortly after I'd landed... disappointment. The left winger I was supposed to replace was going on LTIR, but one of the *other* injured forwards—one who'd been listed as week-to-week—had suddenly been available. I'd dressed and skated during warmups but watched the game from the owners' box. The next morning, I was on the plane again, and the following evening, I was playing in Everett in the PHL like normal.

When I'd been called up this time, I'd been so afraid that would happen again, but it didn't. Two nights ago, in Vancouver, I'd *finally* hit the ice for real. That had been the coolest experience. I'd only played about six and a half minutes, but I'd done my rookie lap and I'd skated alongside players I admired, and I'd even managed a secondary assist.

But tonight was the game I'd *really* been looking forward to.

Not only would I be once again playing for the Rainiers, not only would we be going up against the Denver Mustangs (my favorite team growing up), but it was Pride Night. How cool was that?

The Rainiers always had incredible Pride jerseys, which were then signed and auctioned off to benefit queer charities. The design for this year's jersey hadn't been revealed yet, but there would be one with *my name* and *my number*, and I *couldn't fucking wait*. Ten years after my parents had cautioned fourteen-year-old me against coming out if I wanted to play pro hockey, I was going to play my second ever major league hockey game on Pride Night after wearing a Pride jersey during warmups.

Maybe it was stupid, but I had literally never been more excited about a game in my life. Not the Junior World Championship gold medal final. Not my first game on the PHL team. Not even my first game at this level.

My first major league Pride game.

Hell yeah.

But when I strode into the Seattle Rainiers' locker room, the jersey hanging at my stall was the usual home jersey. Blue with gray and black. No rainbows. No Pride insignia. All the sticks along the wall had white or black tape on the blades and handles.

At first, I thought maybe the equipment managers had made a rare mistake. They worked like a well-oiled machine, though, and our head equipment manager was known throughout the league for being one of the best.

Like, the guy literally traveled to other teams—from youth on up to pro—to help them get their equipment crew running efficiently. I didn't imagine he'd make (or allow) a mistake like this. Especially not when he was vocally out and proud himself.

Christian Hayes dropping the ball on Pride Night? Yeah, right.

And when I found his face in the room, my heart sank. The first time I'd seen him in a video about equipment crews, someone who worked with him had commented that he now understood what it meant for someone to light up a room. For all I'd been told to play down my sexuality if I wanted to make it in the league, Christian wore his like a badge of honor. He was flamboyant and hilarious, and whenever he was photographed or videoed, everyone around him was laughing.

Rumor had it there'd been precisely one homophobic player in Seattle, and it hadn't been Christian or even his father—Jack, the team's general manager—who'd nipped that problem in the bud. It was the Rainiers themselves. Despite being older than a lot of the players, Christian was everyone's honorary little brother, and no one tolerated anyone giving him shit. In one interview, Seattle's captain, Alex Condit, had said Christian could singlehandedly keep up team morale even in the face of a crushing loss just by being himself.

So to see him standing off to the side tonight with his arms crossed over his hoodie and his eyes downcast—that hit me right in the feels. Hell, everyone in the room seemed to be thrown off by the crestfallen expression on the guy the team reporter called "Seattle's very own ray of sunshine."

My heart sank even deeper as the mood in the room settled heavily on my shoulders. I'd admittedly had the worst crush on Christian since the first time I'd seen him in videos, and in person—oh, God, I was lucky I remembered how to tie my skates. He was gorgeous, built lean and powerful like a hockey player since in addition to the physical demands of his job, he apparently worked out with the team, including occasionally joining them on the ice outside of official practices. He had a smile that could stop traffic and crystal blue eyes that had their own online fan club.

No, really—there was a page somewhere called "Have you SEEN the eyes on Seattle's equipment manager?", and for good reason. He was just... fuck, he was so beautiful, and he had an infectious laugh and the kind of personality that made everyone around him smile.

Except tonight.

Ugh. Seriously? What the hell is going on?

That answer came soon enough. As the guys and I were starting to put on our gear, Coach Baldwin walked into the locker room. He gave us his usual pre-game speech, then followed it with, "I know we had Pride Night on the calendar, but Jack Hayes has made the decision to cancel it."

And... that was that. No explanation. Nothing. The GM—the man whose gay son worked with the team—had nixed Pride Night.

I didn't think a locker room had ever been as silent as it was after Coach's speech. There was nothing but the usual sounds of gear rustling, creaking, and rattling. No one talked, though there were some very puzzled looks being exchanged among my teammates.

There were also a lot of sympathetic glances thrown toward our equipment manager. Christian was focused on tightening a screw on someone's visor, but even his intense concentration couldn't mask how obviously upset he was.

Fuck. I was disappointed to have Pride Night canceled,

but it must've been an extra slap in the dick for him. His own *dad* had made the call.

My disappointment started to ebb in favor of anger. Sure, my folks had urged me to be cautious about coming out, but that had been well-intentioned. They loved me, supported me, and accepted me; they'd just been able to read the writing on the wall and had been concerned about a gay son being able to break into the world of professional sports. After all, that world hadn't always been what I would call welcoming to queer people.

Christian's dad actually had power and clout in that world. He had the ability to make statements and huge demonstrations of public support. He was in a position to make a difference for men like us.

Men like me. Men like his own *son*, for God's sake.

And he'd made the call to cancel Pride Night.

Fuck.

That.

Noise.

I finished tying my skate and put my foot down. Then I cleared my throat and called out over the unusually quiet locker room, "Hey, Christian?" When he glanced at me, I gestured for him to come to my stall.

He acknowledged me with a nod and nothing else before continuing to adjust the helmet in his hand. Normal, apart from the lack of a smile or a chirped, "Be right there!"

A few minutes later, as I was pulling on my jersey, he appeared.

"Hey, what do you need?" He sounded polite but exhausted, as if it took everything he had just to show up.

I met those sad blue eyes as I tugged at my jersey. "Do you have any rainbow tape?"

Christian's back stiffened and his eyebrows jumped. "I,

um... Yeah. Of course." Sighing, he let his shoulders fall. "But since we're not doing—"

"Can I get a roll?"

His eyes widened. "Are you... Are you sure?"

I nodded. "Yeah. I'm sure."

He studied me incredulously. I fully expected him to question me. Had I not heard that Pride Night was canceled? Did I want to get fined? Or more likely, since I was a PHL player, sent the hell back down to the minors with no hope of ever getting called up again?

I set my jaw, ready to fire back that I didn't give a damn. Let 'em fine me. Let 'em send me back down. I hadn't worked my ass off to get this far—while being openly gay—only to cower now that I had a chance to stand up for people like us.

Little by little, something brightened in Christian's expression. One corner of his mouth turned up as the faintest glimmer of rebelliousness sparked in his eyes. Without looking away from me, he called over his shoulder, "Hey, Marty?"

"Yeah, boss?" came the response from Marty, who had just finished adjusting someone's skate blade.

A grin came fully to life. "Can you toss me a roll of rainbow tape?"

I sensed some of my teammates glancing our way. Marty shot Christian an uncertain look, but when Christian gave him a nod, Marty shrugged. He handed the skate back to Hanson, then stepped out of the locker room for a second. He returned, and my heart did a little flutter when a roll of tape flew across the room.

Christian caught it and held it out. "Rainbow tape."

I smiled, wondering if anyone else could hear my heart pounding as I took the roll from him.

Then I sat down and, pulse still absolutely thundering, grabbed my stick and started pulling off the black tape.

I was halfway through wrapping the rainbow tape around the blade when Wilcox, who sat at the next stall over, nudged me. "Can I have that when you're done?"

My hands froze mid-wrap, and I looked at him. "Yeah?"

"Hell yeah."

By the time I'd handed the roll to Wilcox, Christian and Marty had brought out four more rolls. I didn't think I'd ever seen Christian smiling brighter than he was as he collected all the discarded black and white tape, and that said a lot. He really was this team's own personal sunbeam, and I decided that watching him brighten up was worth any shit that came my way over this. There would be shit, too; Jack Hayes had an incredibly low tolerance for insubordination, and all of us slapping on rainbow tape after he'd canceled Pride Night definitely fit that category. Once he found out I'd been behind it...

Oh, yeah. There'd be hell to pay.

But Christian Hayes was smiling. I think he even had tears in his eyes.

Bring it, Jack.

I regret nothing.

CHAPTER 2

CHRISTIAN

Not gonna lie—I was tearing up while the Rainiers skated out onto the ice for warmups.

I mean, okay, I've always been an emotional guy, and I will totally cry watching sad or romantic movies. I *bawled* during *Red, White & Royal Blue*—do *not* judge me.

But watching this team take the ice with rainbow-wrapped sticks had me choked up in ways Hollywood could never.

Because they weren't just being allies tonight, showing solidarity to me, the queer players in the league, and their queer fans. They were being allies when it could cost them professionally.

My father was going to be furious, and this was not a man who was above trading or waiving players over petty shit. Last season, one of the second pair defensemen, who'd been coming up on free agency, had answered a reporter honestly about whether he was going to stay in Seattle. All he'd said was, "I like playing here, but it depends on if they want to re-sign me." Dad had taken that as a swipe at the slow progression of contract negotiations, and he'd promptly traded the guy for a couple of *fifth* round draft picks. People still wanted his ass fired over that, and it wasn't the first or last time he'd fucked over a player that way.

Everyone on the Rainiers' roster knew about that. Hell, the guy who'd been traded? His old D partner was still here, now playing in the top pair, and he'd rainbowed the fuck out of his stick tonight.

Go ahead and punish us, the whole team seemed to be daring him. *You can't trade or waive us all.*

Standing behind the bench as I watched them all fall into their warmup routine, I had to work to swallow. My ex had cynically believed they all just kissed my ass because I could fuck with their gear and make their lives hell. Which, okay, that was true. There was a reason hockey players deeply respected their equipment managers.

But there was a big difference between being courteous and thanking us for our work, and defiantly putting rainbow tape on their sticks when they knew their GM would have their heads for it.

Coach Swanson, the defensive coach, stepped up beside me and leaned in to be heard over the music and the crowd. "Uh, I thought your dad canceled Pride Night?"

I nodded, fighting a smile. "Yeah, it's canceled." I scanned the crowd, which was full of rainbow hats, rainbow flags, and a few rainbow warmup jerseys from previous seasons. "I don't think the fans got the memo."

Swanson looked around, pursing his lips. "No, but the players did." I could read between the lines of his curt tone: *Why did you give them rainbow tape anyway?*

I shrugged. "We put black and white tape on the sticks. The guys asked for rainbow."

I sensed him looking at me, and when I turned, his brow was knitted together. I couldn't decide if he was disgusted by the rainbows, or if he was worried about the inevitable backlash. Could've been a bit of both; he was old school, and I'd never gotten the impression he was completely comfortable with me. Whenever he could, he went to the other three members of my crew instead of me, despite me being the head equipment manager.

He was also a bit on the spineless side. Oh, and he'd had his job threatened by my dad several times when the power play was a mess last season, so I suspected he wasn't comfortable with anything that might provoke my father.

I turned back to the team, who were setting up for line rushes. "I'll take the heat for it."

I didn't have to check to see if he was scowling. If I had to guess, he'd make himself extra scarce when Dad came down after the third period.

As the players started line rushes, I searched the numbers and names until my gaze landed on one in particular.

Mathis. Number sixty-one. Left winger on the fourth line.

The first time he'd joined the team, he'd caught my eye because he was cute as hell. The first time he'd laughed at something a teammate had said, I'd almost dropped the skate blade I'd been replacing two stalls over from his. He was a little taller than me—five-ten or so, I thought—with dark hair that curled when it was wet and the darkest eyes I'd ever seen.

I was well-accustomed to being around hockey players in various states of undress, but I'd admittedly let myself steal a glance at him the other night. How was it that I was used to men with six-packs and thighs for days, but one look at his lean, powerful body had screwed with my head? My crew and I had a very well-practiced and efficient routine for moving gear in, out, and around the locker rooms, and I'd lost a step solely because my gaze had landed for all of half a second on his naked back. The perfect shoulders. The sculpted arms. Jesus. What did I do for a living again?

Here behind the bench, I shook myself and pulled my attention away from him before a camera busted me staring. And blushing.

What the hell?

And like, he was seriously cute *and* hot, but then tonight...

"Do you have any rainbow tape?"

My heart had done things in that moment I still couldn't define. It wasn't that I thought he'd been doing this as a show of support for me and the queer guys in the league. After all, he was one of them himself. But the absolute balls it took? Especially for a player from the minors who could easily be sent back down, waived, traded, or released after his contract ended? The guys who came up from the minors, even if it was only for a game or two, knew they had to shine, shine, shine because this was their chance to prove they had what it took to come up permanently. Some of them only got one shot during their entire career, and that one chance could make or break their entire dream of playing PHL hockey.

And Theo Mathis was willing to risk that to make a statement with the tape on his stick.

I couldn't help but admire that.

Admire? Is that what kids are calling it these days?

I shivered, grateful that the long sleeves of my hoodie covered up the goose bumps currently prickling along my arms. I mean, yeah, I did admire the guy, but that admiration only fueled the fire that burned a little hotter every time he caught my eye.

He's a little young for you, don't you think?

Eh, he was twenty-four. I'd be thirty-one soon. That was doable.

Well, it would be if I ever hooked up with the players on my dad's team, which I absolutely *did not.*

Theo skated up to the bench, leaned over it, and retrieved his water bottle. Helmet off, he sprayed some on his face, then ran a hand through his dripping wet hair.

Unaware of my body temperature jumping several degrees, he squirted some water into his mouth, put the bottle back in its slot, and skated off again.

I had to fight the urge to slump back against the glass.

Okay, I didn't *usually* hook up with players on my dad's team.

But if Theo was interested, I would absolutely make an exception tonight.

CHAPTER 3
THEO

This season

"Come on, come on!" I shouted at the TV. "Shoot the puck!"

"What are you waiting for?" Cams flailed his arms beside me. "Dude, shoot!"

There were six of us crowded around the TV in Ricky's condo, all of us pleading with our teammate two thousand miles away to just shoot. The fucking. *Puck.*

Seattle was playing in Buffalo tonight, and halfway through the second period, they'd gone 0-for-4 on power plays. They were drawing penalties like crazy, but could they get the puck into the net? No, they could not.

Right now, the second power play unit was on the ice. Three of the guys on that unit were teammates of ours here in Everett who'd been called up, and they were just passing, passing, passing while the seconds ticked by. It was one of the NAPH players, Rusanov, who finally broke the cycle.

He passed the puck to Wilcox, who fired a beautiful one-timer from the blue line. The puck flew through a dense screen of players and slammed right...

...into the goalie's glove.

We all sat back with groans of frustration.

It was a good thing Seattle's penalty kill was holding its own, because the power play was a disaster. Though in their defense, the team was down quite a few key players, including three from the top power play unit and two from the second. Why? Because the injury fairy had visited Seattle early this year, putting four players on LTIR before the end of November. Three more were week-to-week and I'd lost track of who was day-to-day.

With Rainiers dropping like flies, guys from my team had been going up and down, up and down, filling in whenever they were needed until someone else got hurt. Right now, the bottom defensive pair and the third and fourth offensive lines were almost entirely my teammates from the Everett Orcas. In turn, our roster had gotten seriously thin, so we'd had to pull up half a dozen players from our HLWNA team, the Bellingham Steelheads. If the flu hit the Rainiers or Orcas, we might have to start grabbing up youth players or some shit.

On the screen, the guy in the penalty box sprang free, and he immediately stole the puck from an unsuspecting defenseman. Then he broke away, sprinting for our goal with no one in front of him and our D-pair scrambling to catch up.

Everyone in the room with me was chanting "Oh fuck, oh fuck, oh fuck!" while the Buffalo crowd cheered, and we collectively winced as the player snapped the puck on goal with his wicked backhand.

And then we were the ones cheering because Jan Stetina had defied the laws of physics and made a *miraculous* toe save. Three replays later, we still couldn't figure out how he'd managed to snap his skate into the path of the puck.

As the players onscreen set up for a faceoff in our defensive zone, Cams muttered, "Now watch—Seattle's going to get a penalty for nothing."

The response from all of us was a mutter of cynical agreement. Seattle had had five power plays (not that they'd been able to convert any of them), and it wasn't even midway through the second period. They were absolutely due a soft penalty, since the refs always seemed to pull that bullshit just to "even things up."

Sure enough, after the officials completely ignored an obvious case of holding and some blatant slashing, they tossed Condit into the box for tripping.

The call was garbage. Even the commentators agreed, since the replay clearly showed the "tripped" player blowing a tire on his own while Condit and his stick were well out of his way.

The camera shifted to the bench, focusing on Coach Baldwin as he shouted something at the refs. Something that involved the words "fucking" and "bullshit" if my lipreading skills were accurate.

But before I could try to make out what else he was saying, movement at the edge of the frame pulled my focus. I shifted my gaze, and my heart jumped into my throat.

Unaware of the camera on him, Christian propped someone's helmet on his knee and worked at the screws on one side of the visor. All around me, my teammates argued over whether or not the penalty was trash, if the refs were being bribed or if they were just incompetent. I was distantly aware of the conversation, but even after the camera had cut away from the bench, the image of Christian stayed on my mind like a spot after I'd stared into a stadium light.

Christian. Holy fuck.

Didn't matter that it had been almost a year—every damn time I saw him, whether it was in the background of an interview or during a game, my whole body reacted. One look at him, and I went right back to the day his dad canceled Pride Night. To the look on Christian's face when I'd asked for the rainbow tape. To that moment long after the game was over and Jack had finished ripping into all of us, when Christian had locked eyes with me in the bar, and I'd seen my own hungry rebelliousness in that grin.

Neither of us had actually come out and asked, but what better way to spite his dad and my GM than to hook up with each other? After all, Jack didn't like gay players on his team, he didn't like his son being gay, and he'd made it crystal clear to his son that if he wanted to stay employed, he'd better not fuck any gay players.

The ten and a half months since that night had been the longest dry spell of my life. Not because I'd ever had any trouble finding hookups—there were, after all, some perks to being a pro hockey player, even at the minor league level. I'd just struggled to find anyone who piqued my interest after Christian. Those who did get my attention lost it as soon as we started making out.

No one kissed like Christian Hayes. *No one.*

I squirmed on the couch, hoping my teammates took it as me getting comfortable and not masking a shiver. As the game continued and Seattle went on the penalty kill, my mind stayed back in my brief stint with the Rainiers. Some days, I regretted what I'd done that night—the tape thing, not Christian—because I knew damn well it meant I was never getting called up to Seattle again. I wasn't playing at the NAPH level again until I was traded or otherwise landed in another club, and Jack Hayes was exactly the kind of GM who'd keep me here until the end of my contract just for spite.

At the same time, maybe it was a good thing I was unofficially barred from the Seattle Rainiers locker room. As much as I ached to play in the majors again, as desperate as I was for another chance to prove I was worthy of a spot on a roster while I was still in my prime, I wasn't so sure I could play hockey in the same building as Christian.

More than once, I'd thought about going to a Rainiers game. After all, Everett was only forty-five minutes out of Seattle. It wasn't like I was in a different time zone. So why not grab a ticket and go to a game? See if I could catch Christian's eye? See if he was down for a rematch?

But I was a coward. And anyway, if he was interested in more, he'd have given me his number or asked for mine. He hadn't, so we—

"Oh fuck!" Cams was suddenly bolt upright beside me.

I shook myself and focused on the screen, and my teammates were mumbling, "Oh, that's not good" as the camera panned across the ice.

As soon as the camera stopped, my heart fell into my feet.

Someone was down. I couldn't see who, but he was down, crumpled by the boards and moving in that tight, uncomfortable way that said he was in a ton of pain. Conscious and able to move his extremities, so that was good, but he wasn't getting up.

One of the trainers crouched beside him, blocking our view of his face and his number.

"Shit," someone whispered. "That looks *bad.*"

I wanted to ask what happened, but I didn't want my teammates to know I'd been zoning out. Plus, I knew the replay would fill us in.

As predicted, the screen shifted to a slowed-down clip of two players going after the puck. Our guy—Hamilton, I realized—lost an edge just as he entered the trapezoid, and as he was going down, he slammed into the boards.

I cringed, absently rubbing my shoulder. Best case, he'd be able to skate it off after a minute or so. Worst case could be an injury to the head, neck, shoulder, collarbone, back—that was a terrible angle to hit, especially at speed.

Eventually, and with a lot of help, Hamilton was able to get to his feet. The pain on his face made my stomach lurch. No blood that I could see, but whatever injury he had, he was in a world of hurt. He had his left arm tucked protectively against his side. Very, very slowly, with a teammate on his right and the trainer helping to cradle that left arm, Hamilton made his way off the ice.

Shortly after that, the game resumed, but everyone in this living room was quiet. I was pretty sure we were all thinking the same thing, but it was Cams who finally said it out loud.

"Looks like someone else is getting called up." He sat back beside me and exhaled. "Because I doubt Hamilton's gonna be playing for a while."

We all nodded solemnly, and my teammates surreptitiously glanced at their phones. There was a quiet hum of excitement in the room that I understood fully. An injury like Hamilton's, that was a tough thing to react to. No one ever wanted to see another player hurt. Not even a rival.

Some bruises or a bloody nose, fine, but no one wished actual injuries on anyone.

Still, when you were playing at the level we were, a NAPH player going down meant one of us was going up. It felt opportunistic and gross to be hopeful about getting the call, but that was the world we lived in. If NAPH players didn't get hurt or weren't seriously underperforming, then we didn't get called up, and if we didn't get called up, we were staying down in the PHL, at least until next season's training camp.

The team had traveled with an extra PHL player in case something like this happened, so whoever got called up would probably take his place as backup. Not playing, just ready in case someone else went down. Which, given the way the season had been going, wasn't out of the question.

That did mean practicing with the Rainiers, though, and sometimes that was enough to catch the coach's eye and have him rotate a player in for a game or two. That was how Foster had earned himself a permanent spot three seasons ago—he'd come up from Everett as a backup, shined in practice, and wound up on the fourth line. Now he was a regular fixture on the third line. Well, when he wasn't out with a concussion, anyway.

Someone was about to get that chance. Someone's phone would be ringing tonight. Someone would be making a beeline for the airport to jump on a charter and meet the Rainiers in whatever city they were playing next.

All I knew was that someone wouldn't be me. Jack Hayes wasn't about to trade or release me because then I could sign someplace else, but he'd also made it clear I wasn't coming back to Seattle. Not after "that stunt with the stick tape."

So here I'd stay, continuing to play on the first offensive

line while I watched teammate after teammate after teammate get called up to Seattle.

Maybe I should request a trade. Get my agent to really work at Jack to let me leave this club. I needed to go somewhere I had an actual fighting chance of seeing NAPH ice, and being blacklisted to the PHL by my own GM wasn't going to help me—

My phone went off.

Everyone in the room jumped, especially me. And all heads snapped toward me.

I peered at the screen. My agent's name had my pulse buzzing in my ears.

Holy shit...

Swallowing hard, I accepted the call. "Hey, what's—"

"Pack a bag," she ordered. "A car is on its way. Your flight leaves in two hours."

"Two hours—I'm in Everett!"

"And you're flying out of Paine Field. You gotta go!"

I was already up off the couch. "All right. I'm on my way." Heart pounding, I shoved my phone in my pocket. I was stunned, sure on some level that I'd just hallucinated that call, but if it had been real, then I only had two hours to get my ass and some luggage to the airport here in Everett. I could decide if it was really happening later. Be shocked and disbelieving later. Right now... "Gotta go, guys."

My teammates didn't even question me. They all knew how this worked, and they just slapped me on the back and shoulder and told me to go, go, go.

Didn't have to tell me twice.

This was the second chance I'd firmly believed I'd never had. The one Jack Hayes had explicitly told me had gone up in smoke the second I'd asked for that roll of rainbow stick tape.

With a huge chunk of his team out and a dwindling roster of PHL players to choose from, he was apparently desperate now. Desperate times called for desperate measures, so he was calling me up.

And I was *not* blowing it this time.

CHAPTER 4

CHRISTIAN

This season was cursed. That was the only possible explanation. Seemed like almost every night, we were putting up nameplates for newly arrived players. Good thing we always traveled with away jerseys for every member of our PHL affiliate; anyone they called up, we had a jersey for him, and my God, we'd been going through that stack this year.

After Hamilton had broken his shoulder in Buffalo last night, there'd been no question we'd be onboarding a new player tonight. Even if the new guy was a healthy scratch (which was likely), he'd be here, dressing for warmups. The backup player we'd brought along on this road trip would definitely get to play tonight. And at least one of our minor league players would be on the team for a few weeks now while Hams was on LTIR. Glad I didn't have to make those decisions, though I'd need to find out who it was so I made sure we were well-stocked with his gear.

That had all been on my mind since last night, and I'd known from the moment Hams had gone down that there'd be yet another new name in the dressing room tonight.

Still, I wasn't at all prepared when we were setting up stalls and Marty hung up a pristine white jersey with the number sixty-one on the back.

And there across the shoulders in dark blue letters: *Mathis.*

I almost dropped the nameplates I'd been carrying. Dad had actually called up Theo? Jesus. Were there any players left in Everett or Bellingham? Because the situation had to be even more desperate than I'd thought if Theo was coming up.

"I don't give a damn if he's the best player in the entire PHL," Dad had ranted. "I don't tolerate disrespect. He can rot in the HLWNA for all I care—he's not coming up to this locker room again."

But here we were, arranging a jersey and a pair of skates in front of a locker stall. And here I was, sliding the nameplate for Theo Mathis into the holder above the jersey.

I stared at the nameplate for a second and gulped. Fuck. Was I even going to be able to concentrate with him in here?

Of course I was. He wasn't the first hockey player I'd fucked and he probably wouldn't be the last, even if I did (usually) avoid sleeping with Rainiers. I didn't even know why I was tripping over my own feet about this, apart from the fact that I'd never expected Dad to call him up.

Well, I could tie myself in knots about that later—my crew had about forty-five minutes to finish setting up the locker room before the team arrived for the morning skate.

Fortunately, this was a job I could do mostly on autopilot, because my mind was almost entirely fixed on Theo. I couldn't figure out why, though. I didn't know why that night had stuck with me the way it had. Casual hookups were nothing new for me, but Theo had stayed on my mind like an ex-boyfriend. Not like someone who'd hurt me or anything—just someone who was living rent-free in my head like he owned the goddamned place.

My memory rewound past that night in my condo, past hanging out at the bar, and back to the locker room at the arena.

I'd been crushed that Dad had canceled Pride Night. They'd been a tradition for years, since the GM who came before him, and the fans and players alike loved them. Everyone wondered why Dad had waited until the very last minute to pull the plug, but I knew why.

"Maybe in the future you'll learn not to get your hopes up," he'd told me in his office minutes after the announcement was made. "My team does *not* endorse that lifestyle."

Only anger had kept me from tearing up. "It's not 'my lifestyle.' It's who I am."

His dismissive shrug had set my teeth on edge. "And you can live your life however you want. I've never tried to stop you." Expression darkening, he'd added, "But that doesn't mean I need to make my team wave rainbows around."

So many reporters asked him, "Why change the policy on Pride Nights now? You've celebrated them in the past."

More than a few had called him a coward in their articles after he'd answered that another team had set the precedent.

"Some of Omaha's players didn't want to wear the Pride sweaters last season. The organization had the courage to let individual players say no. This season, Seattle has the courage to say that we're a hockey team, not puppets for political statements."

Ugh. Fuck him. And fuck our president of hockey operations, too, for leaving it in Dad's hands and not caring enough to do anything about it. He didn't even care about the disrespect to the team's fans.

Standing there in that locker room, staring at the jerseys we'd hung up minutes after pulling down the Pride jerseys, I'd felt lower than I had in a long time. Dad hadn't just canceled Pride Night, he'd made sure *I* had to physically *remove* it. He'd waited until the jerseys and nameplates were up and the players were about to start coming in.

Fuck the fans, apparently. Fuck the queer players and the allies. Fuck his own son, but that was no surprise.

I'd had die a little inside with every nameplate I took down and every jersey I pulled off a hanger and stuffed in a bag. Try to stay collected and professional as I slid the everyday nameplates into place while Marty and Jake hung up the regular home game jerseys. By the time players had started coming in, the locker room looked exactly the same as it did before every game.

It was the first time I'd given serious thought to going to work for another team. I was at a point in my career where I could go to work for any club in the league if I wanted to, and I wouldn't have to put up with my asshole father anymore. I wouldn't even have to live near him, though it would suck to be far away from my mom and sister.

I'd had my resignation letter planned out in my head as I'd adjusted Sorenson's visor, when...

"Hey, Christian?"

Mathis. The kid from the minors.

"Be right there," I'd replied, and a moment later, I'd gone to his stall. "Hey, what do you need?"

He'd looked up at me with the most beautiful brown eyes I'd ever seen, and he'd said the words that had started putting the whole night back on the rails: "Do you have any rainbow tape?"

Within minutes, every roll of rainbow tape we had was making the rounds as the team—the *whole* team—replaced the white and black on their blades. A few had even candy-cane-striped their stick handles with colorful tape.

The resignation letter in my head had gone up in smoke as I'd watched the whole scene play out. Every man in that room knew they were in for an earful from my dad, but they did it anyway. For their queer teammates. For themselves. For me. There were a lot of reasons why I sometimes considered giving up this job—most of them relating to him—but there were so many *more* reasons I hung on. Twenty of those reasons—twenty-two including the pair who'd be healthy scratches—had rainbow-taped their sticks right in there in front of me.

"Jack Hayes can go fuck himself," they'd said with every bright stripe they laid down on their sticks. *"We're doing this."*

When warmups started, they'd marched out of the locker room, one after another, colorful sticks in hand. The crowd had gone nuts. My heart had gone wild. Even after they'd switched back to regular tape for the game (which they would've done anyway), I think I spent that whole game smiling like a fool.

Sometimes I went with the players to the bar after a game. Sometimes I didn't. A lot of times, if we were getting ready for a road trip, I was too busy. Even if I wasn't busy, I was often exhausted and had a reservation for one in my bed.

They always invited me and my crew, though. Without fail. And that night, I'd said yes, because I'd wanted to be surrounded by these amazing men. They were my family. The queer guys were fearless in the face of a man with a lot of power over their careers. The straight guys were relentless in their support. I'd put up with my dad's bullshit until the end of time if it meant staying in this locker room, and hell yes, I'd join them at the bar.

Theo had also joined them. When I'd eventually left the bar, he'd left with me, and I still revisited that night now. I didn't know if it was the lingering euphoria from the game, the rebelliousness of hooking up with someone I shouldn't touch, or if the chemistry really was off the charts between us. Maybe some combination of the three. Whatever the case, he'd rocked my world, and from his dazed expression afterward, I was pretty sure I'd rocked his, too.

We'd both known he'd be sent down the next day. There'd been no way in hell Dad would keep Theo up after the tape. So, why the hell not? Wasn't like he'd be back in this locker room again, so we could hook up and go our separate ways.

I just hadn't thought the sex would be so good I'd want a rematch. By the time I had, he'd already been gone, and we hadn't exchanged numbers. He'd only be forty-five minutes away, but that didn't mean I could find him again.

Social media had been an option. Going to an Orcas game, too.

But cowardice, thy name was Christian, and anyway, he obviously wasn't interested because *he* hadn't asked for *my* number either. So I'd left well enough alone, and the only time I'd seen him again was at training camp. When that had come, I'd pointedly avoided looking at him until curiosity had gotten the best of me, at which point I'd discovered *he* was pointedly avoiding looking at *me*.

Probably because he'd been loudly warned that his career was on thin ice over the stick tape incident, and he was wisely keeping his head down. The last thing he needed was Dad finding out he'd hooked up with me.

Yeah, that night had *definitely* been a one-time thing.

Oh well, I'd told myself. *It was just a hookup.*

Which totally explained why, all these months later, I still jacked off thinking about him and I was completely off-balance after seeing his name above a locker stall. Was I even going to be able to walk straight when he showed up? Probably not. Good thing I didn't have to skate.

"Hey, Christian?"

Not Theo calling me from the locker room this time. No, this was a different voice, carrying over noise and power tools and echoing in that strange way voices did in concrete-lined hallways. When had I come out here?

I shook myself and turned to see Marty eyeing me. "Hmm? What?"

He tilted his head. "I was going to ask you the same thing."

"Huh?" But then I realized that at some point, I'd apparently been so lost in thought, I'd come out into the hall and turned on the skate sharpener but hadn't gotten any further than that. I was just standing here like a dumbass, a piece of steel in my hand, while the sharpener waited for me to do something with it.

Cheeks burning, I cleared my throat. "Sorry. Just, uh..." *Being an absolute idiot about a player I'll never touch again.* "Tired, I guess."

Skepticism creased his forehead.

"I'm good," I assured him. "It was just a long night." At least I had that excuse to fall back on. Even the equipment managers who'd been doing this for twenty years could still be utterly wiped after traveling between back-to-back games. Last night, we'd had to go straight from the arena to the airport, load the plane, fly to Washington, D.C., unload the plane, and come to the arena to get everything set up.

Now we were back, bright and early for the morning skate, and we were probably running on ten hours of sleep between the four of us. Such were road trips.

Marty let it go and left me to continue sharpening steel.

Alone in the hallway, I pulled myself together. Fortunately, there wasn't much left for me to do; we always sharpened skates the night before so everyone had fresh blades in the morning. This was just the box of backup blades. We rotated through this box and two others, so every player always had at least two sharpened blades ready to roll before a game.

I'd just finished the last one when the first set of footsteps announced the arrival of the Seattle Rainiers. Condit was always among the first, and he always carried a tray of four cups of coffee—one for each equipment manager.

"Oh, you're the best," I said as I took mine.

"You're welcome." He flashed the charming smile that the camera so loved, and then he continued into the locker room while I took a careful sip. He even knew how we all liked our coffee, and mine had exactly the right amount of sugar. It was nice to be appreciated.

After Condit, the rest of the team trickled in, including the guys from the minor team. Perry, a defenseman who wasn't even old enough to drink yet, was sporting a hell of a shiner thanks to a fight last night. I shuddered thinking about that brawl. The other guy had richly deserved it, but he'd also had six inches and a good forty pounds on Perry. I'd had visions of the kid being added to the growing list of injuries.

Perry had held his own, though, and I suspected he was wearing the black eye as a badge of honor.

Too bad that no amount of fighting could undo that asshole boarding MacKenzie late in the third period. We'd already lost Hams to a broken shoulder, and then Mac had gone down. Last I'd heard, he was still being evaluated for an upper body injury. As bad as he was weaving when he'd come off the ice, he'd probably be down for at least a few days on concussion protocol.

Maybe you'll get to play tonight after all, Theo.

My own thought almost made me spit out my coffee. Jesus. All mental roads were going to lead to him, weren't they? Was I even going to be able to do my job when he walked in?

I didn't have a lot of time to ponder that, because a moment later... there he was. Some dark hair stuck out from under his Seattle Rainiers beanie, and he was laughing at something Brody, one of the other PHL guys, had said. His smile... Fuck me. As much time as I'd spent fantasizing about the night we'd spent together, it was that sweet, lopsided smile that made my knees shake this time.

God, he's cute.

I'm so fucking doomed.

Right then, he looked my way, and he stumbled a little. Probably just as well—then he could tell Brody that was why he was suddenly turning bright red.

He did give me a quick, shy smile, though. Then a second glance—a fast down-up—before he dropped his gaze and continued past me, his cheeks turning even redder.

As soon as he was gone, I closed my eyes and leaned against the cold cinderblock wall. I wanted him again. Plain and simple.

But... we couldn't.

He probably wouldn't, no matter how much desire I was pretty sure I'd seen in his eyes. The fact that he'd been called up at all was nothing short of a miracle, and I wouldn't ask him to risk this tenuous second chance for me.

One time had been reckless enough. I had no idea if my crew or the team had ever caught on that Theo and I had slept together. I had no idea if he'd told anyone. What I did know was that if that information made it back to my father, Theo and I would *both* be out of a job. Dad had fired my sister from the accounting department shortly after they'd had a tiff over something, and he'd axed my brother-in-law from the PR team after Aiden dared to stand up for his wife. So, cutting his own son loose was *not* out of the question. I'd been treading delicately ever since last season's Pride Night anyway, and if Dad caught wind that I'd put my hands on one of his players? Hello, unemployment.

Sometimes it was tempting to let him fire me, or to just bail. What stopped me was remembering that while I did work *for* my dad, I didn't work *with* him all the time. If I had, I'd have jumped ship ages ago. As it was, he was an intermittent and mostly avoidable pain in my ass at an otherwise amazing job that I did *not* want to lose.

I pushed out a breath and rolled my shoulders, wondering when they'd started getting so tight.

No matter how hot Theo was, no matter how distracting he was, I *had* to keep my distance. This job was more important than getting laid. And anyway, he'd only be up for a little while. I could deal with that. Even if he stayed up for a month or two, it wouldn't be forever.

I'd just keep my head down.

Do my job.

And try not to lose my damned mind over that beautiful, off-limits man.

CHAPTER 5
THEO

"Mathis." Jack Hayes's sharp voice cut through the noise in the locker room and sent my heart into my throat. When I met his gaze, he gestured for me to join him in the hallway.

I swallowed, my hands still on the shin pad I'd been pulling on. Oh, fuck. This couldn't be good.

I didn't dare keep the GM waiting, so I hurried after him. I was mostly dressed—everything except skates and jersey—and I strode across the room, pretending not to notice my teammates glancing my way. Did they think I was about to get my ass chewed? Because I was pretty sure I was about to get my ass chewed, and not in the fun way.

As I stepped out into the hall, I felt weirdly naked despite all the protective gear I was already wearing. Something told me I wouldn't have felt much better had I been decked out in goalie pads. No amount of equipment would shield me from the things Jack Hayes could do to me with the stroke of a pen.

It didn't help that he was huge. He'd been an enforcer back in the day, and his sheer size had been enough to intimidate even the meanest players. In his fifties and no longer in his gear, he was as narrow as any of us, but he was still almost six foot six. In that moment, I wished I was one of those guys who put my skates on before my shin pads; at least that would give me a couple extra inches instead of facing him down from my usual height of five-foot-ten.

Not that it would actually help, but I'd take whatever I could get right then.

He glared at me for an uncomfortably long moment. I was vaguely aware that the hallway around us had gone quiet. There'd been staff members moving around, and someone was cutting a stick while someone else rifled around in a trunk for something. Now everything had fallen silent and the people had scattered like startled mice. There was no one around except the two of us.

"Listen, kid," Jack said in his don't-fuck-with-me tone. "Before you touch that ice with my team, there are some things we need to get straight."

I gulped and nodded but didn't say a word.

"Coach Baldwin specifically asked me to bring you up," he said through his teeth. "In fact, he's been wanting you to come up ever since Alton went on LTIR."

Some part of me knew I should've been downright giddy over that. The head coach wanted me here? Oh, hell, this was definitely my time to shine so he might want me to *stay* here.

But the excitement that desperately wanted to bubble up kept simmering beneath the surface, because Jack wasn't finished.

"Quite frankly, the way you play, I would've happily brought you up. In fact..." He half-shrugged. "I'd have encouraged him to keep you after training camp."

Whoa.

A tiny bit of excitement tentatively swelled in my chest.

Then Jack's expression darkened, and he leaned in enough to make me draw back. "But I haven't forgotten that stunt you pulled last season." He inclined his head. "Do you know what stunt that was?"

I nodded.

He raised his eyebrows, clearly encouraging me to go on.

I cleared my throat. "I, um... I put rainbow tape on my stick. After you canceled Pride Night."

"Yes. You did." His jaw worked. "And that kind of disrespect is going to keep you in the PHL for the rest of your career. Or maybe all the way down to the HLW, if I decide to send you down there."

"I, um... I know." I swallowed. "I'm sorry." I wasn't. Not at all. But I was admittedly scared of this guy already, and he was determined to show me that my hockey career was on the edge of a knife that *he* controlled.

"If Coach Baldwin wants you to stay up while he sends down one of the other boys," Jack went on, "then I'll allow it. Now that you're here, if you prove to him you can play at this level, then I'll let him make the call." He stabbed a finger at me, very nearly hitting my chest protector. "But step over that line again, kid—give me *one reason* to believe you're even thinking about disrespecting me again—and I won't just send you down. I will make sure no GM in North America puts your name on another roster. Am I clear?"

That wasn't an empty threat. There'd been rumors for several years now that he'd had a player blacklisted for something or another. I didn't know if the rumors were true, and no one was clear on the offense that had pissed off Jack, but that player was tearing it up in Europe now. Absolutely North American caliber, but effectively banished to the other side of the Atlantic.

Slapping Jack Hayes in the face was... costly.

I fought the urge to draw back farther. Where there'd been uneasy excitement earlier, there was a deep chill now. One that had me on the verge of shivering. I was genuinely shocked I didn't see my breath as I said, "Yeah. You're clear."

He glowered for what felt like an entire twenty-minute game period. Then he gestured into the locker room. "Get your ass dressed."

I mumbled a thank-you and beat feet into the locker room. I kept my head down, my face burning as I hurried to my stall to finish putting on my gear. There were some murmurs, but it was hard to tell if they were about me or just the guys talking to each other. The room was definitely quieter than normal. Less banter. Less chirping.

Condit was the one to break the ice, so to speak. He came up as I was lacing up my skates, and he gave my boot a tap with his stick. "Good to see you again, kid. You're not too jetlagged, are you?"

I managed a laugh as I sat back. "Nah. I'm caffeinated enough to keep me going."

He studied me, then chuckled, tapped my skate again, and headed for the sheet.

I followed a moment later, my stomach a mix of excited butterflies and panicked nerves. I was *terrified* of Jack Hayes. Everyone knew he was one of the most ruthless GMs in the league, absolutely willing to trade or send down anyone who couldn't produce or wouldn't toe the line. Making myself persona non grata in his eyes probably qualified as a career-limiting move.

But I was here. I was on the ice, ready to prove myself worthy of a spot at this level. That was going to be a lot harder for me than for my other PHL teammates because the GM hated me, but it was what I had to work with. Fear and threats be damned—a long as I was playing with the Rainiers, I was going to *shine*.

The morning skate went well enough. I was still starstruck by some of the big guys, same as the last time I came up, but I focused on this sport I'd been playing since I was little, and I held my own. I even put a couple of pucks behind Jan Stetina, the star goalie. Okay, so he was taking it easy in order to avoid injury before tonight's game, but still—there was something immensely satisfying about getting a shot past one of the NAPH's top netminders. I'd take it.

Aside from that conversation with Jack Hayes, I felt pretty good about everything, honestly. Even though I probably wouldn't be playing, if I could impress the coaches enough during practice, maybe they'd tell Jack to call me up again. A boy could dream, right?

As I stepped into the locker room, though, my gaze landed on one of the equipment managers, and my heart skipped.

In same instant my eyes found Christian, he looked my way, and I almost stumbled on my skates. Cheeks suddenly on fire, I quickly averted my gaze. I had no idea if he did the same or if he was staring at me, and I was afraid to look.

He was going to make things complicated, wasn't he? Not directly or deliberately, but just by existing. By being here. My first time with the Rainiers, he'd distracted me the same way some of the really hot players did—just by being hot and making me wish we could hook up.

This time...

Oh, God. This time, we *had* hooked up. I knew what that man's mouth could do. What his kiss tasted like. What it tasted like after he'd sucked me off. How my scalp burned while he gripped my hair and what he sounded like when he came.

And I was supposed to play hockey while he was here?

Fuck my life.

I shook myself and focused on getting out of my gear. My career was too important to me. I wasn't going to risk it by getting all stupid over a man I never should've touched in the first place.

A man I regretted never touching again.

A man I desperately wanted to touch—

Mathis. For fuck's sake. Get it together.

Way too much on the line. Had to focus. *Had* to.

Though this was a different locker room, a different level, and a different team, my routine stayed the same. I peeled off my practice jersey and tossed it in the laundry bin, then started on all the various pads and protectors.

I was down to my base layer and had just toed my skates under the bench when Coach appeared at my stall. "Mathis, you're dressing tonight."

I blinked. "I am?" I'd expected to be here as a backup. Dress for warmups, sure, but not the game itself.

He nodded grimly. "Hams and Mac are both down for a while, and I'm healthy scratching Brody." He clapped my shoulder. "Next man up."

"Oh." I gulped. "Okay. Yeah. I'll be ready to roll."

He gave a sharp nod and clomped away.

I stood there stupidly for a moment, disbelieving this was actually happening. I'd fully expected to just be here as a backup while the team was on the road, but now this? Holy fuck. I was excited, but also nervous as hell for a million reasons. Especially since Brody was a healthy scratch, which probably meant Coach wasn't impressed with his performance. Coach was hard up for players, but he was still more than willing to bench one of us if we weren't up to snuff.

No pressure, or anything.

Well, I hadn't expected a lack of pressure at this level. As far as I was concerned, this was my time to shine.

Or fall flat on my face.

One of the two.

I let my gaze drift toward Christian, who was poring over something on a clipboard with one of the other equipment managers.

Having him this close by—that ridiculously sexy man with the mind-bending kiss—definitely tipped the odds in favor of me falling flat on my face. He'd been a distraction and a half for the last several months, even when I'd been playing in Everett.

Now I had one and only one chance to prove to the Rainiers that I was worthy of a spot on this team, and Christian was... here. In the same locker room. On the same bus. On the same plane. In the same hotels.

Goose bumps sprang up under my thin shirt as I tore my gaze away from him.

Oh, man.

I was so fucked.

Last season

"That took some serious balls, kid." Condit clinked his beer glass against mine. "Standing up to Jack is not for the faint of heart."

I laughed nervously. "Probably not for the professionally ambitious, either." I rolled my eyes as I brought my beer up for a sip. "Pretty sure I just shot myself in the foot."

Nobody at the table piped up with any dissent, so... yeah, I'd probably fucked myself pretty hard with what I'd done tonight.

I didn't regret it, though. There were kids at that game tonight. Probably a few who were queer—some who may not have even known it yet—and they didn't deserve to wonder why their favorite team had canceled Pride Night. If the tape on my stick made just one kid in the audience feel like they belonged there, then whatever fallout came my way was a hundred percent worth it.

It would still suck, though. No doubt about that.

I set my beer down as I scanned the faces at the table. I wanted so badly to play with these guys again. Some of them were future Hall-of-Famers. Some were just incredible players who I'd admired from the minors and juniors.

Still think it was worth it?

Before I could think too much about that, my gaze landed on the one man at this table who hadn't skated tonight.

Christian Hayes.

And in that same moment, his gaze landed on me. We were at opposite ends of the long table, so in theory, he could've been just looking in my general direction, but no... our eyes *locked*. And I *felt* it.

I also felt it when he grinned behind his beer glass. And I remembered how crestfallen and hurt he'd been in the locker room earlier tonight. When he'd been visibly crushed that his dad had nixed Pride Night.

Oh, fuck yeah, the tape was worth it. Whatever fallout came, I'd take it, because Christian had been smiling all damn night.

Now that we were out of the locker room, with the game behind us and some alcohol flowing, he was still smiling, but there was something different to it now. Every time we looked at each other, one corner of his mouth would lift, and something would spark in his eyes that made me squirm in my seat.

I'd never in a million years forget the way his eyes had lit up when he'd realized the rainbow tape was happening despite Jack's bullshit. The way they watched me now, though? That was something else entirely. Something that simmered—smoldered, really—as if this wasn't the time or place to let it out.

Something that seemed to echo what had been tingling along the length of my spine ever since I first laid eyes on Christian.

What could I say? He was one of the hottest men I'd ever seen, and considering he was surrounded by hockey stars, that said a lot. He just had this smile and these beautiful eyes, and I loved the way he lit up the room just by strolling into it. He was one of the very, very few men in that room I *hadn't* seen naked, but even fully dressed in workout pants and a hoodie—his usual uniform when he was working—he pulled my attention away from every ass and six-pack in sight. Not that I made a habit of checking out my teammates, but when there were men in various states of undress everywhere you looked, you saw things.

And he's probably the most attractive man in the building because he's the absolute last *one you have* any *business touching if you value your career.*

Ooh, right. That. Christian's dad had waaay too much control over my future in hockey for me to fuck around with his son.

Then again, I thought as I "accidentally" caught Christian's eye across the table, *I probably torpedoed my hockey future the minute I put that rainbow tape on my stick.*

So what's the harm in getting naked with Jack's son while I have the chance?

And looking in those eyes... oh, fuck. I *did* have a chance, didn't I?

I took a deep swallow from my drink just to cool myself down. When Christian smiled at me before taking a sip from his own glass, my body temperature skyrocketed all over again.

That was probably the last time I'll ever play for Seattle.

If he's game tonight...

Why the hell not?

CHAPTER 6

CHRISTIAN

This season

My job meant seeing hockey players the way the public didn't. For all people thought it was sketchy to have a gay guy in the locker room since I'd be perving on all the players, everyone who worked with a hockey team knew that was stupid. Anyone who worked in a locker room (even those wielding cameras) quickly got used to seeing the players in various states of undress. I'd been doing this for so many years, it didn't even register on my radar. Sure, I'd notice a tattoo sometimes, and there was that one goalie whose dick was so big it probably even turned some of the straight guys' heads. Otherwise, naked men caught my eye in here about as much as towels and stick tape.

Theo Mathis, though? I couldn't even concentrate when he was *dressed*.

I'd thought he was cute the first time he'd walked into the locker room, wide-eyed and starstruck. Now he seemed a little more confident in himself, even if he was obviously and understandably wary of my dad, and—I mean, who was I kidding? I couldn't look at him without remembering the sparks that had flown when we'd touched.

The night we'd hooked up, I'd fully expected him to get sent down the next day. Hell, I'd been sure that while we'd been flirting at that bar and then fucking around in my condo, my dad had already made the necessary calls and signed the necessary forms. When Theo turned his phone back on, there would be a message from his agent saying to get his butt back to Everett.

And knowing my dad, Theo would never darken a locker stall in Seattle for the rest of *either* of their careers.

So what was the harm in hooking up? Wasn't like we'd ever cross paths in a locker room again.

But it had been *so damn good*. This man's kiss had been living rent-free in my head ever since, not to mention his other oral skills, and I'd been kicking myself for not getting his number. Especially since he'd been wrung out from the game and I'd been wiped from the long day, so we hadn't even had enough left in us to fuck. The whole time I'd had his dick in my mouth, I'd imagined how spectacular it would feel in my ass, but we just... hadn't had anything left. We'd gone our separate ways, and then he'd been gone, and that was that.

And now he was back. He was *here*. He was undressing in the Rainiers' locker room while I had to pretend I still knew how to do my job.

At least my current task wasn't a difficult one, and as a bonus, it meant getting my butt out of the locker room.

I wheeled the cart full of sweaty, stinking practice jerseys into the laundry facility. As soon as I was in the room, I shut the steel door and paused to just exhale. I *had* to pull my damn head together. There was way more at stake right now than Dad ripping into me for having a crush on a player. When that had happened, there hadn't been any backlash on the players. Just Dad flipping out at me.

"Do you want to keep this job, Christian?" he'd demanded. "Because you are far more replaceable than you think."

"Yes, I want to keep my job. And I'm not doing anything."

He'd glared at me. "So I'm just imagining you checking out—"

"Yes!" I'd thrown up my hands. "Just because I'm gay doesn't mean I can't be respectful and keep my eyes where they belong."

"Bullshit. I saw the way you were looking at Barker."

I'd blinked. "What? I'd just finished patching his socks and I was making sure the patch held." I'd shown my palms. "He knew exactly what I was doing."

That argument had lasted a good hour and a half. In the end, he still hadn't believed me that I didn't and wouldn't perv on players. He'd threatened my job a few more times, and I'd finally just agreed not to look at any of the guys because then he'd feel like he won and we could be done with it.

Sometimes I wondered why he didn't fire me. Maybe because the coaching staff and players loved me? They were very vocal about that—about all the equipment managers, but especially me. I could have as much of an ego as the next person, but I wasn't stupid—they weren't singing my praises because I was God's gift to equipment management. They just knew Dad wasn't thrilled about me being here.

In the present, I sighed and pushed myself off the door. As I loaded jerseys into two machines—two smaller loads took far less time than one giant one—I let my brain wander to the man who was currently the target of my dad's ire.

Theo wasn't supposed to be here. He wasn't supposed to come back. That was the whole reason I'd said "to hell with it" and hooked up with him; because I didn't dare touch a player who would be staying with the team or coming back any time soon. In fact, the one other time I'd slept with a player had been Kessler. We'd circled each other all season, and then he found out the night before the trade deadline that he was heading for Edmonton the next day.

Theo and I had both believed his time in Seattle was as finished as Kessler's had been, so why the hell not?

And... here we were.

"Fucking hell," I muttered over the sound of the washing machines. I rested my hands on the now-empty laundry cart, closed my eyes, and let my head fall forward. I needed to get back to the locker room—there was a shitload of work to do between now and tonight's game—but I needed a goddamned minute.

Theo was here. There was no telling how long he'd be here. With the ever-growing list of injuries and the revolving door between the Rainiers and the Orcas, it was impossible to guess. If he impressed Coach Baldwin, then he might be here for the bulk of the remaining season, as long as there was cap space and room on the roster. If his performance was tepid or some of the injured players rallied faster than projected, then the problem could resolve on its own.

I winced. I didn't want Theo to go back down. I mean, I did in the sense that I didn't think I could stay sane around him. But I also wanted the best for his career, which meant staying up at this level for as long as possible. I really didn't want to be selfish about this. At the same time... Fuck. I didn't know what outcome I really wanted. Was it too much to ask to just stay sane no matter what? Probably.

One thing was for sure: I would be stupid to imagine there was any chance of us crossing that line again. I'd seen the shell-shocked look on Theo's face when he'd come back from that little one-on-one with my dad, and I could read between those lines. Dad had undoubtedly warned him not to fuck up again. He'd threatened him within an inch of his career, promising grave professional consequences if Theo didn't toe the line. I didn't have to be a mind reader or even overhear the conversation to know that. I knew my dad. I knew Theo's expression because I'd seen it on other players' faces, and I'd worn it myself.

I wanted to pull him aside and tell him not to be afraid of my father's bullshit. Theo was a good hockey player, and it wasn't his fault Dad was an asshole on a power trip. I wanted to tell him everything would be fine if he just played hockey and kept his head down (well, metaphorically; he needed to keep his head *up* on the ice).

But I couldn't do that.

One, because I was afraid that if we so much as made prolonged eye contact, people would immediately see through to that scorching hot night last season.

And two, because I would be lying. I knew my father. I knew he'd be scrutinizing Theo's every move, looking for a reason to give him a one-way express ticket back to the minors. I knew Dad could and would ruin a player's career over the smallest slight, especially if there was any perceived disrespect toward him personally.

God help this team if Dad ever managed to take over as president of hockey operations. Right now, Bruce Collins was in that position, and he was the only one who had a leash of any kind on Dad. Not a very tight one, and not one he used very often, but a leash. The owners wouldn't lift a finger to rein Dad in; they just didn't care enough about anything except winning. As long as the Rainiers held a respectable position in the standings and made a valiant run at the Cup each season, they were completely hands off.

Dad with the full power of the presidency *without* Bruce to talk him down? Yeah, I would probably go looking for a job on another team at that point. As if I hadn't already considered that a few million times.

So there wasn't anything I could do to reassure Theo that he wasn't skating on dangerously thin ice. I couldn't even risk being seen talking to him unless it was *obviously* about equipment, or Dad might decide there was something between us and lash out professionally at Theo.

He was here. I was here.

And if either of us valued our careers, we'd pretend like hell we didn't notice.

Fuck my damn life.

CHAPTER 7

THEO

It never ceased to amaze me how quickly players moved within the league. Not just up and down between the PHL and NAPH, but between teams.

Last night, just hours after we'd returned from the five-game East Coast road trip, there'd been an announcement that Seattle had made a trade. The Rainiers had sent Langley and a third-round draft pick to Montreal in exchange for Yury Grekov, a spectacular young defenseman.

Langley had played in our last road trip game and he was on the flight home. This morning, all his gear and his nameplate were gone, and in what was previously his stall, the new guy was suiting up for the morning skate. He might even play in tonight's game if Coach decided he meshed well with the team.

Everyone seemed impressed as hell that Jack had managed to swing that deal. Langley was good and all, but Grekov had been tearing it up for Montreal. He'd racked up half a dozen goals in between taking on the role of heavy-weight enforcer, and he was excellent at drawing penalties while he deftly avoided taking them. Though he'd been a fourth-round pick, commentators and players alike had been marveling at what an overlooked talent he was, and how much potential he had for a spectacular career as a defenseman. How Jack had acquired him for so relatively little, I had no idea.

Guess that's how he keeps his job—he's an absolute pustule of a human being, but he's damn good at being a GM.

Grekov had a translator with him, and he also had that wide-eyed, fish-out-of-water look some guys had when they didn't speak English. It was overwhelming, being surrounded by people speaking in another language, and it showed.

There wasn't much I could do when the new guy was Swedish, Finnish, or French Canadian. A Russian like Grekov, though...

I pulled on my jersey and crossed over to his stall. "Hey, welcome to Seattle," I said in Russian.

Grekov sat up straighter, his eyes lighting up. "You speak Russian?"

I nodded. "Da."

He exhaled. His translator chuckled, looking a little relieved himself. He was probably glad Grekov had someone who could translate for him on the fly, especially out on the ice, since it wasn't like the translator could stick with him during games.

I gestured over my shoulder toward my locker stall. "I have to get my gear on, but when we're out on the ice or on the bench..."

Grekov smiled. "Thank you."

I left him to continue getting dressed, and I headed back to my own stall. Halfway there, though, I paused. Then I changed direction and went looking for Coach, who was just coming into the locker room, peering at something on an iPad.

"Hey, Coach?"

He looked up from the iPad. "Hmm?"

I tipped my head toward Grekov. "The new guy doesn't speak much English. Or any—I'm not sure. But I speak Russian, so as long as I'm here, it might make it easier for him if we sit near each other on the bench, but since he's defense..."

Coach glanced past me, pursing his lips. "We'll keep his translator out there for when he's on the bench. But if you guys can sit near each other and still talk to your linemates..." He half-shrugged.

"Perfect. Thanks, Coach." I headed back to my stall to finish getting dressed.

Grekov's translator would keep him filled in with whatever the coaches, trainers, or referees said, but we also talked amongst ourselves on the bench. Reviewing plays. Strategizing. Chirping or reassuring, depending on what the moment called for. I knew from one of my old Finnish teammates that the bench could get incredibly lonely for someone who couldn't banter or talk hockey with the guys sitting next to him. Even if someone could translate, there was no substitute for someone who spoke your own language well enough to shoot the shit and joke around. Too much of that just got lost in translation.

Rusanov eyed me as I geared up. "How the fuck do you know Russian?" he asked in the same language.

I shot him an innocent look. "Your sister talks in her sleep."

He swore and threw a balled up sock at me. "Oh, fuck you."

I laughed and threw it back.

Condit watched us both. "Do I even want to know?"

Yanni was Czech, but he must've known at least a little Russian because he said, "Mathis was saying he learned Russian by banging Rusanov's sister."

Rusanov responded with what I could only assume was some Czech swearing—I kind of vaguely recognized it from a previous teammate who'd taught me a few phrases—and the sock flew at Yanni's head. Yanni and I cackled.

Condit shook his head as he started putting on his shin pads. "You know what? Never mind. I don't want to know."

Rusanov gave me and Yanni the finger as he said something I didn't understand. Must've been Czech.

Two stalls down from Condit, Abrahamsson barked a laugh. "Language!"

"How the fuck do you know what it means?" Yanni asked. "Do they teach Czech curses in Sweden now?"

"No," Abrahamsson deadpanned. "I learned it from your mom."

That had the whole locker room howling enough that I didn't hear Yanni's response.

Right then, Jack walked into the room, and the laughter died away faster than a crowd going silent when a ref was about to announce the result of a video review. One minute, we were loud and raucous. The next, I could hear Yanni adjusting one of his pads from eight stalls away.

Jack looked around, then gestured for Coach and the defensive coach to step out into the hallway. After they were gone, some of the conversation tentatively started up again, but the banter was dead and the raucous vibe was gone.

Ugh. At least he hadn't said or done anything. Just walked in like the Grim Reaper of Fun, then walked out, and the mood didn't recover. I hated to imagine what would happen if he came in and ripped into all of us or something. Especially since I'd heard he was not at all above doing that.

Damn. He must be fun at parties.

Well, fun vibe or not, it was time to focus on hockey. That would shake us all out of this sudden funk.

I was just grabbing my gloves off the bench when Christian appeared beside me.

My brain skidded to a halt, because... Christian. I was still so damn stupid over him, and any time he looked at me or especially when he spoke to me, I lost my train of thought.

And he'd asked me something. Hadn't he? Shit. What had he said?

I frantically rewound and—thank God—found the moment he'd spoken.

"So, you speak Russian?"

I nodded. "Yeah."

"Okay." He nodded sharply. "I'm going to shuffle locker stalls. Move you and Grekov closer to Rusanov. It'll be a lot easier for him if you're all next to each other."

"What about Yanni?" I tipped my head toward the goalie. "Seems like he speaks some."

Christian snorted. "Yeah, 'some' as in all the curses and insults."

"Ah, so he'd just be a bad influence."

"Pretty much. So we'll keep Grekov with you and Rusanov."

"You think we'll be much better?"

"No." He flashed a grin that shouldn't have been that cute. "But either way, that's Coach Baldwin's problem."

I laughed. "All right, sounds good." I gestured at my gear. "You want me to pack any of it up for—"

"No, don't worry about that. I still have to check a few things and air out your skates between now and the game, so just..." He waved his hand at the stall. "Leave it like normal after practice."

"You sure? If I can make it easier—"

"You're good." His smile made the floor tilt. "I've got it."

He walked away before I could say anything else. I didn't think he was bailing on the conversation, really—he had a clipboard in his hand and went straight to one of my other teammates, so I suspected he was just really busy.

I wondered if he knew what happened to my brain every time I saw him. Or every time he made eye contact with me. Or spoke to me.

I shook myself and pulled on my gloves. I needed to get a goddamned grip. It was one time. *One. Time.* Christian had undoubtedly moved on, and I needed to do the same thing.

I just wasn't sure how to do that. How the fuck was I supposed to move on when the man I'd literally been dreaming about for months was constantly *right there?*

Same way I'd handled coexisting with the crushes I didn't dare flirt with. Same way I stayed sane around straight men who were hot enough to make me stumble over my skates *and* my words. Just... focus on other things and move on.

I chanced a look around the room and found Christian talking to Marty with his back turned to me. With those workout pants perfectly hugging that beautiful ass.

Fuck me. It would be so, so much easier to forget him if I'd never been able to touch him. The straight guys were an exercise in frustration because they were a hundred percent off limits. The queer guys who weren't interested in me—same thing.

But Christian was off limits and I'd had a taste of him. Literally.

I shivered, biting my lip as I headed out to the ice. That one night with him had been a mistake. A hot, sexy, amazing mistake that I'd be dreaming about for years to come.

A hot, sexy, amazing mistake I wished like hell I could make just one more time.

Last season

I WAS LOSING MY DAMN MIND, SITTING HERE IN THIS bar. I couldn't decide if I was more starstruck by my teammates or just—

Oh, who was I kidding? I *was* starstruck, but the Rainiers at this table had nothing to do with why my tongue kept sticking to the roof of my mouth or why my brain kept going blank. I hoped they didn't notice. I was pretty sure the object of my distraction did notice, though, because every time his eyes flicked my way, the corner of his mouth would twitch like he was hiding a smile. Then my face would suddenly be so hot I had to be redder than the goal light, and he'd let the smile come to life, and...

Jesus Christ. Why was I so stupid over Christian Hayes? Yes, he was hot as hell, but so were half the guys I played hockey with. All night long, though, I'd been in teenager-with-a-crush mode. It was honestly a miracle I'd made it through the game without blowing a tire or crashing into a ref.

Ever since he'd broken into a smile when he'd realized I

was serious about the Pride Tape, he'd given me goose bumps just by glancing in my general direction. In that moment, he hadn't just been sexy, he'd been sweet and genuine. Someone who'd been deeply hurt but was suddenly finding a reason to smile again. I'd suddenly wanted more than anything to do whatever I could to give him more reasons to smile.

And maybe a few reasons to scream.

Oh, my God. Theo. Get a fucking grip.

I drank some more beer and rolled it around in my mouth, letting the cold make my teeth ache and distract me. It didn't last. The smart thing to do would be bow out and head back to my hotel. Maybe jerk off a time or two before passing out for the night. Maybe just... not sit here at a table with the man who was turning my brain to liquid.

Did I bow out and head back to my hotel? No.

Did I do the smart thing and put some space between me and Christian? No.

Was I getting a fucking grip and pulling myself together? Also no.

As the night went on, the guys at the table peeled away to head home. With each man who left, we'd all move chairs so we could hear each other and didn't have to shout across the long table.

By about one-thirty, we were down to four people.

Condit looked at his phone and sighed. "I should go. I have to get the kids up for school."

Wilcox wrinkled his nose. "Really? The morning after a game?"

"She puts them to bed and doesn't mind if I stay out with you idiots." Condit got up and pulled on his jacket. "Me getting them ready for school while she sleeps in seems like a fair trade."

"Ugh. No, thanks."

Christian rolled his eyes but didn't say anything.

Condit shook his head. "Yeah, come talk to me when you've got a wife busting her ass while you're gone most of the time." He smacked Wilcox's shoulder. "Let me know how that goes for you."

Wilcox grunted something. "I'm going to go close my tab."

He and Condit headed up to the bar, pulling out their wallets as they walked.

As soon as they were out of earshot, Christian, muttered, "Sometimes Wilcox wonders why he's still single." He brought his beer up. "I just can't begin to imagine."

"Right?" I laughed. "You'd think women would be falling all over him."

He chuckled, meeting my gaze over the rim of his glass.

And that was when I realized that... it was just the two of us.

The rest of the team was gone. Nothing remained but a couple of mostly empty beers and this weird silence that seemed to vibrate between us.

I was alone with Christian.

Oh, fuck. I had no idea what to say. I was usually fairly smooth with guys—enough that I didn't make an ass of myself and could even make a connection—but there was nothing smooth about me when I was around Christian.

And it didn't help that he kept looking at me like *that*.

Absently swirling his beer like a fine wine, he narrowed his eyes a little. "So, how was your first stint in the NAPH?"

I laughed nervously. "'First' kind of implies there will be a second time, don't you think?"

He pursed his lips and shrugged. "Sure. But I saw you

play tonight." His smile made the world sway. "You've got talent, Theo. Lots of it." He toasted me with his glass before bringing it up for a sip. "Don't sell yourself short."

My face was burning. "I... I mean, I think I'm good enough. But, um... I also think I might've landed on your dad's shit list tonight, you know?"

Christian's smile fell, and he stared at the table. Sighing, he nodded. "I wish I could tell you he'll let it go. But I know him."

Well, that was encouraging. "Great," I muttered. "So much for ever playing in the NAPH for real."

Christian studied me for a moment, his forehead creased. "Do you think it was a mistake? The tape?"

I gave it some actual thought, because I didn't want to just answer off the cuff and put my foot in my mouth. Absently rotating my glass on the table between my fingers, I sighed. "No. It wasn't a mistake. I stand by what I did." I swallowed hard. "But I know the fallout is probably going to suck."

"I'd love to say it won't be as bad as you think. With my dad involved, though..."

"Yeah. I know."

We were quiet for a long moment. Then he nudged the inside of my ankle with the toe of his shoe. "I'm glad you did it."

I searched his eyes.

He smiled, and it was a softer, friendlier expression than those teasing grins he'd been throwing me all night. "You took a huge risk to stand up for people like us. It wasn't just an empty gesture or lip service, you know? You knew going into it that there would be blowback, but you did it anyway, which means that all the queer fans who were in the stands tonight got to feel seen. That's not a small thing, you know?"

Swallowing hard, I nodded. "I'm glad the other guys followed suit, though."

"Me too. But someone had to take the first step, and it took some serious balls to do that." He nudged my foot again, this time running his up the inside of my leg. "Just... don't think it went unnoticed, you know?"

I almost didn't understand the words because the touch of his shoe was scrambling my brain. Fortunately, I caught up, and I managed a smile. "Thanks."

We shifted to lighter subjects after that, and all the while, my foot and the inside of my calf itched with the absence of that fleeting contact. God, I wanted to touch him. Really touch him. Every time he bit his lip, I wanted to know what his mouth tasted like. Every time he traced his fingers down the side of his glass, I wanted them on my back or—

Fuck. I was so losing it over him. Maybe because it was just more pleasant to drool over him than imagine my future after tonight. Or maybe because I was still feeling a little spicy and rebellious after my admittedly career-derailing move in the locker room. I didn't usually have this much courage with someone I'd just met, but why not run with it while it lasted?

Especially since... oh, hell. This was *not* one-sided.

I kept holding his gaze longer than was professional or platonic, and he held mine right back. When I leaned over the edge of the table, closing some of the space between us, he did the same, and oh, fuck me, his eyes absolutely flicked toward my lips more than once... same as mine kept flicking toward his.

He was the first to actually make contact beyond

nudging my foot under the table. I completely lost track of our conversation when he casually but boldly rested his hand on my forearm. Then it was gone as he reached for his glass instead. A few minutes later, he did it again, frying my brain just like the first time.

And a little while after that, with my heart absolutely slamming into my ribs, I laughed at something he said and nudged his wrist with the back of my hand. The way his eyes narrowed and his lips curled—fuck, it was almost predatory, and my whole body was on fire with need.

The second time, I was more deliberate about it, putting my hand more decisively over his forearm just like he'd done earlier. Christian exhaled, and I thought a little shiver went through him. He went for his drink as if he needed the cold, not the alcohol.

Goddamn, was he as into this as I was? Because every signal said he was.

And I could've done this subtle—and not-so-subtle—flirting all damn night, but unfortunately, we couldn't stay much longer. The bar closed at two, and we didn't want to keep the employees past the ends of their shifts.

"Guess we should get out of here," I said hoarsely as the staff started putting up chairs at other tables.

Christian looked around. "Yeah. Yeah, I guess we, uh..." He bit his lip as he made eye contact again.

It wasn't until after we'd settled the bill that he spoke again, presumably finishing the thought he'd cut off. As we pulled on our jackets, he met my gaze, his eyes narrow and smoldering. Then he made a not-at-all-subtle gesture of raking his eyes up and down my body. "So, um... My condo is a couple of blocks from here. Not much of a walk." He tipped his head toward the street and flicked up one eyebrow.

I gulped. "Uh." The Orcas had practice tomorrow. So did the Rainiers. Whether I got called up or sent down, I had to be at one rink or the other at nine. It was already almost two.

But those eyes... those lips...

I licked my own lips. "Sure. Yeah. I can walk you home."

He laughed softly. "Such a gentleman. Let's go."

The thing about Seattle was that a walk of "a couple of blocks" didn't always tell the whole story. If it was north-south in downtown, it was probably fine. But east-west, or any direction in some of the other neighborhoods? That could get dicey. Not because the streets were dangerous—they were just fucking *steep*.

As we stepped out of the bar, I had visions of us trudging up a near vertical hill while I was at half-mast and losing my damned mind. I was seriously debating if it was too cold for us to just step into an alley and start undoing zippers.

I was pleasantly surprised, however, to realize we were on a blessedly flat stretch of road. The only slope was the very gently decline into the condo's underground parking garage, and then we were in the elevator.

Oh, thank God. We're almost—

The doors hadn't even closed before Christian cupped my face in both hands and kissed me. We both stumbled, staggering back until I hit the wall, and I wrapped my arms around him.

Holy shit. I'd encountered some good kissers in my life, but Christian? I'd had concussions that didn't make the world list and spin the way this man's kiss did. He was explorative without being invasive, hungry without being too demanding. His body fit perfectly against mine, and the way his fingers slid through my hair sent goose bumps down my spine. Oh my God, I wanted him.

The ground jerked slightly beneath my feet. Then there was a quiet *ding*.

Before I could make sense of anything, Christian broke the kiss and grabbed my hand. "Let's go."

Go? Go where?

Ooh. Right. Elevator. Condo.

Bedroom.

I followed him, somehow managing to keep my feet under me, and he fumbled with his keys at the door. I was tempted to slide a hand over his ass or kiss the back of his neck or something, just to wind up him, but that would only delay us getting into his condo and out of our clothes.

"Stupid fucking—" He huffed. Then the lock finally clicked, and he shoved the door open. "Thank you. Jesus Christ."

He let me into his condo. As soon as I'd crossed the threshold, he grabbed on to me just like he had in the elevator, and just like that, we were kissing again. Hungrily. Greedily. I managed to kick the door shut, and then I nudged him back until his shoulders met the wall. He whimpered as I kissed him deeper and harder. His fingers ran through my hair. His hard-on rubbed mine through our clothes. His tongue teased mine as his little moans made my knees weak.

When I went for his throat, he murmured, "Holy shit..."

"I want you so bad," I mumbled against his neck. "I... God..." I rutted against him, driving moans from both of us.

"M-me too." He dragged his fingers up my back. Then he purred, "You know, it took some serious balls to stand up to him like that."

Serious balls? Stand up to—

Oh. Right. My mind had gone blank and the whole evening had disappeared, but I remembered now. And he'd mentioned it in the bar, but there was something different about his tone this time.

"Seemed like... Seemed like the right thing to do." I swallowed. "Standing up for us."

"Uh-huh. It was." Christian bit his lip. Then he slid his hand over my crotch, and I shivered so hard I almost lost my balance. Grinning, he said, "For the record, I'd have hooked up with you in a heartbeat anyway, but after tonight? Well..." He nudged me back a little and started undoing my pants. "I want to rock your fucking world."

And then he went to his knees and, right there in his living room, did exactly that.

CHAPTER 8

CHRISTIAN

This season

Even though I'd watched them interact in the locker room, I still stared as Theo and the new guy clomped past me on the way the ice. They were chatting away in rapid-fire Russian.

I couldn't believe Theo spoke Russian. Fluently, too, from the sound of it; he spoke with ease and confidence. There were none of the uncertain pauses or moments of intense concentration that I'd expect from someone who still had to work to speak a new language. Grekov's translator was walking with them, but he wasn't saying anything, so Theo must've been holding his own.

Yeah, I was definitely putting them together in the locker room, and no, I absolutely didn't get a little flutter in my chest as I watched them. Because it absolutely wasn't cute as hell to see Grekov light up at the sound of someone effortlessly speaking his own language, and it wasn't at all sweet or endearing to watch Theo make sure he had someone to talk to on the team.

Oh my God, they're adorable.

What if they started flirting in Russian? Would I even notice? Because I'd noticed with all the Russian speakers over the years that inflection and tone could be hard to read for someone who didn't know the language. One staff member a couple of seasons ago had intervened when he'd seen two teammates arguing in the hallway. Turned out they were just having a very animated conversation.

So if Grekov and Theo started flirting, I probably wouldn't even notice unless one of them blushed or something.

And what the fuck does it matter if they do *flirt? Idiot.*

I shook myself and headed down the runway to take my place on the bench for practice. Some days, I was busy the entire time—replacing skate blades, adjusting visors, fixing goalie helmets. Other days, everyone's gear did what it was supposed to do without breaking. Those days were deceptive. It made for an easy practice, but it often meant something was going to wait until the game to break. If I didn't have to do much right now, I'd spend the rest of the morning and part of the afternoon scrutinizing every strap, skate, and screw to see if something was about to fail.

Today was somewhere in the middle. Almost everyone's gear was working the way it was supposed to, with the exception of Yanni's mask (which needed a new strap midway through practice). It was pretty quiet on the equipment front, which meant tonight would probably be a shitshow.

It also meant that, for the time being, I could mostly hang back and watch the guys practice. As it often did lately, my gaze kept sliding to one player in particular. Watching him skate. Watching him shoot.

Today, watching him talking with Grekov in between drills, both of them laughing and carrying on as easily as the guys chatting in English. Though Grekov was a defenseman, he stuck close to Theo through practice whenever they weren't actually skating. Any time one of the coaches was explaining a drill or something, Theo was leaning in close, speaking quietly to Grekov, who was nodding along.

I couldn't help smiling. I'd seen a lot of players come through here who spoke little to no English. They picked it up eventually, but it took time, and even when they did, sometimes they still felt left out. I always felt bad for the guys when they joined us at bars or whatever, and I could just see it in their eyes that they really wanted to be part of the conversation, but they couldn't. The pop culture references. The slang. The figures of speech. It had to be a lot.

And of course, the heavy accents and even heavier intoxication didn't make anyone any more intelligible. I still remembered one outing a year or two ago when we'd had a Finn, Korhonen, who was just starting to get the hang of English. We'd all been drinking, and Halko had been absolutely shitfaced. After Halko had been carrying on for a while, Korhonen looked at me and said, "I thought I was getting good at English, but..." He'd waved a frustrated hand at Halko.

I'd laughed and clapped his shoulder, and I'd had to fight hard not to slur myself as I said, "Oh, no, you're good." Gesturing at Halko, I'd said, "He's so fucking drunk, *none* of us can understand him."

Korhonen had been visibly relieved, but not nearly as much as Grekov, who'd lucked into a pair of teammates who spoke his language, even if one of them would only be here for so long.

I'd once heard that the way someone could tell if they were fluent enough to speak like a native was if they could tell a joke and if they could understand when someone else told one. From the way Grekov and Theo kept making each other chuckle... Yeah. Theo definitely spoke like a native, and that seemed to put Grekov seriously at ease.

And no, it didn't make me jealous.

Not in the slightest.

Not at all.

"Hey." Marty bumped my elbow. "You trying to see how much that strap can take?"

"Trying to—" I looked down, and I realized I'd been playing with the strap I'd removed from Yanni's goalie mask. And by "playing with it," I meant, twisting it tighter and tighter between my fingers.

Face hot, I relaxed my fingers and let the elastic unwind itself. "Nah. I'm..." I couldn't find an explanation, so I just shrugged it away and cleared my throat. "As soon as they're done, I'm shuffling stalls around." I glanced at Marty and pretended not to notice his puzzled expression. "Mathis is fluent in Russian, so I'm going to put him and Grekov next to Rusanov."

"Oh. Okay. No problem."

Fortunately, he either decided to drop the subject of what I was doing with the strap, or he got distracted by something else (which was more likely; the work of an equipment manager was never done for very long). Either way, he let it go and disappeared back into the locker room.

On the ice, the players wrapped up some special teams work, and then the offensive coach wanted to run the forwards and defensemen through some drills. The goalies got a much-deserved break after twenty minutes of fighting off the power play, and they both skated up to the bench for some water.

Easton, the backup goalie, pulled off his mask and wiped his face. "Okay, am I concussed? Or did I just see Mathis talking to the new guy in Russian?"

"No, you're not concuss—well, you might be, but those two chatting in Russian? Yes."

He flipped me off, probably for the concussion remark, then turned to watch the other players. "Well, that's good. Especially with Bondarev still out."

I nodded. Bondarev was on the second defensive pairing, and he'd be out for the rest of the season thanks to hip surgery. And Klokov had taken a leave of absence for personal reasons; no one knew if or when he'd be back. So for a Russian speaker who struggled with English, that left Rusanov... and Theo.

Theo, who was already mercilessly attractive.

Theo, who was the last man I had any business wanting.

Theo, who was putting a new player at ease just by giving him someone to shoot the shit with in his own language.

I suppressed a string of curses that might've even made some hockey players wince.

I wanted him. Plain and simple.

But if I valued either of our careers—and I did—I couldn't fucking touch him.

I WAS ALWAYS RESTLESS BEFORE A GAME, BUT NEVER like this. Sometimes I wondered if it was just the team's energy rubbing off on me; Marty theorized that most hockey players had some variety of ADHD, so there was a lot of energy in that locker room. Especially if they'd all had to sit through a meeting or review film or something. When they were all gearing up and champing at the bit to hit the ice, the room damn near vibrated with their collective itch to *move*.

He might've been right. About them, and also about it rubbing off on me. Mostly, though, it was the pressure of my job. Not a bad thing by any means—I loved what I did, stress and all. Maybe I *was* a little like the players in that regard. I was always wound up and ready to go, go, go. There was always something for the equipment managers to do, and when we hit a lull—which we usually did in the hour or so before a game if we'd done our jobs—it made me twitchy. It made me worry I'd missed something, and it also made me want to just get the game going so we could start addressing problems as they came up in between packing and staging gear for a road trip.

I needed the chaos. I thrived on it. The calm before the storm was too calm with too big a storm ahead, and I needed that storm to *get here* so I could *do stuff*.

That was my normal, but now the stress felt less like restless excitement and more like... well... *stress*.

The Rainiers' locker room was my happy place. It was where I did my job, and I did it well. But lately... fuck. My dad stressed me out like always, but he wasn't the issue these days. Not all of it, anyway.

There was a man in that locker room right now. A man whose moans still echoed in my ears after all this time. A man whose eyes occasionally locked on mine and still burned with the same hunger they had when I'd slid my hand into his pants. Goddamn, I wanted him again so damn bad.

I'd been trying to find an outlet for this horniness, but it just wasn't happening. None of the hookup apps were offering up anyone with a prayer of putting Theo out of my mind. I could get an orgasm or three out of it, sure, but I could do that with my hand. I'd be thinking of Theo either way, so what was the point of involving someone else?

And now, here I was, in this locker room with fuck all to do for the next hour and a half. Every skate blade in the building was sharpened, including the spares. Every hole in every jersey, sock, or pants was mended or patched. Every helmet, skate, and piece of protective gear was in working order.

So... fuck it. I needed to get out of here for a bit. If someone needed me, they had my cell.

For now, I wandered the arena's ice level.

I knew this facility like the back of my hand. Every room and closet behind every door. I knew where I was relative to the stands, too; if I walked out to the ice from anywhere, I'd know exactly where I'd pop out, whether it was by the Zamboni gate or a random spot between two sections of seating. It was like a second home to me. Hell, I probably knew it better than I knew my own condo building.

It was cold, shadowy, and familiar down here. Quiet in a way—not many voices or activity, but the hums and vibrations of all the systems that kept the air flowing and the ice frozen.

Usually, a walk through here settled me. It burned off some nervous energy and helped to center my scattering thoughts. By the time I made it back to the locker room, I'd be as calm as I ever was before a game.

Tonight, I'd made three laps and still felt like I was this close to coming unglued.

I found the area where the Zambonis were parked when they were out of use. In a couple of hours, they'd be rumbling to life and making their slow, methodical rounds to resurface the ice. For now, they were silent, tucked into an alcove beside the ice crews' buckets and snow shovels. Both had brightly colored wraps advertising sponsors—a car dealership on one, an investment firm on the other—but the colors were dull and lifeless back here beneath the half-hearted glow of some fluorescent lights.

I'd driven a Zamboni at the practice rink when my dad had coached in the minors when I was a teenager. I kind of missed that. There was something deeply satisfying about turning a scuffed-up sheet of ice into a smooth, shiny surface. If I hadn't scored the gig as an equipment manager, I'd probably still be driving one to this day.

Ah, well. I liked my job. It was more stress, but it was also more money, and it was more satisfying in its own ways.

More frustrating, too, because it meant being in the locker room with the smoking hot hockey player I couldn't fucking touch.

Groaning to myself, I leaned against a Zamboni and rubbed my temples. At least there weren't any cameras back here. The last thing I needed was someone watching me standing here losing my stupid mind and feeling sorry for my stupid self.

It wasn't beneath me at all to crave something I couldn't or shouldn't have, and a hot, gay hockey player was absolutely on that list. Dad had warned me when I took this job that the players on his team were off-limits. So were the farm teams. So were visiting teams. He'd probably blow a gasket if I dated someone playing in a beer league. So, yeah, there was a certain amount of forbidden fruit action going on here. A certain temptation to have what had been explicitly roped off.

But I couldn't make myself believe that was the only thing that kept drawing me to Theo Mathis.

Was the sex really that good, though? Or was I just remembering it fondly because it had been hot and rebellious?

That night with him had been furtive as only one-night stands could be. Feverish and frantic, both of us determined to wring every drop of pleasure we could from the one and only time we'd have each other.

But now he was back. Even if we did say "fuck the rules" and had a rematch, would it be as hot? Would it be as fun?

Probably. Especially because I'd actually get that amazing dick in my ass this time, and—

I swore under my breath. I was so fucking stupid. I was—

Footsteps approached. They tapped against the concrete and echoed off the walls, and I prayed like hell they belonged to Theo at the same time I prayed they didn't. It was the Zamboni drivers, right? It had to be. Who else would be down here?

I looked up right as the interloper turned the corner and came into view, and—

Oh, fuck me.

Theo was dressed in a black Rainiers' hoodie and matching track pants, and he was as unreasonably sexy in those as he was in a suit or his gear.

And from the way he locked eyes with me, he hadn't found me by accident. Sliding his hands into the front pocket of his hoodie, he came a little closer, out of the shadows and into the blanched glow of the overhead lights.

Fluorescents weren't flattering for anyone, but they didn't make him any less hot. I didn't imagine there was much that could.

"Uh. Hey." I pushed myself off the Zamboni and slid my hands into my own pockets. "What, um... What are you doing down here?"

He shrugged. "Just going for a walk."

I moistened my lips. "Yeah. Same."

We held each other's gazes. Neither of us spoke. Neither of us moved.

I shifted my weight. "Shouldn't you be getting ready for the game?"

"Shouldn't you?"

God, the restlessness was going to drive me out of my mind. "Everything's done." I forced a nervous laugh. "Until someone breaks something while they're getting dressed, anyway."

Theo's chuckle was almost soundless, and it didn't last. He dropped his gaze and chewed his lip, but he didn't retreat.

Fuck. Now what?

The fluorescent lights buzzed above us. The ventilation system hummed along with other unseen machinery—probably everything keeping the ice at precisely the right temperature. Elsewhere, voices and movement echoed, but they were all far away, and we were tucked back from the main hallway. No one was stumbling across us in this little alcove with the Zambonis.

Just like Theo hadn't stumbled across me. Because he'd clearly come looking for me, but now that he was here, he didn't seem to remember why. Or maybe he'd lost his nerve? My mouth had gone completely dry and my brain was almost blank except for *I want you*. That helpful little mantra kept running through my head like a flashing neon sign, as if my mind wanted to catch my mouth off guard and make it say the words out loud.

It was Theo who finally broke the silent standoff. "Listen." He let his shoulders fall as he fixed a plaintive look on me. "I don't want to make it something it isn't, but the last time I was here..." He chewed his lip and furrowed his brow as if he didn't know what to say.

"We can't do it again." Why didn't I sound convinced? "We... shouldn't."

"I know," he whispered. "But it happened. And now we're both here, and..." He shook his head, breaking eye contact.

I studied him, not sure how to read his expression. Did he regret what we'd done before? Hell, probably. He should have. I didn't want to, and in some ways I didn't, but I did regret doing something that had him stressed out and miserable now.

I took a breath. "Do you regret it?"

"No." He didn't even hesitate. "I don't."

I blinked. "You don't?"

"No. Do you?"

I opened my mouth to speak, but hesitated. I hadn't even been able to answer that definitely for myself. Now he wanted me to give him a straight answer? Fuck. Anything I said threatened to either make the tension between us unbearable, or make things unbearably awkward. And we did have to function together to some extent for as long as he was playing for the Rainiers.

But hadn't I also been losing my damned mind ever since that one night we spent together? We'd already crossed into forbidden territory and turned the tension between us up to a nine. Was I really going to make it worse if I told him the God's honest truth?

I swallowed, which took some work. "I don't regret it. I just..." I stared at the concrete between us as I pushed a hand through my hair. "Sometimes I think it was a mistake because now I can't fucking concentrate around you. And other times... Other times, I think the only mistake was not getting your number before you left."

The hitch of his breath was so subtle, I might've imagined it. It might've been a random noise from one of the many systems functioning above and around us. But I didn't think so.

I cautiously met his gaze, and he was staring back at me with wide eyes.

He swept his tongue across his lips. "So we're... on the same page."

"Are we?"

Theo nodded slowly. "I've been kicking myself all this time because I should've gotten your number." He gave a quiet, bitter laugh. "We both knew I was going to be gone the next morning. I, um..." His expression turned sheepish, and now he was the one staring at the concrete as he shyly murmured, "I figured since you didn't ask, you just wanted it to be a one-time thing."

My shoulders sagged. Hadn't I made the same damn assumption? "That's what I thought, too. And I mean... I also knew it was a really, really bad idea." I swallowed. "It still is."

"Yeah. I know." He rubbed the back of his neck and sighed. "But it's been stuck in my head ever since, and now that I'm here..."

Fuck. My heart was pounding so hard it was almost painful. "So what do we do?"

Theo was quiet for a moment. Then he pushed his shoulders back and looked me right in the eyes. "Maybe we stop frustrating ourselves."

I gulped. "So... hook up again?"

"Why not?" He shrugged as if it were really that simple. "It was fun the first time."

My voice trembled as I said, "It was, but if we get caught, you're fucked as a hockey player. You know that, right?"

"Yeah." He swallowed. "I do." He stepped closer. "But I have a feeling I'm fucked as a hockey player either way. As long as your dad has a hand in things..." He frowned and shook his head. "So why hold back on the things he *can't* control?"

I... could not argue against that logic. I knew I should. There was a lot on the line for both of us if we were busted together. I didn't want to lose this job, and I also didn't want to be what derailed Theo's hockey career.

But I couldn't get any of that past the tip of my tongue. Especially because Theo was close now. Really close. Close enough I could reach out and touch him. Close enough that when we both exhaled, the faint clouds of our breath mingled in the space between us.

Fuck it.

"God, I want you," I growled as I grabbed the front of his hoodie. I hauled him to me, and Theo met my kiss so readily, so aggressively, he may as well have been the one who'd initiated it. Then he shoved me back against the Zamboni, and my knees and spine went weak because holy fuck, this man was hot.

Pinned between him and the ice resurfacer, at the mercy of the kiss that I'd been dreaming about for months, all my fear and anxiety melted away. Oh, the risks were still there, and I knew we were taking them. I just didn't give a shit. I was too hungry for this man and everything his aggressive kiss both promised and demanded.

Damn it, did we have to do this here? Couldn't we have waited until we were someplace we could start tearing off clothes and going to town on each other? Okay, no. No, there'd been no more waiting. I wanted him and couldn't wait another minute to have his mouth and his touch. The rest...

Well, I couldn't wait for that either, but I didn't have much choice.

Theo touched his forehead to mine and ground against me, his hard-on unmistakable through the soft material of our workout pants. "I don't care what your dad thinks," he panted. "I want you. I've been wanting you for months. What he doesn't know won't hurt us."

I whimpered softly, my knees trembling beneath me. When had anyone—hookup, boyfriend, or anyone in between—ever made me feel so irresistibly desired? And how the hell I could I resist that? Especially when I'd been losing my stupid mind over him already?

"Well..." I swallowed hard and met his gaze. "We could skip going to the bar after the game."

Interested sparked in his eyes. "Yeah? What do you suggest instead?"

"I was thinking we go back to my condo and you fuck me until I cry."

His lips parted and his eyebrows rose. Then he closed his eyes and tilted his head back, exhaling a thin cloud. "Fuuuck."

"What? You don't like that idea?"

"No, I do." He brought his gaze back down to meet mine, his eyes full of fire. "I'm just not sure how I'm going to get through the game when I know I'm gonna be balls deep in your later."

I shivered. "Sorry?"

"Uh-huh. Sure you are." He pulled me in close again. "Honestly, I only had two regrets last time."

"Oh yeah?"

Theo nodded. "One, the part where I didn't get your number. Two?" He rutted his hard dick against mine again. "I never got to fuck that ass of yours."

I whimpered softly, holding on to fistfuls of his hoodie. "God, Theo..."

He claimed another long, bruising kiss. When he relented this time, we were both even more out of breath. "After the game. Please. I can stop and get condoms. I can—"

"I've got them." I licked my lips, almost grazing his. "Haven't needed them in a long time, but I've got them."

He drew back enough to meet my gaze. "You haven't needed them?"

"No." I slid my hands up the smooth front of his hoodie. "I haven't been laid since that night with you."

He blinked. "Really?"

"Mmhmm. What can I say?" I wrapped my arms around his neck. "No one else has turned my head."

Theo's eyes widened. Then he growled into another deep, hungry kiss—one that promised tonight would absolutely be worth all the months of blue balls.

"We should get back to the locker room," he mumbled against my lips. "Gotta... Gotta get ready for the game." He kissed me again anyway.

After a moment, I managed, "We should go. The Zamboni drivers will be..."

He pulled back and glanced past around us as if he'd forgotten where we were. What we were leaning against.

Licking his lips, he met my gaze. As he loosened his embrace, he said, "After the game?"

I grinned. "After the game."

CHAPTER 9

THEO

It would be a genuine miracle if I made it through this game without falling on my face, bursting into flames, or both. Especially with Christian constantly there, standing along-side the bench between the backup goalie and the stick rack, waiting to jump into action if anyone's gear broke.

Just getting back to the locker room had been an exer-cise in frustration. We'd both wanted to calm down a little before we stepped out into the flow of foot traffic. The workout pants we both had on would absolutely incriminate us if anyone glanced below the belt.

But how in the hell was I supposed to calm down with Christian right there? Especially after we'd made out against that Zamboni? And made plans to get naked after the game? After we'd come out and said I'd be fucking him after this?

Fortunately, we'd both pulled ourselves together enough to discreetly slip away. He went left and I went right, both of us following the hallway that went all the way around the arena. My direction meant going the long way, which was fine by me—more time for my dick to completely settle down.

Though it did settle down pretty quick when I stepped out into the hall and almost crashed into the Zamboni drivers on their way in.

One of them cocked a brow. "You lost, kid?"

"I, uh..." I cleared my throat and laughed, my face suddenly hot. "Still learning my way around the building. Guess I made a wrong turn." I looked around. "The locker room is..."

"That way," the other said tersely, gesturing down the hall. "Ain't no reason for you to be back here."

"No, no. Sorry. Like I said—made a wrong turn." I laughed nervously. "Thanks for pointing me in the right direction!"

Then I got the hell out of there, my heart thumping with every step.

Oh. Fuck. *That* could've been awkward if we'd kept making out an extra thirty seconds or so.

I walked the perimeter of the arena, then took a second lap just to pull my head together and calm down. As excited as I was about hooking up with Christian later, it was just that—later.

Between now and then, I had to have my head in the game. Hockey wasn't one of those games someone could play with their mind someplace else. It required all eight mental cylinders or else things went wrong. Sometimes catastrophically wrong. Skating at upwards of twenty miles an hour, staying aware of the other nine skaters on the ice, maneuvering around those other skaters, and controlling a puck, all while others tried to steal the puck and knock me on my ass, meant engaging every available brain cell. And that was before factoring in things like finding a shooting lane, predicting the goalie's reaction, shooting to get around that predicted reaction, actually taking the shot, and maybe finding the back of the net.

There was no room for thinking with my dick.

By the time I made it to the locker room and started gearing up, I was mostly in game mode. Even when I glanced at Christian, I kept my head together and focused on my pre-game routine.

Shooting the shit with Grekov helped. We'd spent part of the morning chatting about Seattle and what there was to do in this area, and he'd apparently looked up a few more places since then. Though I was fluent in Russian, I didn't speak it as often as I spoke English. It took a bit of a mental shift to get into the flow of conversation with someone, and that shift helped me pull my focus away from Christian.

"What about the market?" Grekov asked as he taped his socks. "Pike Place?"

"It's worth visiting." I sat down on the bench and started taping my own socks. "I'd wait until the summer, though. It's a farmers' market more than anything, so there's more selection, you know? But go during the week. It's too crowded on the weekends."

Grekov nodded along as I spoke. "So, summer. Good idea. And the Space Needle?"

I told him what little I knew about visiting the Space Needle. I hadn't been up in it since I was a kid, and that was back when they still had the rotating restaurant. From what I'd heard, that had been converted into a glass-bottomed observation deck. Some people I knew thought it was worth visiting. Some didn't.

"Busy on weekends?" he asked.

I chuckled. "Everything worth doing is busy on weekends. Trust me."

He laughed. "Maybe you come with me?" He pointed his chin toward Sam, his translator, who was doing something on his phone a few feet away. "Give him a break."

"Pfft. He doesn't need a break."

Sam looked up from his phone and cocked a brow at me. I responded with an innocent shrug, which prompted an eyeroll.

Snickering, I nudged Grekov with my glove. "You're on. When we actually have some downtime, we'll hit the Space Needle."

He smiled broadly, and I returned it. As we finished putting ourselves together for the game, I made a mental note to look up some of the other places a tourist might enjoy. Wasn't there an observation deck on the Columbia Tower that was even higher than the Space Needle? I'd have to look that up.

Right now, though, I had a game to think about.

First things first: warmups.

And on the way to the tunnel, I glanced to my right without thinking.

And almost tripped.

Goddamn. One glance into those mischievous blue eyes, and I was right back to stupid.

Fuck my life. I *had* to get it together. Later tonight, I could forget about hockey and get naked with Christian.

Right now, I needed to forget about getting naked with Christian—*oh my God*—and focus. On. *Hockey.*

I followed my teammates down the tunnel, and as soon as my steel met the ice, my mind *was* on hockey. Skating. Passing. Shooting. *Hockey.*

Okay. Okay, I had this. I could do this. I wasn't doing so hot about getting pucks into the net, but at least I was staying on my skates and hadn't, like, let go of my stick or something. Maybe that meant I could really keep my head together for the game.

By the time line rushes started, I was pretty confident I wouldn't make an ass of myself tonight.

But holy fuck, every time I so much as glanced toward the bench, I was lucky I didn't lose an edge.

Fuck me. I could still taste his kiss. I swore I could still feel his hard-on pressing against mine. I couldn't really—my athletic cup didn't feel nearly as good as Christian's hard dick rubbing insistently against—

I stumbled, then bumped into Sorenson as he skated by. We both staggered a little, but he caught himself on the boards and I somehow managed to get my dumbass upright.

"Easy there, Mathis." Sorenson smacked my shin with his stick. "You hiding whiskey in your water bottle or something?"

"Pfft. I wish. Sorry, man!"

He tapped my leg again. "Don't worry about it." As he skated away, he threw over his shoulder, "Dinner's on you next time we're on the road!"

I just laughed. Seemed like a fair trade.

Warmups ended a few minutes later. On the way into the locker room, I caught Christian's eye, and the little shit smirked at me. I chuckled and rolled my eyes.

As I listened to Coach's pregame speech, I sent up a prayer to anyone who was listening that we won this thing in regulation. Knowing my luck, we'd end up in one of those protracted shootouts where nobody could get that decisive goal, and it was just shooter after shooter after shooter. What was the league record for shootouts, anyway? Like nineteen, twenty rounds?

Fuck that. Regulation win tonight, or else I was going to wind up banging Christian in the parking garage.

The first period didn't instill much faith that this was going to be settled in sixty minutes. They scored. We scored. They got a power play. We got a power play. They scored. We scored. By the end of the second period, it was 2-2. Both teams had the same number of penalty minutes. Both goalies had made exactly eleven saves.

We still had forty minutes of hockey, and this sport was chaotic enough that anything could happen during that time. All it would take was one side tilting the ice and hammering a goalie, and the score could become promisingly lopsided (ideally in Seattle's favor). But given my postgame plans and the decidedly even game so far, I wasn't holding my breath that things would change.

Five minutes into the second period, I was eating those words.

The first two minutes were more of the same from the previous period, but then Philly got a breakaway at the worst possible moment. Our defensemen had been out for almost the full two minutes. They were gassed, and thinking the action was well into our offensive zone, they'd gone to the bench for a much-needed line change. In the same moment, Condit did a badly timed drop pass, probably expecting one of his wingers to be right behind him. Unbeknownst to him, one of Philly's forwards had swooped in. He stole the puck and flew toward our end of the ice.

There wasn't much our skaters could do. They were way too far behind him, and he was one of those guys who was both fast as hell and deadly with the puck.

Yanni was ready for him, glove and stick both poised for whatever came his way. The player wound back for a slapper, and Yanni dropped into the butterfly position, probably anticipating a low shot.

As soon as the goalie went down, the player switched to his backhand and chipped it right over Yanni's left shoulder.

Goals like that weren't great for morale. A turnover in the middle of a line change that left our zone undefended—that had everyone off their game for a couple of shifts. We pulled it together and found our game again, but not before their rookie scored his first NAPH goal, making this a two-goal game. Fuck.

We rallied, though. In the minute and a half after that rookie's goal, we peppered their netminder with eight shots on goal. Another shot pinged loudly off the crossbar. That sound could throw a goalie off his game, so this might be our chance if we kept hammering him with shots.

I hit the ice a few seconds after that crossbar shot. Condit and Wilcox were tied up the defensive zone; they'd been out for almost a minute of very intense play and were probably running out of steam. They'd tried to peel away for a line change, but only Sorenson had been able to get off the ice. We needed a whistle, or we needed to get the puck out of our end so our exhausted forwards could get to the bench.

That was when I realized Philly was so focused on a puck battle in the corner, they hadn't noticed me. Grekov and I were both behind their D with nothing but open ice between us and their goal.

Condit got the puck free and started up the wall. I tapped my stick to call for the puck, and he sent it my way. Their defenseman noticed me and charged toward me, so as soon as the puck hit my tape, I passed it to Grekov... but my damn stick snapped in half.

I shouted, "Fuck!" as the bottom half of the stick went flying. Before it had even landed, I dropped the handle to the ice, kicked the puck toward Grekov, and sprinted toward the bench.

Christian was ready and waiting, holding out a new stick handle first.

Our eyes locked for a split second as I grabbed the stick *—oh my God, you're so pretty—*and I gave him a nod of acknowledgment before I tore after my teammates.

Grekov was charging toward the other end of the ice with Rusanov. Condit and Wilcox both sped toward the bench, and I hurried after Grekov and Rusanov, confident that fresh bodies were on their way.

Rusanov had the puck now. He shouldered his way through a much smaller forward, but a huge defenseman was coming his way, so he passed the puck to me. Abrahamsson appeared in the zone, and I passed to him. We cycled it, keeping the Philly players moving while we tried to find or open a shooting lane.

I once again called for the puck, and Abrahamsson sent it to me. The puck hit my tape but now there was too much traffic in front of the net, so I passed to Grekov. I thought he'd send it to Rusanov, who was wide open, but instead, he wound up and fired a one-timer at the net.

The puck whizzed past everyone in front of the goal and sailed right through the netminder's five-hole.

Before the light even went on or the horn sounded, the crowd roared to their feet as Grekov fist-pumped.

Now we had some serious momentum going, and Coach shouted at us to "Keep it up, keep it up!"

We did, too. The ice tilted hard in our direction. There was usually a brief delay—a minute or two at most—between when a goal was scored and when the arena announcer called it out. The situation room sometimes needed a little time to figure out who got the primary and secondary assists and the precise time on the clock when the puck crossed the goal line. So we were usually well into another shift when he'd bellow, "The Seattle goal!" followed by the names of the players responsible for it.

Tonight, before he'd even had a chance to announce Grekov's goal, Sorenson put another puck into Philly's net.

Awesome. Now the score was tied. We could focus on getting and widening a lead instead of digging ourselves out of a two-point hole.

Except... now the score was tied. Again.

So help me if this game goes into fucking overtime...

JUST MY GODDAMNED LUCK—AFTER A SPICY BACK-AND-forth game, time ran out when the score was 6-6.

It *would've* been 5-4 in our favor if the refs had been halfway competent. Early in the third, Coach Baldwin challenged Philly's goal for offside. On the replay, it was blatantly clear that the play was offside; the defenseman's skate had cleared the blue line enough that there was a *painfully* obvious strip of not-blue ice between his skate blade and the line when his team's puck carrier entered the zone. It wasn't even questionable—it was offside. Full stop.

But *nooo*, the refs said it was onside, so the goal stayed, *and* we were assessed a bench penalty for delay of game. That gave Philly's power play a chance to rack up another point and put us back into a two-point deficit.

Sheer anger drove us to pocket two more goals, one of them with only twenty-three seconds left on the clock, and tie up the game.

So now... overtime.

Goddammit.

There would be no never-ending shootout tonight, though—nineteen seconds into overtime, Philly's star center scored, and just like that, it was over.

I was bummed that we'd lost. We still got a point, which was great, but losing sucked.

Secretly, though? I was just glad the damn game was over. All I had to do was get the hell out of here and finish what Christian and I had started up against that Zamboni.

And... also I had to ignore him as much as possible so I didn't telegraph to everyone in the room that I was painfully horny.

Just breathe. Get a shower, get some food, and then go get Christian. Just. Breathe.

That would've been a lot more doable if Christian had been someone who was easy to ignore. But even for the guys who weren't quietly lusting after him, he was very noticeable.

At one point, Christian put his hands on his hips and looked around the room. "Where is my Coach bag? Has anyone seen my Coach bag?" He huffed melodramatically. "That bag is expensive, gentlemen! Where is—*ooh,* there it is!" Then he picked up the gear bag marked *Coach Baldwin.*

Everyone in the room chuckled. Christian hoisted the giant bag onto his shoulder, struck a pose, and strutted out of the room like a model on a runway, leaving the team in stitches.

As I watched him go, warmth rushed into my face, but it wasn't a blush. It wasn't embarrassment. It was straight-up *heat.* I was hot from the game, but now I was even hotter from watching him goofing around and being, well, him.

Goddamn. I could not get out of this place and into Christian's bed—into Christian—fast enough.

I still had to shower and shove some food into my face.

Both of those especially needed to happen before I went to Christian's place. I was just impatient. Restless with need. Now that I no longer needed to concentrate on hockey, my mind was free to grab on to all those fantasies I'd had about him since the first night.

Except I didn't need to get an inopportune hard-on, so I made myself concentrate on hockey just so I wouldn't embarrass myself in the locker room or the showers.

All I had to do was shower. Get dressed. Eat enough that I wouldn't pass out.

And then get the hell over to Christian's condo.

Almost there...

CHAPTER 10

CHRISTIAN

The Rainiers weren't heading out on the road and didn't have a game tomorrow. That meant this was one of those nights my crew and I weren't scrambling to get everything packed up and either on the truck or laid out for the morning skate. The laundry was dealt with. The big fans were set up to air out everything in the dressing room. I did a walkthrough to make sure everything was where it needed to be, made a note of a few small tasks that could be dealt with tomorrow, and gave my crew the green light to head out for the night.

"Nice job, everyone," I said as the four of us headed for the garage. "See you at the rink."

This was when some of us would go join the team at a nearby bar to celebrate a win or commiserate over a loss, but a lot of times, we'd just head home to enjoy one of those relaxed and relatively early nights that didn't come as often as people thought. These multi-game home stands were the best, especially when the games weren't back-to-back.

I didn't go to the bar tonight. I headed straight home, my heart pounding the entire way. That little interlude beside the Zamboni had me way too spun up for polite company, and I just hoped and prayed Theo didn't come to his senses, realize this was a terrible idea, and bail.

It *was* a terrible idea. It had been the first time. It was beside the Zamboni. It definitely was right now.

But oh my God, I wanted him.

I was just walking in the front door when my phone pinged, sending my pulse skyward. Silently pleading with him not to have second thoughts, I looked at the screen.

Theo: *Leaving now. Be there in 15.*

Oh, yes. Oh, thank God, yes. Fifteen minutes sounded like torture at this point, but I could wait.

Christian: *Door's unlocked. You still remember the way to my bedroom?*

I chuckled at my own text. He probably didn't remember much about my condo, but it wasn't exactly a labyrinth and he wasn't stupid. I doubted he'd have any trouble finding my bedroom, my bed, or me in it.

A moment later, he replied:

Theo: *If I get lost, I have Google Maps.*

I snorted. Smartass.

In the bedroom, I put some condoms and lube on the nightstand, and then stripped out of my clothes. I loved foreplay as much as anyone, but the foreplay between us had started the moment he'd arrived in the Seattle locker room. I was tired of waiting. I needed this man to dick me down, and I needed him to do it the minute he walked in the door.

So, I got to work. I bottomed enough—mostly on my own with toys these days—that I didn't need a lot of prep, but tonight I got myself ready like it was the first time. Naked and already a little out of breath, I lay back on my bed with my legs apart. I fingered myself until I was long past ready; I was tempted to use a toy, but decided I wanted to be on this edge when he arrived—hungry for more and ready to lose my damn mind with the need for something bigger. I wanted Theo to be that something bigger that finally stretched me as much as I needed. I wanted him to be what finally took me from turned on to losing my damn mind.

By the time my front door opened and the air pressure changed, I was so keyed up, I actually whimpered. My toes curled and I bit my lip, slowing my strokes as the anticipation threatened to make me go off too soon.

The footsteps coming down the hall were almost inaudible over my thundering heart. Then Theo stepped into the room, and he stopped dead. He stared at me, slack-jawed, which gave me the perfect moment to stare right back at him. The players always wore suits going in and out of the arena, and he was still wearing his. It was navy blue with a near-black tie, which he'd loosened a little. Oh my God, he looked good.

He found his breath and met my gaze. "Fuck..."

"Good idea," I murmured.

He huffed a soundless laugh and crossed the room, undoing his tie the rest of the way. "Any other night, I'd watch you play with yourself like that, but this time..." He shook his head as he climbed onto the bed. "If I'm not balls deep in you in the next thirty seconds—"

We both cut him off as our mouths came together. I raked my free hand through his hair, and he growled against me as he fumbled with his belt and zipper.

"Get these clothes off," I pleaded between kisses as I tugged at his shirt. "Now."

His lips curved against mine, and the jingle of his belt

buckle and the sound of his zipper had me arching off the bed. Yes, yes, please, yes.

As much as I didn't want to stop kissing him, it was kind of necessary if he was going to get naked, so I didn't protest when he sat up. He leaned over me to snatch the condom off the nightstand. He started to get up again, but paused, and then guided his dick to my mouth.

Fuck. Oh, fuck. I loved the slide of his hard cock between my lips and over his tongue. The salt of his skin and his pre-cum.

"God, yeah," he whispered, rocking in and out. "Been thinking about your mouth for *months*."

I moaned around his dick and looked up at him, finding those dark eyes fixed on me and smoldering with a need so intense, I was probably going to be buying a new bed after this.

Bring it, baby. Fuck me until your *neighbors complain.*

Theo pushed a little deeper, almost to my gag reflex. Then he groaned and withdrew. "Can't wait." He tore the condom wrapper with his teeth. "This is gonna be quick, but—"

"Don't care." I withdrew my fingers and spread my legs wider, my whole damn body vibrating as I watched him roll on the condom.

He was between my thighs and guiding himself in when it clicked in my brain that he hadn't even bothered undressing. In the same instant he thrust inside me, I realized that... Oh, sweet Jesus, he was sexy like this. Dressed but disheveled, his tie a mess and his shirt partway undone but his jacket still on his shoulders, and his face the very picture of need as he pounded into my ass. I thought we'd been frantic and needy before, but letting go of all that pent-up need had us clawing at each other, grinding and thrusting and panting.

I pumped myself furiously as Theo fucked me deep and hard, exactly the way he had in my fantasies. Nonsense rolled off my tongue—probably pleas for more and curses because it was so good I didn't think I could take anymore—but all I heard was Theo's sharp, rapid breaths as he hauled both of us higher with every thrust.

I grabbed his lapels and pulled us together—dragging him down as I hauled myself up—into a messy, breathless kiss. His moan made my spine tingle. His rhythm came apart, but I didn't care and I didn't think he did either. Not when he was plowing into me and we were kissing and my whole body was ready to come unraveled.

Theo wasn't kidding that this was going to be quick, either—in no time, he broke the kiss with a gasp as a violent shiver ran through him. I dropped back onto the bed and rolled my hips, and he cried out and drove into me as hard as he could, shoving me up the mattress as he forced himself as deep as I could take him.

Then he moaned and slumped over me, holding himself up on his arms. His tie and jacket brushed my chest. His breath rushed past my cheek.

"Oh, my God," he slurred.

"Uh-huh." I trailed my hand up his side.

He brushed a kiss across my lips. "Next round will be longer. Promise."

"Mmm. Baby." I lifted my chin for another kiss. "Quickies are fun."

"I know, but—"

"I mean it." I grinned. "And if that had been much longer, we probably would've needed medical attention."

He laughed and sank into a longer kiss. He relaxed over

me, so hopefully my joke had eased his embarrassment over going off so fast. It really hadn't been that fast. A quickie, yes, but he was hardly a minuteman. And seriously, as keyed up as we'd both been after avoiding each other for so long, anything longer than a quickie would've killed us both. Or at the very least, had us both moving uncomfortably at tomorrow's practice.

He touched his hot forehead to mine. "Let me get rid of this. Then it's your turn."

I bit my lip, arching under him. Every nerve ending in my body was still humming from being railed by Theo. The orgasm those beautiful eyes promised? Hell, medical attention might still be on the table.

He didn't keep me waiting long, and he still didn't bother getting undressed. He climbed onto the bed, shoved my thighs apart again, and—

"Oh, my God!" I grabbed handfuls of the sheets as I pushed myself deeper into his eager mouth. Then he had two fingers inside me, and he thrust them in and out as he moaned around my dick. "Jesus Christ, Theo..." I squirmed and arched, murmuring curses and God only knew what else as he masterfully drove me into the stratosphere. Sometimes I tried to hold back my climax just so I could ride out the buildup a little longer, but I didn't stand a chance this time. I was completely and blissfully at Theo's mercy, and before I knew it, I was shouting and thrashing and coming.

He gently brought me back down to earth, and by the time the smoke had cleared, he was beside me, an arm slung over me as he lazily kissed me.

"Holy fuck," I murmured when I came up for air. "Your mouth should win awards."

Theo laughed. "Are there competitions for that?"

"If there are, you should enter. You'd win them for sure."

He grinned against my lips, and we made out a little more just because... I mean, why the hell not? I was still vibrating all over from that orgasm, and Theo's mouth seriously was incredible.

There was one *minor* detail that needed addressing, though.

"You, good sir, still have clothes on," I slurred.

"What can I say?" He nipped my lower lip. "Getting you off was more important than getting naked."

I laughed drunkenly at the corniness of the line and curled closer to him. "Well, now that you've accomplished that mission..." Our lips met again, and we indulged in another long, lazy kiss.

We'd get cleaned up. Get him out of his now rumpled suit.

In a minute.

CHAPTER 11
THEO

After we'd cleaned ourselves up, we returned to Christian's bed. I'd been fully dressed while I'd fucked him, but I was completely naked now, molded to his gorgeous body as we kissed lazily.

I loved the way his hands were constantly on the move, sliding over my chest, my arms, my back—he was so tactile, and I couldn't get enough. He seemed to enjoy me doing the same thing, too. I just couldn't help touching him all over. Fingers through his hair. Palms down his back. Trailing my hand along his thigh before hooking my fingers behind his knee and pulling it up onto my hip. The way he whimpered against my lips when I did that—goddamn, he was so sexy.

Eventually, we relaxed onto the pillows, still holding each other close and touching as if we needed to be absolutely sure this was real. His eyes were a mix of satisfied and sleepy, which made me grin. I loved the way a man looked when I'd left him blissed out, and the fact that it was *this* man—that was just the icing on the damn cake.

"I really should've gotten your number last time," I murmured.

He laughed softly. "Same. I'd have made the drive to Everett for this."

"Totally worth coming down to Seattle." I lifted my head for brief, light kiss. "I'd do the driving. No point in making you sit in traffic after I fucked your ass like that."

Christian chuckled, squirming a little. "You think I'd be that sore?"

"Depends on how many rounds you'd need before you had enough."

He bit his lip, almost muffling a soft moan. "Does that mean you're going to drill me again tonight?"

I lifted an eyebrow. "Are you saying you haven't had enough?"

"Baby." He grinned. "I haven't had a dicking down like that in a long time. You better believe I'm game for more."

"Good. Because I haven't had anywhere near enough of that ass tonight." I pulled him back in for a long, lazy kiss, reveling in the way he shivered and whimpered. Fuck him again tonight? Oh, hell yeah. "When you're ready for more," I mumbled between kisses, "just say the word."

"Believe me, I will."

We made out for a little while, but neither of us was trying to wind the other up. Not quite yet. No, we just lazily kissed and touched, which I loved. I'd had hookups where we'd both come, then play on our phones until we'd both recharged. We'd go another round, and then we'd either go to sleep or one of us would leave.

It had been way too long since I'd been with someone who enjoyed everything in between. It wasn't affection like if we were boyfriends—just touching and tasting while things were quiet. Maybe we'd be screwing again in five minutes. Maybe it would be an hour. Either way, I had no complaints.

As we had earlier, we eventually relaxed onto the pillows. We were still absently touching, but the conversation meandered to whatever came to mind.

After a while, Christian propped himself up on his elbow and studied me. "Can I ask you something completely unrelated to you banging my brains out?"

I barked a laugh. "Yeah, of course."

He trailed his fingertips up the middle of my chest. "How did you learn Russian?"

"My mom." I ran my palm along his forearm. "She's lived in the U.S. since she was sixteen, but my grandparents and most of my extended family on that side don't speak much English. And she also wanted us to know her language."

"Huh. Your name definitely didn't give anything away."

I chuckled. "Yeah, apparently my parents argued about that. A lot. My dad wanted to name me after my grandfather, but my mom wanted to give me the Russian version, which is Fyodor."

"How did they settle it?"

"To hear them tell it, they never did," I muttered. "My mom and her side of the family call me Fedya—that's the diminutive of Fyodor—and the other side calls me Theo." I laughed. "Mom says Dad filled out the birth certificate while she was still drugged up. Dad says Mom told him 'name him whatever you want as long as you take him away and let me sleep for a couple of hours.'"

Christian laughed. "I mean, sleep deprivation sucks. I could see giving up naming rights for a kid in exchange for a nap."

"Right?" I rolled my eyes. "She loves to remind me that it's my fault. If I hadn't put her through such hell in labor, I'd have a respectable Russian name."

He arched an eyebrow. "Like, a legit guilt trip? Or is she just messing with you?"

"Oh, she's just messing with me. It's totally her sense of humor." I chuckled. "Like when I was being a stubborn teenager, and she'd tell me"—I mimicked my mother's accent—"'You can't be difficult delivery *and* difficult teenager, Fedya. Go clean your room.'"

Christian snorted. "Did that work?"

"Most of the time, yeah." I rolled my eyes. "And sometimes when I was being a pain in the ass, she'd say, 'See, this is why I let your *father* name you. Because you are *clearly* his son.'"

"Your mom sounds like a spitfire. I love it."

Nodding, I laughed. "She keeps us all in line, believe me."

Christian laughed, but it faded, and his expression turned a little sad as he broke eye contact.

I touched his face. "What?"

"I..." He deflated a bit. "I was just going to say my mom can be spicy like that too. Just... not with my dad."

I sobered too. "Really? I mean, I know what your dad is like, but is he a jerk at home, too?"

He laughed bitterly. "You think he's only an asshole when he's on the clock? Trust me—he's the same at home. And I think it wears on my mom as much as it does my sister and me." Before I could respond, he sighed. "I'm sorry. I'm sorry. We were joking, and I derailed it and—"

"No, it's okay." I laced our fingers together between us. "Having a dad like that would bum me out, too."

He met my eyes again. "Are you out to your parents?"

"Oh, yeah. My dad was a little surprised just because I don't think he was paying attention, but my mom was all,

'Of course you're gay, Fedya. I knew you were gay when you were five.'"

A laugh broke through Christian's sudden funk. "She said that?"

"Yep. And my dad was like, 'When he was five? What?' And she just sort of rolled her eyes and told him that was why his father was convinced she was a Russian spy. Not because she did anything to suggest she was a spy—just because my dad's too oblivious to notice if she did."

Christian chuckled. "Family dinners in your house must be entertaining as all hell."

"They are. Believe me." I sobered a bit. "I, um... I'm guessing it didn't go over well when you came out."

He blew out a breath, watching his hand running up and down my arm. "No. In fact, I came out to my mom when I was thirteen, and she flat out told me not to tell my dad until I was eighteen."

I stared at him. "Seriously?"

Grimacing, he nodded. "She knew he'd kick me out, and there wouldn't be anything she could do to stop him."

"But she stayed with him? Knowing he'd throw out one of her kids?" I paused. "Fuck. Sorry. I shouldn't be so judgy about your family."

"No, it's okay. And honestly, I get it—they got together back when my dad was still playing hockey. She was twenty, he was twenty-five, and she signed an *ironclad* prenup. She didn't think anything of it at the time because she loved him and didn't care about his money." Christian sighed. "Now she's in her fifties, she hasn't worked since she was nineteen, and if she leaves, she has nothing. Even if my sister and I try to help her out... I mean, she's gotten used to the life he gave her. She's unhappy with him, but she's scared of life after him. So... she stays."

"Wow," I said. "That's really sad."

"Right?"

I chewed the inside of my cheek. "Can I ask you something personal?"

Christian's eyebrow flicked up, a hint of his mischievous spark coming back to life in those gorgeous blue eyes. "We're naked in bed and I can still feel what you did to my ass. I think we're beyond 'something personal,' aren't we?"

I laughed, shivering at the memory of everything I'd done to his ass, not to mention everything I still planned to do to it tonight. "Okay, fair. I guess I'm just wondering..." I turned serious again. "Why do you work for him? He obviously treats you like shit. Why put up with it?"

"Because I love my job," he said simply. "Every time I think I want to leave, I look at all the guys in the locker room and all the people I work with, and I just... I can't. I don't want to." He swallowed. "I had to sneak around dating boys when I was a teenager so my dad didn't find out I was gay. I've had to walk on eggshells around him at home my entire life and at work for the past several years. But... I mean, I guess I stay with the job for the same reason I'm here with you tonight: I won't let him take away the things I enjoy. I like my job. And..." He slid his hand up my chest. "I like *this*."

"I like it, too," I whispered. "But if your dad finds out..."

"I know." He gave a subtle nod. "Believe me, I know. And... doing this tonight is one thing. If you don't want to take the risk of doing it again, I promise I'll understand."

I searched his eyes. "What if I do want to do it again?"

Some hope flickered across his expression. "Do you? Even with everything that's at stake?"

"Yes," I said without hesitation.

"Are you sure?" His brow pinched. "You've experienced firsthand what happens if you cross my dad. And I promise you, sleeping with his son is going to piss him off a lot more than putting rainbow tape on your stick."

"I know. And I know we shouldn't do this." I curved my hand beside his neck. "But... I mean, last time was so good, and *this* time..."

Christian gave a soft little moan a second before our lips met. "It was so good," he slurred between kisses. "It's... God, it's really good." He carded his fingers through my hair. "I just don't want to fuck up your career."

"You're not. *I'm* making the choice. I know what's at stake." I ran my fingertips along the edge of his jaw. "And I want you."

He shivered. "Me too."

I claimed his mouth again, and he melted against me, letting me tease and explore as he held on like he thought I might pull away. Rationally, we both knew I *should* pull away, and that this was a stupid, reckless thing to do.

I wasn't interested in rational. I was interested in Christian. Now that I'd finally satisfied that craving I'd had since the first time we'd hooked up, I wanted more. I couldn't get enough.

And as I pulled him closer, my cock thickening between us, I couldn't wait to be buried inside him again.

"Remember when we did this the first time?" I mumbled against his lips. "When we were—when we didn't have enough for a second round?"

Christian arched against me, rubbing his hardening dick alongside mine. "Uh-huh?"

"That's not gonna be a problem this time."

He whimpered softly and claimed my mouth. He slid a hand between us and stroked me to full attention, muffling all my gasps and moans with his lips and tongue. I'd already come once tonight, but his hand and his kiss had me trembling and needy like I hadn't gone off in weeks.

I finally broke the kiss and panted, "I want to fuck you again."

The choked little sound he made had my toes curling. "Please?"

"Yeah?"

"Uh-huh," he whispered. "Not as hard this time. Slower. I'm a little—"

"Sensitive?" I brushed my lips across his. "I'll be careful. I promise."

He slid a hand into my hair and kissed me, letting it linger for a moment. When he broke away, I pushed myself up and reached for the nightstand.

After I'd put on the condom and lube, I kissed him again and murmured, "Turn over."

Christian shivered, biting his lip. "On my side or my stomach?"

"Whichever." I teased his nipple with my thumbnail. "However you like it."

He flashed me a grin. Then he rolled onto his stomach, and I followed. I settled over him and guided myself in. I pushed in carefully, and he took me easily, both of us moaning as I slid deeper. Christian buried his face in the pillows and pressed his back against my chest. I dropped a light kiss on his shoulder, but that wasn't enough, so I let my lips skate up the back of his neck as I kept slowly rocking in and out of him.

"Oh, God," he whispered, tilting his head forward. "That feels so... Oh my God."

I kissed along his hairline as I rocked in and out of him, slowly and smoothly. As fun as it was to slam into him and fuck him so hard I pushed him up the mattress, this was sexy as hell. Hard and fast was fine and good. Slow and easy, though, meant I could feel *everything,* and I loved this. Loved the heat of our bodies touching from our feet to my lips on his neck, all while I moved inside him. Loved the scent of him as I kissed his neck and shoulder. Loved how every shiver and tremor reverberated from his body through mine.

Christian shifted a little under me, moving his weight to his right arm. I thought he was going to reach under us to jack himself, and I started to lift myself up so he could move, but he reached back and carded his fingers through my hair. I shivered, groaning softly as I bit his shoulder.

"Jesus Christ, Theo," he whined, rolling his hips to egg me on and—I guessed—rut against the sheets. "Oh, God, you feel amazing."

"Mmm, so do you." I kissed the back of his neck again. "Can you come like this?" Then I bit his earlobe. Not hard, but enough to make him gasp.

Arching under me, he nodded. "Y-yeah. I..." He brought his arm back down. "Lift up a little?"

I did, holding his hip and pulling him up with me.

As soon as he had room, he pushed a hand beneath us, and I sucked in air as he clenched hard around me.

"Oh, *God,*" he moaned. From the motion of his shoulder, he was stroking himself at the same speed I was riding him.

I struggled to stay slow. The need to piston into him hard and fast until we both screamed was almost irresistible. But I wasn't about to hurt him, so I was going to stay slow and careful unless he wanted it harder. And it didn't matter how fast or hard I fucked him—much more of this and I was absolutely going to come.

"I want you to come this way," I pleaded, trying like hell to hold on to my rhythm. "I want to feel it."

The strangled sound he released almost sent me into oblivion, but I bit my lip and tried to keep my own orgasm back.

"A little harder," he whispered shakily. "A little—ungh, baby. A little more. Just—ooh, fuck, yes, like that!" He bucked under me, clenching hard around my dick, and suddenly I was crying out as I rode both of our orgasms until we collapsed onto the mattress

I managed to keep from resting my full weight on him, holding myself up on shaking arms as we both tried to catch our breath.

As the smoke cleared, our earlier conversation—the one we'd been having when we'd gotten lost in each other again instead—drifted back into my mind.

"Listen," I panted against his neck. "I know we shouldn't do this. I know we're risking a lot. But I can't help it." I pressed a kiss just beneath his ear. "I want you."

Christian moaned softly and squirmed under me. "I want you, too." He twisted around just a little, and I shifted to one side so we could make eye contact even like this. Even with my dick still buried inside him.

His eyebrows knitted together. "You know we're both fucked if we get caught, right?"

I nodded. "I know. But with as much as I've been kicking myself since last time..." I half-shrugged.

He studied me. Then, little by little, a smile spread across his lips. "Well then. Good thing you won't be leaving without my number in your phone this time, eh?"

I laughed and kissed him.

"Oh, yeah," I murmured. "A damn good thing."

After that, Christian and I grabbed every opportunity we could to hook up. Not on the road, of course, because that was just too damn dangerous, but if the team was in Seattle and we weren't scrambling off to the airport? Hell, yeah. We usually went to his place because it was closer to the arena and practice rink. The team was putting me up in a hotel in town, but there were other players staying there, as well as some of the journalists who came to town to cover games. Not a good place for a clandestine hookup.

When there was a day or so between games, we'd sometimes go up to Everett to my apartment. I would've done that anyway—hotels got old, and it was nice to sleep in my own damn bed—but it was even better when I was sharing that bed with Christian.

"I thought it was kind of stupid, them getting me a hotel room," I told him one night while we were in my bed, "but the first time I didn't have to drive all the way back up here after a game... I stopped questioning it."

"Good call," he said with a grin. "And it's really not that far. So when you do get sent back down..." The grin broadened as he trailed his fingers up the middle of my chest.

Toes curling, I leaned in for a soft kiss. "So, you'll want to keep doing this? Even when I get sent back to Everett?"

"Are you kidding? Were you not there twenty minutes ago when you had me coming so hard I almost passed out?" He teased my nipple with his thumbnail. "Fuck yeah, I'll drive up here."

I laughed as goose bumps broke out along my arms. Then I thought more about what he said, and my amusement dipped. "I'm surprised they haven't sent me back down yet."

"I'm not," he said without hesitation.

"Really? The injured guys are trickling back, and—"

"And you're tearing it up out there." Christian smiled. "Hell, Eppley's back and Coach Baldwin still has you on the third line instead of bumping you down to the fourth."

Huh. Okay, yeah, he had a point. Eppley had been on the third offensive line for the past three seasons. He'd been back for a week now, and I was still in his old spot while he was on the fourth line.

"No, you probably won't be up forever," Christian said gently. "But I think you've been impressing everyone. I have a feeling they'll send back the other forwards before they send you down."

My heart fluttered. "You think so?"

"I've been watching how this team operates for a long time. When Baldwin finds someone who gels with his guys and his system, he holds on to them."

"Well, damn. And here I thought I'd be the first one to get bumped when people started coming off the injured list."

"If my dad had his way, you probably would be."

I grimaced. "Yeah. Probably."

"But Baldwin isn't afraid of my dad," Christian insisted, "and he'll stick to his guns." He laced our fingers together and kissed the heel of my hand. "I highly doubt you're going anywhere any time soon unless all the guys on LTIR magically recover."

Considering one was out for the rest of the season and two others *might* be back in time for the playoffs—holy shit. Yeah. I might be here a while.

As long as I didn't piss off Jack Hayes.

"Do you really think we'll be able to keep this"—I gestured at Christian, then myself—"out of your dad's sight?"

His smile was both sexy and reassuring. "If I didn't, we wouldn't be doing it." He must've seen my uncertainty, because he went on, "My dad can't be everywhere all the time. He's literally only been to my condo like three times, and one of those was because my mom dragged him there to check on me while I was sick." He rolled his eyes. "Trust me, he isn't going to be creeping around the parking lot or anything. And aside from what we did over by the Zambonis, we haven't touched at the arena or practice facility."

I tensed a little. "And there's... You're sure there's no cameras back there, right?"

Christian huffed a laugh. "Trust me. The Zamboni drivers and the facilities staff have been trying to get some back there for *ages*. Dad always pulls strings until whatever funds they would've allocated for cameras get redirected to something he thinks is more important in the locker rooms."

"Seriously?"

"Uh-huh. That's literally the only reason I know there's no cameras in there—because I've had to listen to my dad go on and on and *on* about it."

"But... why? I mean, what's the point? Cameras aren't that expensive, are they?"

Sighing, Christian rolled onto his back. As I propped myself onto my elbow beside him, he scrubbed a hand over his face. "That's the thing with my dad—it doesn't have to be logical or reasonable. It makes perfect sense to put cameras in the Zamboni bay, and it wouldn't cost much at all. But like three or four years ago, one of the facilities guys got into it with my dad over something. I don't even remember what, just that Dad's been bound and determined to make their lives difficult ever since."

"Does he even have that kind of power?" I asked, absently running my free hand down Christian's chest. "I didn't think the club had that much clout over the arena."

"It doesn't, and no, he doesn't either." Christian tsked. "But some of his flying monkeys do work for the arena, and they're in positions to veto things like that. So they keep doing it to keep him happy."

"All because a facilities staffer pissed him off?"

"Mmhmm." He met my gaze. "Man's got a vindictive streak, if you hadn't noticed."

I laughed. "You don't say." I chewed my lip. "But... we can still fly under his radar, I think. You're right—it's a big city, and it isn't like we're fucking in the locker room showers."

Christian grinned. "You have to admit—that *would* be kinda hot."

Rolling my eyes, I said, "Uh-huh. Right up until some of my teammates walked in and started heckling us."

The laugh that burst out of him made my whole body warm all over. "They would, too, wouldn't they? Can you *imagine?*"

"Yes, I can." I mimicked Rusanov's voice, "'Wow, Christian really *can* manage Mathis's equipment.'"

Christian was howling now. "Oh my God. I can so picture that." He tried to turn serious as he said, "And then Yanni would be all, 'You can't hold his hips like that—that's goaltender interference!'"

I cackled. "I mean as long as they don't let the reporters in..."

We both let the laughter take over for a moment. Yeah, our teammates would definitely heckle and chirp if they caught us in the shower. Talk about performance anxiety, too. Goddamn.

But God help us if the GM caught us.

I shoved that thought back as I gathered Christian in my arms. As amusement shifted to affection, and playful kisses shifted to something much sexier, I pushed all thoughts of Jack Hayes out of my mind.

"You know," Christian murmured between kisses, "the locker room shower is out, but yours isn't so bad." He arched an eyebrow. "Feel like banging me up against the wall?"

If my dick hadn't already been well on its way to hard, it was now. "I'll bang you anywhere you want as long as you come as loud as you did earlier."

Christian licked his lips. "Sounds like an even trade."

"Mmhmm. Shower?"

"Shower."

CHAPTER 12

CHRISTIAN

Unfortunately, while Theo and I did manage to spend a lot of time together, we couldn't spend *every* night that way, and not just because hockey was demanding.

Once a month, as long as the Rainiers were in town—and weekly during the off season—my parents expected my sister, her husband, and me at the house for dinner. I would've loved to be conveniently unavailable or just not bother answering my phone, but seeing us on a weekly basis made my mom happy. Sometimes I thought it was one of the only things that made her happy.

For that reason alone, I dutifully took my usual seat at my parents' ornate dining room table tonight.

I had to bite back a laugh as I sat down. It wasn't the first time I'd been at this table while I could still feel the sex I'd had the previous night or earlier in the same day, though that hadn't happened in a while. It was, however, the first time the man who'd ridden me into oblivion had been on my father's payroll.

All through grace, I fought the chuckle that desperately wanted to bubble up. I'd stayed at Theo's place last night.

We'd started the day with some coffee, followed by some lazy sixty-nining while we waited for the DoorDasher to drop off our breakfast. It was as decadent as it was forbidden.

And my dad didn't have a clue.

That wasn't to say I was involved with Theo to rebel against my dad. I wanted Theo. I wanted his body against mine as often as possible, and I just... wanted to be around him. I liked him. It was still way too soon to know if this would be friends with benefits and nothing more, or if there might be something else here. I was happy either way. If we didn't end up dating, then I hoped we ended up being actual friends in addition to those benefits, because he seemed like a really good guy.

So, no. I hadn't spent last night or any other with Theo as a fuck-you to my father.

But I'd have been lying if I said that fuck-you didn't exist and wasn't satisfying as all hell. He hated it when I had boyfriends. He hated being reminded that I was queer, as if anyone could ignore it once I opened my mouth. If he found out I was dating a player from his club? Ooh, he'd be livid.

If he found out that player was the one who'd defied him with the Pride Tape?

Yeah, like I said, the fuck-you was *definitely* satisfying.

"So." My father peered at Aiden, who sat across from me beside my sister. "How is the job search going?"

Aiden chewed as if the chicken my mother had prepared was tough and overcooked. It wasn't. I suspected he was just trying to hold back all the things he wished he could say to his father-in-law. For a moment, he stared at his plate. Then he cut his eyes toward my dad and managed to keep his tone even as he said, "I have some promising leads."

"Good." Dad smiled that smile that made everyone in the locker room twitchy with nerves. "Well, if you need a reference..."

Most people would follow that with "Let me know" or "Hit me up." Dad just left it vague, and I didn't imagine I was the only one in the room who could infer what he'd left unsaid.

"Use me for a reference, Aiden. I dare you."

Aiden smiled tightly, offered thanks, and then shifted the conversation to compliment my mom's cooking and ask if she minded sharing the recipe. "How did you get the sauce to thicken up? Last time I tried to make one like this, I followed all the instructions, but it still came out all watery."

That had me grinning behind my wineglass. Aiden was good at not directly antagonizing my father, but he knew which buttons to passive-aggressively push. Dad *hated* when we talked about Mom's cooking. He especially hated when anyone other than him was being asked for their advice or expertise. For all Dad had been an excellent hockey player and was (for the most part) a genius general manager, there wasn't much else he was good at. He despised when there was a discussion he couldn't contribute to or couldn't dominate by being the expert in the room.

Maybe Dad had fired Aiden and derailed his career, but he couldn't hold a candle to Aiden's or Mom's skill in the kitchen.

It was also annoying, this dining room power struggle. I'd heard that most families had normal conversations over dinner instead of pissing matches, but I don't know. That sounded fake to me. This was all I'd ever known. Hell, I'd been out of my element the first time the Rainiers had invited me to join them for dinner. There was shit-talking and chirping, of course—that came with the territory of being around hockey players—but it was all good-natured. Nothing was barbed. No compliments were backhanded. No one was being criticized for real. It was just... fun and relaxed, with everyone talking about whatever and no one taking over the conversation.

This? Dad trying to domineer while the rest of us found ways to subtly subvert him and antagonize him? It wasn't normal, but it was *my* normal, and I still found it exhausting.

I was honestly surprised Aiden didn't bow out of these dinners more often. Once in a while, he was hung up working on one of his occasional freelance gigs, but most of the time, he showed up with my sister. He never looked happy about it, and if looks could kill, my dad would've been in the ground a long time ago.

I didn't think Chelsea browbeat him into coming. Knowing her, she insisted she could go alone. Was it pride that kept him showing up, week after week? A refusal to let Dad think he'd won somehow? Masochism, maybe? I had no idea, but here he was, looking as miserable as ever in the same room as my parents.

My mother was in mid-sentence, explaining how she'd tweaked the recipe to make the sauce a little sweeter, when Dad said, "Christian, I understand there were some issues with a shipment or jerseys from the manufacturer." He stabbed a piece of chicken. "What was that about?"

"Uh..." I glanced at my mom and brother-in-law. They both subtly shook their heads and focused on their food. Chelsea met my gaze and shrugged. It wasn't like they didn't know this game, or that they thought there was any point in pushing back. Better to just play along so we could all get through dinner and get the hell out of here. I cleared my throat, absently dragging a green bean through the sauce in question. "Just, um... The ones for Military Night, yeah. There were a few seams that weren't done right." I gestured dismissively with my fork. "Marty and I fixed them just in case the replacements don't come in time."

"What do you mean, if they don't come in time?" he growled.

"The manufacturer is expediting them," I said. "They'll go out today—tomorrow at the latest—via express shipping, but they're coming from Canada, so we needed a contingency in case they get hung up in customs."

"I see." He picked up his wineglass. "And why did it take until *yesterday* for this problem to come to my attention?"

It didn't even make me panic anymore when I could tell Dad was sniffing around for a reason to make something my fault. I was so used to that from my childhood that it hadn't been a surprise when he started doing it as my boss. After one season of that bullshit, it barely registered anymore beyond mentally acknowledging that's what he was doing.

Soo predictable.

I sipped my own wine. "The jerseys came in yesterday afternoon. Marty and I found the problem right away, and we prioritized contacting the manufacturer and figuring out if we could fix the jerseys we had in hand." I half-shrugged. "Once we had the situation under control, I emailed you and Bruce to keep everyone in the loop."

"I need to be notified about situations like this," he snapped. "I need to be notified immediately. Not after you've crossed off items on your to-do list. Is that clear?"

A few years ago, I'd have been sweating bullets, knowing I was in a no-win situation. If I notified him immediately without first addressing the issue directly, then I'd get chewed out for bringing him problems and not solutions. When I notified him after we'd figured out and implemented a solution, then I was leaving him out of the loop and only telling him as an afterthought.

"I can't win!" younger me would be saying. *"There is literally* no way *for me to win!"*

Older and wiser me understood how true that was, and I'd saved myself a lot of stress by simply accepting that, no, there was no way for me to win. These days, I just resolved the situation as efficiently and effectively as possible, and then let Dad rant, rave, and threaten me over not running to him the moment I discovered the problem. Yawn.

I took another drink of wine and let myself sound bored as I told him, "I'll let you know next time."

"There had better not be a next time," he growled. "Or that manufacturer can pound sand."

It was a struggle not to laugh. Especially when Aiden—who'd worked for the club long enough to know how things ran—pressed his lips together to fight back his own amusement.

Sure, Dad. Sure. You're going to fire the jersey manufacturer. The one with the ten-year, multimillion dollar exclusive contract with the NAPH. Good luck with that.

Dinner mercifully didn't last much longer. Mom's desserts were always blessedly simple and small, so they hit the table just a few minutes after the dinner dishes were cleared away and they didn't take long to eat. I was pretty sure that was by design, too.

Chelsea and Aiden left shortly after dessert. It was my turn to linger and help Mom clean the kitchen, and no, my sister and I absolutely did *not* have a standing agreement to take turns being the one who had to stick around. Never. Not at all.

Of course we were both—along with Aiden—more than happy to help Mom with the post-dinner cleanup. We never wanted to bail on her. The issue was my dad, and who got to get the hell away from him first.

The one upshot was that Dad didn't do kitchen cleanup. It always ended up being time we got to spend with Mom, chatting about whatever while we scrubbed pots and pans.

"We have a dishwasher, Beth," Dad always snidely reminded her. "You don't need to wash them by hand."

"It's fine," she'd tell him. "I don't like putting my good dishes in the dishwasher."

Sometimes I thought she used the fine china on family dinner nights specifically so she'd have a reason to wash them by hand. That meant time with whichever sibling stayed behind, and a good twenty minutes or more without my dad.

God, we were dysfunctional.

I was elbow deep in soapy water when my mom asked, "How is work going?"

Again, lines I could read between: *"How are you holding up working for your father?"*

I shrugged, focusing intently on scrubbing a plate that was already spotless. "I like what I do."

She sighed as she dried a large pan with a dishtowel. "I'd miss you if you moved away, but I won't be upset if you decide to go work for another team."

I swallowed hard. "I like it here. I don't want to leave Seattle." I glanced at her. "And ninety percent of the time, I'm working with everyone *but* him. It's really not that bad."

Her forehead creased in that way that said she knew I was lying and she wondered why I bothered.

I pushed out a breath and put the plate aside so I could

start on another. I wasn't actually lying. Everything I'd said was true... except the part about *"it's really not that bad."* Because... it *was* that bad. I always tried to gaslight myself into believing it wasn't but who was I kidding?

The thing was, when I was in the zone and focused on the gear and the game, I loved it. That was my happy place. The problem was that I always knew Dad was watching. During games, he was in the owners' box with a bird's eye view of the bench. At the practice rink, he was always lurking somewhere nearby. In the locker room, he could come storming in at any moment to throw a shitfit about whatever had his panties in a wad.

Yeah, I'd learned to live with it, but I was lying if I said it didn't stress me out.

Or that it didn't stress me out more now that I was screwing one of the Rainiers.

I swallowed the bile rising in the back of my throat. I wondered if Theo understood just how attractive he was. How strong his magnetism was if he'd drawn me to him despite my fear of my dad's wrath. Because whether I wanted to admit it out loud or not, I was afraid of my dad. I was afraid of what he could do to me professionally. How he could humiliate me in front of the staff and the players.

It wasn't that bad? Bullshit it wasn't.

But I did like my job.

And I did like the man who'd curled against me this morning while I was still half-asleep. Enough to risk both of our careers? Fuck. Now I was having second thoughts.

My mother was still waiting for an answer, though, so I cleared my throat as I put aside another plate. "It's stressful. It is. But... I really do love my job."

"You could love it on another team," Mom said softly, as

if she didn't want her voice to carry to wherever Dad was. "I just don't want you to be miserable."

"I'm..." I couldn't say I wasn't. Not entirely. "I'll put out some feelers during the off season." Was I lying? I didn't even know.

"Okay. Just... don't feel like you have to stay there if you're unhappy."

I met her gaze. I wanted so, so bad to tell her that the same applied to her.

We'd had that conversation before, though, and all it ever accomplished was upsetting her. I knew where she stood and why. I knew why she didn't leave. Maybe that was why she was so adamant about me looking elsewhere—I had choices that she didn't, and she wanted me to use them.

Maybe I would.

But it wouldn't be tonight.

Eventually, we finished up the dishes, and we chatted in the kitchen for a little while before I had to head out. There was practice tomorrow, after all, and the day started early.

I was almost home free—in the foyer with my car keys in hand—when Dad appeared.

"Christian." He beckoned. "Before you go..."

My throat constricted. This probably wasn't good. Though I didn't want to, I pocketed my keys and followed Dad out of the kitchen, down the hall, and into his office. There, he closed the door, which was also a bad sign.

I stood there silently and waited. He had something to say, which meant I needed to let him start the conversation. Lesson learned the hard way.

After a painfully long silence, he finally did so. "I just want to make sure we're on the same page." He folded his arms and leaned against his desk, giving me that pointed look that said I needed to be reading between the lines.

"Um." I swallowed. "The same page about... what?"

He gave an annoyed little sigh, apparently frustrated that, at the age of thirty-one, I had *still* rudely refused to develop the ability to read his mind. "On the job, you're my employee. You understand that, correct?"

Okay, those lines I could read between:

When we're at work, you're my underling—not my son.

Gritting my teeth, I nodded. "Of course. I'm just like any other member of the staff." To a point, I was fine with that. I hated when people thought I only had my job because of nepotism. And like, yeah, being the GM's son had definitely given me a step up when getting the job. I knew that. But the respect I'd earned? My status as the head equipment manager? Those had nothing to do with my dad and everything to do with how I did my job. I believed firmly that I should be treated like any other employee, not the son of the general manager.

I wasn't stupid, though—when Dad reminded me of my place, he thought I was a step or three *beneath* everyone else on the payroll. I had to toe the line more than anyone. Bow and scrape so Dad knew I was grateful for the position he'd bestowed upon me through benevolence and pity.

"Because you're my son," he went on, "you and I are both under a lot of extra scrutiny. People don't like nepotism and favoritism, after all."

The only thing that kept a sarcastic laugh from escaping was how unnerved I was by this line of conversation, not to mention how irritated I was by it. "I know. I've known that from the beginning."

"Right. So I would suggest you keep that in mind going forward. Don't let this jersey nonsense happen again. You find out there's a problem, you let me know immediately. Am I clear?"

I gritted my teeth. For as much as we were supposed to be speaking as boss-employee right now, I had the distinct impression he was envisioning me as a seven-year-old who hadn't done his chores.

"It won't happen again," I said blandly.

We locked eyes. I couldn't read his expression, but somewhere deep in my gut, a cold ball of lead started to swell.

Dad despised being crossed. He was this pissy over me not reading him in about the jersey debacle, and he'd have been equally pissy if I'd come to him before I'd had a solution. There was no winning with him.

The thing that suddenly worried me was the card I *wasn't* showing him. The one that was fun to play in the moment, but suddenly seemed like a reckless gamble when I was standing in his angry crosshairs.

What if he found out about me and Theo?

He already had his finger on the trigger, ready to send Theo back down, fire me, or both at the slightest provocation. He was just waiting for a reason to pull it.

Shiiit.

Fortunately, Dad was apparently satisfied he'd made his point, and he dismissed me. I got the hell out of that house like it was a fire, hurrying down the front steps to my car, which was parked in front of their six-car garage.

Sitting down to dinner with my body still aching from sex with Theo had been a rebellious little fuck-you to my dad. Sitting here now in my idling car in front of my parents' house, I felt sick.

Theo and I both knew what we were risking if we kept sleeping together. The professional consequences would not be minor for either of us, and I didn't imagine we'd have anyone on our side. No one had pushed back against Dad for canceling Pride Night. No one except for Theo, and then the other players who'd put on the rainbow tape after him.

The owners? The president of hockey operations? The league? The players' association? Nada.

So there was no way we could count on anyone to have our backs if Dad found out that Theo and I were hooking up. Or dating. Whatever the hell we were doing. The players who'd been supportive enough to put on the tape and who were protective of me when we went out to bars weren't necessarily going to like the idea of me screwing one of their teammates. That was how it worked with allies sometimes. They were supportive—even vocally so—right up until something made them uncomfortable. Then all that support was gone so fast, I wondered if it was ever there at all.

We couldn't bank on any support. We could probably bet on some serious backlash, though.

No matter how I sliced it, this thing we were doing—it was a really, really bad idea.

I pulled up his contact and started writing out a text.

Christian: *Listen, I'm sorry. This has been super fun and hot, but the more I think about it... I just can't put either of our jobs on the line like this. Let's just call this a fling and stop before we get caught.*

For long minutes, I stared at the message, my thumb hovering over the Send button. This was the right thing to do. Really the only thing to do if either of us valued our careers, which we did. We weren't in so deep that there'd be hurt feelings or resentment. Disappointment, sure, but it wasn't like we'd started getting emotionally involved with each other.

I chewed my lip, still reading and rereading the words I'd written.

I had to do this. I needed to. For his sake and mine. It sucked that my dad had that much power over me—over us—but it wasn't like I could change that reality. If Dad found out and decided to derail Theo's career and fire me, the people above him didn't have enough backbone between them to overrule him. And hell, they'd probably support the decision.

So why can't I send this damn message?

Because Theo deserves to hear it in person.

Ah. That was it.

I deleted the message and tossed my phone onto the passenger seat. As I backed out of my parents' driveway, I reassured myself that was the problem. We needed to talk about this face to face. That way there'd be no misunderstandings or mixed messages. Nothing lost in the translation.

Tomorrow, I'd look him in the eye and tell him everything I'd written, and then we could move on with our careers intact.

And I spent my entire drive home trying to make myself believe that.

CHAPTER 13

THEO

"Okay, but *which* mountains?" I asked as the practice rink's doors banged shut behind Grekov and me. "There's two different ranges."

"What? No." He shot me an incredulous look. "The mountains." He gestured behind us. "The ones I see across the lake."

"Right?" I glanced at him. "To the east or west?"

He pursed his lips. "East, I think?"

Nodding, I said, "Okay, those are the Cascades. You can get there in a couple of hours. The ones to the west are the Olympics. I think it's like... three hours, maybe? Depending on if you take the ferry or the highway?"

Grekov huffed with annoyance. "They look so much closer."

"Uh-huh. But there's traffic, because it's Seattle, and—I mean, they're not as close as they look. Mount Rainier looks close, but it's not."

He furrowed his brow. "Mount Rainier. Is that where they get...?" He tugged at his hoodie, which, like mine, had *Seattle Rainiers* screen-printed across the front.

"Yep!"

He nodded. "Is that the one that blew up?"

"No, that's St. Helens. It's to the south. And then there's Baker up north."

"Is Baker also a volcano?"

"Yep."

He muttered some Russian curses. "How many volcanos does this place have? Why do people live so close to them?"

"Why not?" I shrugged. "They don't go off that often."

"But they *could!*" He flailed his hands. "What kind of insane people build cities next to three volcanos?"

"Five, actually."

He eyed me. "What? What do you mean, five?"

I ticked them off on my fingers. "Rainier, Baker, Adams, St. Helens, and..." I furrowed my brow. "Crap, what was the last one? Oh! Glacier Peak."

"Bullshit."

"Nope. Google it."

He eyed me as if he thought I'd finally admit I was yanking his chain. When I didn't, he tsked and rolled his eyes. "Fine. What kind of insane people build cities next to *five* volcanos?"

I shrugged. "Americans?"

Grekov pursed his lips. "Okay, now it makes sense."

"Hey!"

He snickered as we kept walking. "You said it. Not me."

"Fuck off."

He opened his mouth, probably ready to either fire back another snarky comment or continue asking about which mountains had the best snowboarding, but a sharp voice halted us in our tracks.

"Mr. Mathis."

We both turned.

Jack beckoned to me. "A moment, please?"

My heart jumped into my throat. I glanced at Grekov, who nodded sharply and then made a quick escape into the locker room. I didn't blame him; he wasn't on any of Jack's shit lists as far as I knew, but the man's reputation as an asshole wasn't a big secret.

Alone in the hallway with our GM, I slipped my hands into the front pocket of my hoodie. "Sure. What's up?"

He peered down at me, his expression mostly neutral but his eyes hard in a way I couldn't quite understand. As if he wasn't angry... yet.

"Listen, kid," he began. "You've been surprising everyone since you've been here." Only Jack could make that sound backhanded. "Coach Baldwin and all the other coaches are *very* impressed with you."

I swallowed. "Thank you. I'm trying my best."

He nodded slowly. "Uh-huh. I see that. We all do." He put a heavy hand on my shoulder. "And I suggest you continue to do so. Remember—*no one* on a team is irreplaceable."

The *"especially not a last resort call-up from the minors"* went unspoken.

Before I could even comprehend that, never mind respond to it, Jack walked away, the click of dress shoes on concrete echoing through the hallway.

After he'd turned the corner and disappeared, I rolled my shoulders and chafed my arms as I released a harsh breath. God, I hated that guy.

And his ominous comments and thinly veiled threats burrowed deeper under my skin every time I replayed them.

Did he know something? Or was that just my guilty conscience?

Either way, was I playing with fire by screwing around with Jack's son?

Yeah, I definitely was, and I'd known it from the start, but it just got a whole lot scarier.

Fuck. What was I doing?

When I'd been called up to the Rainiers, I hadn't expected to be here this long. A handful of games at most. But I was still here. And while bonding with teammates was something I'd known since early childhood, I somehow hadn't expected to form any kind of bond with the guys at this level. That was stupid, of course. *All* teams bonded to some extent, even those who were just together briefly, like the national teams assembled just for specific international competitions.

I think I just hadn't let myself entertain the idea of forming any kind of attachment to the players at this level. Not unless and until I actually made it on to a roster and stayed there. Getting called up to fill in for injured players—we all knew how that worked. It was temporary. I wasn't going to get in tight with the guys any more than I did when I went to training camp, which I did every season.

But here I was, firmly ensconced on the third line of the Seattle Rainiers. I chirped with the guys. I hung out with them in bars. I sat with them on planes and buses. I knew the names of their spouses and kids. I'd made friends with these guys, especially Grekov.

If I lost my place here, I wasn't just losing my shot at playing for the Rainiers and potentially at the NAPH level at all. I was getting pulled away from these men.

That was part of hockey. People got traded. Free agency happened. It was just something everyone accepted and lived with even though it was hard. So no matter how clean

I kept my nose, there was no guarantee I'd stay in Seattle or that I wouldn't see any of my friends traded away.

I accepted all of that. But there was a big difference between the normal volatility of hockey rosters and being an impulsive dumbass who decided to wildly increase his odds of getting yeeted off a team.

I pressed my head back against the cold wall and closed my eyes. I was a fucking idiot. I'd been working for this my entire life. Over the past handful of weeks, I'd been finding the place I'd wanted all this time—a place on a NAPH team with NAPH players who treated me like I was their peer. I was starting to forge real friendships with some of these guys.

Was I really going to throw that away? And was I really going to throw it away for some casual sex?

Wow, I was an idiot. An absolute dumbass who apparently had no sense of professional self-preservation. My homophobic GM hated me, so what did I do after provoking him with rainbow tape? Start banging the hell out of his son at every opportunity.

That had to stop. I had to break things off with Christian. The sex was fun and everything, but there was just too much on the line. For both of us.

I didn't want to call this off, but I had to.

First opportunity to talk to him alone, I was ending things.

My chance came when I saw Christian wheeling a cart full of laundry out of the locker room. The equipment managers never let dirty laundry fester for very long, so it was a safe bet he was going to put it all in the machines now, not just drop it off and leave.

After I gave him a brief head start—long enough to get into the laundry facility down the hall—I slipped out of the locker room. I glanced up and down the hall to make sure no one else was around, then pushed open the door and stepped inside.

Christian was just shoving an armload of practice jerseys into a washer. He glanced my way, did a double take, and nearly dropped the jerseys. "Theo! What the—" He paused to push the rest into the washer, then faced me. "What are you doing? If someone sees us in here—"

"A player and the equipment manager in the laundry room?" I circled my finger in the air. "Is this the kind of place people are going to think someone is hooking up?"

He quirked his lips. And I mean, a laundromat or a laundry room probably wasn't a bad place for a hookup. A laundry room with a cart full of jerseys that smelled like a whole army of sweaty hockey players on top of the lingering smell of socks? Not so much.

So no, if we got caught in here, no one would think anything was happening. And anyway, I'd come in here to make things *not* happen anymore. Hockey smells or not, there wasn't going to be anything spicy going on in here right now.

Except...

Gazing into his startled eyes, all my resolve died away.

I came in here to tell you we can't do this.

But... I can't do that.

What the fuck?

Christian met my gaze but quickly broke eye contact. He seemed to be very pointedly avoiding my gaze as he pulled some more jerseys out of the cart and put them into the washer. "So... What's going on?"

"I, uh..."

Yeah, Theo. What's going on?

And why is he *on edge?*

Fuck. I couldn't find my breath, never mind the words. I knew what I came to say—what I needed to say—but I couldn't do it. What the hell?

Christian glanced through the window on the door, then turned to me, guard firmly up. "What's going up? You seem kinda... rattled, I guess?"

So do you, I didn't say out loud.

"I..." I pushed out a shaky breath and rubbed the back of my neck, wondering when those muscles had knotted up. What was I even supposed to say? How was I supposed to explain any of this?

"Theo. Look at me."

For the first time, I didn't want to do that, but I did what I was told. Christian's eyes were soft and full of concern. I could also see the glowing embers of the fire that always came to life when we were truly alone. Facing him now, I couldn't justify what I'd intended to do when I'd walked in here. I still knew all the reasons why I needed to end this, but for all I'd worried about the friendships and camaraderie I'd be losing if I lost this team, I hadn't thought about what *else* I'd be losing. *Who* else.

We're just hooking up. Why is it so hard to let you go?

Christian narrowed his eyes a little, like he was trying to read me. "What's going on?"

As my resolve died away, I wiped a hand over my face. "So, your dad stopped me on my way into practice."

Christian stiffened and his eyes widened. "Oh yeah?"

I nodded, and I told him about the brief exchange,

finishing with, "I can't decide if he's just fucking with me or if he knows something."

Christian chewed his lip and shifted his weight uncomfortably. "I don't think he knows. I feel like he'd confront me or..." Folding his arms, he shook his head. "Unless he's just enjoying playing games. I... God, I don't even know. Maybe he doesn't have a clue and he's just still messing with your head over the whole Pride Tape thing."

I sighed and leaned against one of the dryers. "I don't know. And... I'm not gonna lie. I came in here because I was going to tell you we shouldn't do this. I've got a lot on the line, and so do you, and I just..."

He tensed, swallowing hard. "Yeah. I, um. I get it. I do. If you can't, then I'll under—"

"No." I shook my head. "I came in here to end things, but now that I'm here..."

Christian watched me, brow pinched. "I don't want this to be a source of stress. You've got a lot of pressure on your shoulders already."

I nodded. "I know. But I just..." I ran a hand through my hair and blew out a breath. "I'm probably stupid as fuck, but now that I'm in here, I don't want to stop what we're doing. Even with everything that's at stake."

"I don't *want* to fuck up your career, though. Or have you resent me if it all blows up, though."

"If it does, it's not your fault."

"No, but if I wasn't in the picture, it wouldn't be an issue."

"And if it was anyone else," I admitted softly, "I wouldn't want to take the risk."

His eyebrows rose.

"I know what's at stake," I went on. "And I know we're

just hooking up and all, and we're probably being stupid as all hell, but… I *like* what we're doing. I like it, and I don't want to stop. Your dad has a ton of power of me and my future. I just can't convince myself to let him have control over this, too."

Christian's lips parted.

"If you don't want to," I whispered, "I'll understand. But I'm going into it with my eyes open. If it blows up in my face, then…" *Then I probably lose the NAPH. And you.* "Then it blows up in my face. But I don't want to stop doing this."

"Neither do I. I don't want to be selfish and ask you to risk your career, though."

"You're not." God, it was so hard not to reach for him right then. "I know what's on the line. I'm making the decision that I *want* to do this. Risk and all."

He held my gaze for a moment. Then he dropped his and leaned hard against the washing machine, looking anywhere but right at me. "To be honest, I was going to break things off too."

My stomach somersaulted. "Oh."

He kneaded the back of his neck and sighed. "My dad was on my back about some things last night. About my job, and…" Dropping his hand, he shook his head. "It's the usual stuff he fucks with me about—getting pissed at me for doing my job one way even though we both know he'd be pissed if I did it the other way, too—but it got me thinking. About what we're doing and what'll happen if he finds out." Christian swallowed hard, and he finally looked at me. "I was going to text you from my parents' driveway last night, but then I thought you deserved to hear it in person, and then you came in here and I saw you, and…" His shoulders slumped. "I can't fucking do it."

My heart didn't know whether to sink or speed up. "You can't?"

"No. I should. We're stupid as hell if we keep doing this. But..." Christian held my gaze even though it seemed like a struggle. "I can't explain it, but I just... can't pull away from you."

"Neither can I," I whispered. "And like, I know it's a risk. But when I was just crushing on you and didn't think this was going to happen, I was a mess, you know?" I laughed nervously. "It's almost like I'd be taking a bigger risk being distracted with my career if I pretended I didn't want you."

Christian chuckled. "So it wasn't just me? Getting distracted?"

"No. God, no. And I'm not saying—I don't want to pressure you or anything. That's not what I meant. I'm just saying that I'd rather put in the work to keep this a secret than drive myself insane seeing you every day without being able to touch you."

His lips parted. "Really?"

I nodded, my cheeks burning. "I don't know if that makes any sense. I just... I mean, what can I say?" I laughed. "I'd rather be stupid than stop."

To my great relief, Christian laughed, too. "Yeah. Same. Maybe I've just been around hockey players too long, but I—"

"Hey! What's that supposed to mean?"

"Uh, that a lot of you are impulsive, reckless, and a little nuts, and I think that's rubbed off on me?"

"Well, damn." I quirked my lips. "I can't even argue with that."

"Right? He smiled, the expression a mix of warm and

hot. "Or maybe I've just gotten too hooked on the things you do to me, and I don't want to give it up."

"Oh, I can relate." Why was I out of breath? "So... does that mean we're still going to do this?"

God, it was stupid and reckless, and I fucking knew it all the way to my bones, but when Christian gave me that sly grin? When his eyes narrowed just right to make my knees weak?

Fuck it. Sign me up for stupid and reckless.

He sobered a little. "We'll just have to be extra careful, though." He threw a wary glance at the window. "Really keep it on the DL."

"I think we've been pretty good about that, haven't we?"

"We have, but my dad..."

I pursed my lips. "He spooked me. But I mean, do you really think he knows anything?"

Christian seemed to consider it. "Probably not, or he'd have made a move beyond his usual cryptic bullshit comments. I think he was just being a dick to me because that's what he always fucking does, and he's messing with your head because he's still pissy about the stick tape."

I rolled my eyes. "Of course he is."

"And he will be for a long time." Christian glanced at the window again, then touched my hand. "So let's just take this as a sign from the universe to really cover our tracks. Go forward as if he's caught the scent and he's suspicious of us, and don't do anything to confirm his suspicions."

"So... same as before."

"Dialed up to a ten, but yeah."

"Okay." I smiled. "I can do that."

"Me too. And speaking of..." Christian took out his phone and checked the time. "It's one o'clock now. I'll probably be out of here around four." He turned an impish smile on me. "My place at six?"

"See you then."

We exchanged grins but didn't dare kiss. Not with that window showing us to anyone who walked by. We'd make up for that later.

As I left Christian to the laundry and went back to the locker room, my heart was racing. I was all the way back to my stall when I realized it wasn't the thrill of sneaking around that had my blood pumping. It was a mix of relief that I hadn't done the stupid thing, and the anticipation of everything Christian and I would be doing after six this evening.

I didn't know what to make of any of that. What it meant about whatever this was between us or how stupid we were really being.

I just knew I liked being with him.

And I was glad I hadn't ended it after all.

CHAPTER 14

CHRISTIAN

"Oh, my God..." I dropped onto the mattress beside Theo, still shaking all over from that orgasm. "I'm not gonna be able to walk tomorrow."

He laughed drunkenly. "So you don't want to go another round?"

"I didn't say that. I just said I wouldn't be able to walk tomorrow." I wiped sweat from my forehead. "If we go another round, though, I nominate you to be on top. My legs are *still* shaking."

Theo grinned. "Pretty sure I can manage that. And make your legs shake again."

I bit back a moan. This man was absolutely insatiable, and he was a spectacular lay. That months-long dry spell between our first and second hookups had been frustrating as all hell, but we'd been making up for lost time and then some. He had stamina to burn, the perfect-sized dick to fuck me senseless without leaving me sore, and... I mean, he was a hockey player. He had some serious strength in his lower body, and he *used it*. Even when I was riding him like I'd just done, he didn't lie still and let me do all the work.

"I should get rid of this." Theo groaned as he sat up. "Shower?"

"Mmm, good idea." I paused. "When I can stand."

He shot me a playful look. "Oh, come on. I didn't make you come that hard."

"Pfft. Says you." I moaned theatrically as I hauled myself up out of bed. My legs were still wobbly, but, yeah, I could stand enough to handle a shower. And hell, if my balance went wonky, I could always lean on Theo. *Such* a hardship.

Though my condo was blessed with an unusually large shower, we didn't need much of the real estate. We cleaned ourselves off, but then spent most of the time kissing and touching under the spray. I didn't have to lean on him to stay upright, but I did it anyway because I loved how I felt wrapped up in his powerful arms. He was leaner than a lot of guys I'd been with, but every inch of him was perfectly toned and tight. I could never get enough of touching him all over while we made out, and he seemed to enjoy that. In fact, he did the same thing—running his hands and fingertips all over my skin. Not just groping my ass or trying to turn me on, either. It was like he wanted to commit every inch of my body to memory.

I was more than happy to let him do it, too.

After a while, I came up for air and met his amazing dark eyes. Sliding my hands up his back, I said, "I'm glad we decided to keep doing this. Even if it's, um... risky."

Theo brushed a few strands of wet hair off my forehead. "Feels weird to think I was going to call it off. But one look at you..." He trailed off, shaking his head.

Some warmth rose in my face. "Really?"

He nodded, a blush in his own cheeks deepening the flush from the hot shower. "I can't really explain it. I was all set to say we can't do this. But as soon as I walked into that room..."

I kissed him lightly. "Must've been that intoxicating scent of unwashed jerseys."

He wrinkled his nose as he burst out laughing. "Oh, yeah. That's it. If that cart had been full of jock straps, we'd be on our way to Vegas right now to elope."

We both collapsed into laughter, which led to more kissing. First playful, then more languid and soft.

"We should get out of here," he murmured against my throat. "Before we use the whole building's hot water."

"Mmm, good point." I shut off the water and we got out of the shower. After we'd dried off, we returned to my bed, slid under the covers, and picked up right where'd left off—touching and kissing.

When he broke away this time, an unspoken thought creased his forehead.

I smoothed his wet hair. "What's on your mind?"

"Uh. Well..." His expression was completely serious now. "Listen, I don't want to rush anything, you know? I don't know what we're doing. What you want out of this. What *I* want out of it." He trailed featherlight fingertips along the edge of my jaw. "Literally the only thing I know is that regardless of what's at stake, I don't want to stop."

I wrapped my arms around his neck and pressed against him. "That's all we really need to know at this point, isn't it?"

"True. I just... I didn't want you to think that what we talked about earlier means we're getting serious. Or that we're not. Or..." He exhaled and shook his head. "I don't know. I guess I just don't want extra pressure on either of us?"

"I know what you mean." I brushed my lips across his.

"And like, we don't need to make any long-term plans or commitments. But you're the only one who's turned my head since that first time we hooked up. I don't see that changing any time soon." I half-shrugged. "So even if it's not serious—nor or ever—I wouldn't be opposed to us being exclusive."

Theo's eyebrows flicked up. For a split second, I thought he might pull away and declare that that was too much, but then his kiss-swollen lips curved into a smile. "I haven't touched anyone since the first time with you, so... Yeah. I'm good with being exclusive."

I grinned back, startled by the flutter of excitement in my chest. It wasn't like we were getting engaged or anything. We weren't getting serious. But still, the thought of being the only man he wanted was heady as hell. "Okay. So... just the two of us. Pretty sure I can keep you satisfied."

His laugh made my whole world a few shades brighter. Sleep with him and only him for the foreseeable future? Twist my arm.

Sobering a little, he searched my eyes. "Do you, um..." His blush was so adorable. "Do you want to keep using condoms?" He carded his fingers through my hair. "Or grab some blood tests and ditch them?"

I considered it. "I don't see any reason to keep using them if we're exclusive."

"Good." His shy smile turned into a wicked grin, and he slid closer to me. "Because I would love to fuck that beautiful ass of yours bareback."

"Mr. Mathis." I tsked, wrapping an arm around him. "You have a filthy mouth."

"Mmhmm." He brushed that mouth across mine. "Are you complaining?"

"Not in the least."

Neither of us said anything after that for a long, long time.

But I definitely kept that filthy mouth busy.

THEO AND I WERE EXTRA CAREFUL AFTER WE HAD THAT talk. We didn't take these risks lightly, and we made sure no one—especially my dad—caught even the faintest scent that there was anything between us.

It was tougher on the road, but we made it work. Sometimes one of us went to the hotel bar with the team. Sometimes both. We didn't make any conspicuous attempts to sit away from each other, but we also didn't try to sit together. On the plane, we'd occasionally wind up in the same card game, but Theo spent most flights with Grekov and Rusanov. They were the only guys on the team who Grekov could interact with easily, so I understood spending as much time with him as possible. I couldn't imagine the isolation of having a language barrier between me and nearly everyone I worked with.

It turned out Grekov did know some English. He wasn't fluent enough to joke around and banter, but he could carry on a conversation if people spoke a little slower and enunciated. In a pinch, he had his translator, Rusanov, or Theo handy to fill in the gaps. As he got more comfortable with the team, he started getting more outgoing with the English speakers, and he seemed to be feeling more like part of the group these days.

Still, it was always helpful to have someone to talk to who was as fluent as Theo or Rusanov.

Not gonna lie—I still found it endearing as hell that Theo went out of his way to help another Russian speaker find his place on the team. Card games. Chirping. Patiently translating during practices and while we were hanging out in bars. A lot of players did that if someone joined the team who didn't speak much English; the Swedes, the French Canadians, the Finns, the Russians—they all had each other's linguistic backs.

But every time I saw Theo bantering with Grekov or translating something on a menu at a restaurant, it melted my heart a little. I didn't care that other guys did the exact same thing. When Theo did it, it was sweet and adorable, and it definitely did nothing to cool my attraction to him.

It also had the added benefit of keeping any spotlight off Theo and me. If any rumors were going to start up about Theo getting involved with someone connected to the Rainiers, it was going to be Grekov, not me. Especially since Grekov was single. Straight? The jury was still out.

Either way, people were probably way more likely to think there was something going on between Theo and Grekov than Theo and me, and that was fine by me.

When we were in Seattle, it was game on at every available opportunity. He stayed at my condo more often than he stayed in his hotel room or his apartment.

Road trips just meant a lot of exchanged grins and racy texts, not to mention fucking like rabbits before we left. Tonight, we were in St. Louis for a game, and the pre-warmup routines were well underway. I was *still* aching all over from everything that had gone down after Theo walked into my condo the night before we left. Every time I moved, I could feel all the things we'd done. I was grinning like an idiot and no one but Theo had a clue why.

He definitely knew, too. Every time I caught his eye, he'd shoot me a smug little grin.

Cocky bastard.

Ah, well. He'd earned the right to be that cocky.

As we got closer to warmups, I noticed we were missing a goalie. In fact, now that I thought about it, Yanni hadn't been at the morning skate, either. Had he been at the team breakfast? I hadn't been paying nearly enough attention to notice.

Now, his locker stall was conspicuously unoccupied, his gear still set up exactly how I'd left it last night.

He wasn't injured, was he? That could be bad. He was our star goalie, and losing him for any length of time could be a disaster. Easton was good, but he wasn't Jan Stetina good.

The answer came when Coach Baldwin asked for everyone's attention.

"A little update to the lineup for tonight." He scanned all his players getting ready in the visitors' locker room. "Easton will be starting in net." With a grimace, he added, "Yanni's brother was injured in a PHL game last night and he's understandably shaken up over it."

A murmur of concern went around the room.

Condit spoke up first. "Is Marek okay?" His voice echoed the worry in all of us; teammates' family members were like extensions of our own families.

Coach nodded. "He took an open ice hit. Lost consciousness briefly, but he was able to get up and skate off the ice with help."

The room released a collective sigh.

"He'll be fine," Coach assured everyone. "But I think we can all sympathize with Yanni's head not being in the game tonight."

Solemn nods all around the room, and then everyone got back to work putting on their gear.

Yesterday must've been a hell of a roller coaster for

Yanni. First the league had announced that his dad was being inducted into the Hall of Fame, then his brother took a scary hit. No wonder Coach wasn't asking him to start tonight.

Yanni did come in and suit up, though, since he'd still be the backup goalie. Even from across the room, he was clearly not in a good place. I didn't blame him. He and Marek were close from what I'd gathered, and Yanni was incredibly protective of his baby brother. One by one, players gave him shoulder smacks and stick taps, probably telling him they hoped Marek was all right.

During warmups, I had my chance to talk briefly with him while I fixed the strap on his mask, and this time, it wasn't about how he somehow went through straps faster than every goalie I'd ever worked with combined. I'd give him grief about that another day.

As I replaced the strap, I glanced up at him. *Way* up, because he had skates on and he was—being a goalie—a giant. "Sorry to hear about Marek. How is he doing?"

Yanni winced. "He's got a terrible headache and his balance is a mess. He'll be fine, though. It's nothing life-threatening, and they're keeping an eye on him."

I nodded. I'd been around this sport long enough to know that head injuries could suddenly decide to become life-threatening, so the teams' medical staff kept a very, very close eye on them. "Well, he's in good hands with the league. Even at the PHL level."

"I know. And his team shares a training facility with the NAPH team, so he's got access to their doctors too. He'll be fine." Yanni frowned. "No idea how long he'll be on the bench."

"He's a Stetina." I handed back the goalie mask. "If he's

anything like his brother, they'll have to *tie* him to the bench."

Yanni laughed with some feeling as he pulled on the mask. "Probably. When I talked to him this morning, he was already bitching about not being able to skate." He rolled his eyes. "Idiot can't even stand up right now, but he's complaining because he's benched."

"Mmhmm, sounds just like his brother."

Yanni flipped me off.

"Rude."

He chuckled and skated away. I laughed too. I was glad Marek was recovering. Poor kid. Yanni would be okay, even if he was still too rattled to tend goal tonight.

I let my gaze drift around the ice. Naturally, it landed on Theo. As if he sensed me watching him, he glanced my way.

And he smiled.

And all those little aches lit up all over my body again.

God, I wanted him.

Was it time to go back to the hotel yet?

CHAPTER 15

THEO

This game was not going well. We were down by two halfway through the second period, and now we were setting up for a faceoff in our defensive zone. Not ideal with their first offensive line on the ice; their right winger already had two goals tonight, and I had no doubt he was itching for a hat trick.

Easton was doing his damnedest to keep us alive, but we'd stupidly allowed too many scoring opportunities. That was especially bad when this team knew all of Easton's tricks and weaknesses.

"Easton is solid," Condit had told us earlier. "But we can't forget that he played for St. Louis for eight seasons before he came to Seattle. Most of the guys there now, they played with him, so they practiced on him. Which means they know how to get under his skin and get past him, and they're going to use that to their advantage."

I'd caught Yanni's eye a few times as he hung out by the bench in his gear and baseball cap. He was clearly stressed out and miserable, and I didn't think it was all because of his brother's injury. This was one of those games when we needed him. Putting Easton up against the team who'd traded him a season ago wasn't necessarily a recipe for disaster, but it wasn't anyone's idea of a good plan A.

Plan B was what we had to work with tonight, though, and it wasn't Yanni's fault or Easton's. They'd both feel like shit if we lost this game, so I was extra determined to unfuck things.

I took my position beside one of St. Louis's wingers. Abrahamsson lost the faceoff, but Grekov poke-checked the puck away from St. Louis's center. He passed it to Foster, and just like that, my line was breaking away, flying toward the offensive zone.

Two defensemen closed in on Foster, so he passed to Abrahamsson, who whizzed around another skater before sending a stretch pass to me.

I was at the blue line and fully intended to send the puck to Foster, who had set up at the edge of the crease. But right as I was about to pass it to him, he and one of the defensemen were trying to jostle each other out of the way, and Foster's stick broke.

He dropped it and skated toward the bench. Abrahamsson was coming around the back of the net.

I passed to Grekov to keep the puck moving. He passed it back to me. We cycled it a few times, and as Foster returned to the zone with a new stick in hand, I skated closer to the net, ready to pass to him or Abrahamsson so they could tip it in.

No lane. No room.

I passed to Rusanov. He passed to Grekov. Grekov passed to me.

Still no lane. Still no—

Wait. The goaltender had lost track of the puck. He was

behind a dense screen of players from both teams, and he hadn't yet realized I had possession.

Abrahamsson and I locked eyes.

I wound back and shot the puck as hard as I could.

I fully expected Abrahamsson to tip it in, but one of the defensemen forced his stick up and out of the way.

Turned out it didn't matter:

Because the puck went in.

The red light came on.

For a split second, I was stunned. It... Had it really gone in?

I'd scored plenty of times in juniors and in the minors, but... had I just tallied my very first NAPH goal?

Abrahamsson, Foster, Rusanov, and Grekov all flew my way and tackle-hugged me against the glass.

"Nice one, kid!" Abrahamsson clapped my shoulder hard with his glove. "This is your first, isn't it?"

"Yeah!" I was laughing from excitement. "First one!"

Then we were skating by the bench for fist bumps with me leading the line for the first time ever. Didn't matter how many times I'd done this on my other teams—this was cooler than the moment I'd scored a game-winning goal in the playoffs in U16.

"Well done, Mathis!" Coach called out.

"Keep it up!" one of the other coaches said.

Our shift was over, so we came off the ice for a breather. As I stepped through the door, I met Christian's gaze.

He was hanging back a little, toolbelt on his hips and arms folded loosely across his hoodie, and...

Oh my God. That smile.

I was so overwhelmed by excitement that I almost —*almost*—grabbed him into a hug. And more than a hug.

The impulse to throw my arms around him and kiss him

right there behind the bench spooked me. As I sat down and took a few gulps of water, my heart was pounding, and not just from adrenaline and excitement.

Holy shit. I have to remember not to do that.

I didn't know if I'd actually have done it. If I had really forgotten myself enough that I would've slipped up, or if it was just a momentary lapse—a pleasant but intrusive thought—that wouldn't have gone anywhere.

Either way, I reminded myself we couldn't do that. Not even if I scored a game-winning hat trick goal in overtime.

That wasn't to say we couldn't celebrate. We'd just do it when we got back to the hotel and I managed to sneak away from my room and into his.

Goose bumps sprang up under all my hockey gear. Would he be game for that?

I chanced a quick look over my shoulder. Christian must've sensed me looking at him, because he flicked his eyes toward me.

Aww, fuck me. That little smile was going to end me.

Hockey, Theo. Focus on hockey.

I faced the game again. We could still win this thing. Condit's line was out now, and they had St. Louis on their heels. If we could keep them in their own end, keep them away from Easton, and get two more pucks into the back of their net, we could beat them.

I tapped my heel rapidly, the skate blade scraping against the bench. I had my first goal tonight. I had something to celebrate with Christian once we got back to the hotel. No way in hell did I want to do this halfway. I wanted a win alongside that goal. I wanted the night to end on a good note for Yanni and Easton.

We've got this, Rainiers. Let's fucking win it.

CHAPTER 16

CHRISTIAN

After a big win on the road, the Rainiers always wound up in the hotel bar until the early hours of the morning. Unless they had to be at the airport, of course, but this time their flight wasn't until late tomorrow morning.

Marty and I had stayed back at the arena with the rest of the equipment crew to finish loading up the trucks, and we'd gone to the airport to load the plane.

That was something we had down to a science, of course; we started breaking things down during the third period and packing them into crates. By the time the team was finished stripping off their gear and showering, all that remained was to grab everything they'd taken off, pack it, and load it. The trucks left the arena less than twenty minutes after the final whistle, and we were back at the hotel by one o'clock.

Unsurprisingly, the players were still in the bar, gathered around a large booth, loud and raucous and drunk after their comeback win. St. Louis had had them on their heels early on, but in the end, Seattle had stomped them 6-3. They deserved to celebrate, especially Condit, who'd managed a hat trick, and a certain winger who'd potted his first ever NAPH goal tonight.

After an eighteen-hour day, I was dragging ass and just wanted to go faceplant in my pillow. Marty and the other guys shuffled toward the elevator, all three of them fully in zombie mode and ready to collapse.

I should've followed. Really, really should've.

But I went into the bar anyway.

"Hey, Christian!" Condit slurred, waving his glass at me. "You joining us?"

"For a few minutes." The guys moved over enough that I could squeeze in on the end of the bench. I caught Theo's eye across the table but didn't hold his gaze, instead shifting my attention to the server who'd come to take my order.

"Yo, now that you're here..." Sorenson said. "Remember that night Langley's stick got stuck between the boards, and then Condit tripped over it and busted his skate?" He flailed a hand at Grekov. "Because he thinks we're lying."

"You *are* lying." Grekov gestured with his beer bottle. "Is bullshit."

"No, it's not bullshit." I tsked. "It was the stupidest thing, I'm telling you."

Grekov eyed me suspiciously.

"Okay, so they were playing in—I want to say it was Long Island?"

"Buffalo," a couple of the guys chimed in.

"Buffalo. Right, right. Anyway..." I waved a hand. "Somehow, the blade of Langley's stick got wedged between the boards behind the goal with the handle sticking up. Condit had no idea, and he comes flying around behind the goal, trips over it, and while he's trying to stay on his feet, he lands weird and manages to snap off his fucking blade." I shook my head and rolled my eyes. "And he broke the stick, too, which is just rude."

"Hey!" Condit crossed his arms. "I didn't see it!"

"Still! Those things are expensive!"

The captain huffed. "Yeah, well, I think I served my penance crawling the hell back to the bench while the game went on."

Grekov's eyebrows were almost to his hairline. "So... is not bullshit?"

"Nope." I shook my head. "I'm surprised no one got a video."

"Oh, there's videos," Condit said. "But you showed up, so now we don't have to find them."

"Lazy asses," I muttered. No one argued.

Grekov did want to see the video, though, so out came the phones.

While everyone was poring over YouTube, I stole the opportunity to steal a glance at Theo. He met my gaze across the table, but quickly flicked his eyes way. Understandable; if he was anything like me, he was terrified that even the most innocent glance lingering a second too long would give us away to the rest of the guys. Didn't matter that they were drunk and busy chirping. We were both paranoid. That was kind of a necessity if we wanted to stay employed by the Seattle Rainiers.

But sitting this close to him, casting surreptitious glances to drink in the sight of him in that navy blue suit, I was going to lose my mind. We'd been on the road for a few days, which meant we hadn't been able to touch.

Despite my long day and the promise of an even longer one tomorrow, and despite the increased risk of being caught, I needed to spend some time alone with Theo. Question was... how to pull that off without his teammates or my coworkers—all of whom were staying on the same floor of this hotel—finding out?

Eh, we could be stealthy. This late at night, the guys peeled away one or two at a time, so it wouldn't be suspicious if we left, and we'd have the elevator and hallway to ourselves. Even if someone else decided going to bed was a good idea, they wouldn't hang out in the hallway forever; Theo could just chill in his room for a few minutes, then sneak into mine.

But we probably shouldn't actually leave together. That would be a little too risky.

I took out my phone and wrote out a text.

Christian: *I'm going to head up to my room in 10 minutes. Room 922.*

Then I sent it, and I fixed my attention on Condit, who was drunk off his ass and animatedly telling a story about when he and Wilcox were in major juniors together. Theo's phone was facedown on the table, and when it buzzed, the vibration made it to my arm. I didn't dare look at him or the phone, though.

He waited a good two or three minutes before he even picked it up to look at it. When he read the screen, he swallowed hard, but otherwise didn't give away that anything had even registered.

He sat back in his chair and casually wrote out a text, sent it, and put the phone down again before turning his attention back to the story Condit was still slurring his way through.

It was absolute torture, pretending I hadn't felt my phone vibrate. Every minute I waited to look at it put more distance between the moment Theo sent a text and the moment I read it, which would throw everyone else off the scent that we were texting each other.

Everyone else who was drunk, laughing, and completely focused on whatever wild story Condit was telling. Literally no one cared about me, Theo, whether we were texting each other, or what we might be texting about.

Still, our jobs were on the line, so we were rightfully paranoid.

After four agonizing minutes, I casually took my phone out of my pocket.

Theo: *I'll wait another 10 after you leave.*

God, yes. I was so, so tempted to send back a teasing message about how I planned to wait for him and what he was going to do to me once he was in my room. I thought better of it, though. I didn't need one of his teammates to read over his shoulder, and if he ended up with a hard-on, it would take him even longer to get out of here and into me.

So I'd keep the teasing to myself.

After a couple of minutes, I drained my drink and got up. "All right, gentlemen. Some of us actually have to *work* for a living, and—"

That got me a chorus of "Fuck you" and "Let's see you skate five miles every goddamned night."

I chuckled. "Yeah, yeah. Anyway, I'm calling it a night. See you boys at breakfast."

"Going to bed already?" Abrahamsson slurred. "But the party is just getting started!"

"Uh-huh. Says the guy who isn't the first to the arena and the last to leave every night."

Immediately, half the guys started making "world's smallest violin" gestures.

I gave the haughtiest scoff I could and shook my head. "Go ahead, boys. Troll the man who decides which chemicals wash your jocks."

That changed their tunes, and they all shouted, "Whoa,

wait" and "You know we were kidding, right?" at my back as I headed out of the bar. I just smiled cheekily and flipped them all off before continuing to the elevator.

I chuckled to myself. I loved the relationship I had with all these men. There was plenty of chirping and trolling, which was basically how hockey players showed affection. I also knew they deeply respected and appreciated me as well as the other equipment managers. More than a few of them went out of their way to thank us for keeping everything running smoothly, and they went all out for us on Christmas, birthdays, and the end of the season.

As I waited for the elevator, my smile fell a bit. All the teams treated their equipment managers that way if they knew what was good for them, but I was also close to these guys. They were like brothers to me, and I felt it every time one of them was traded, retired, or signed elsewhere. I worried when Yanni's brother got hurt or when Foster's wife's pregnancy had some complications last year. People said that "we're like a family" was a red flag for a toxic work environment, but in hockey, teams and organizations really *were* like family.

And the relationships I had within this family were arguably more loving and functional than the one I had with my own father.

Was I being stupid, risking this camaraderie so I could screw one of their teammates? And how would they feel if they found out? They were all completely fine with my sexuality, and in my time with the team, there'd been two openly gay players who'd passed through without any issues (aside from my dad being a dick). But would that good will extend to a player and an employee hooking up? Would they be okay with two of their teammates hooking up?

Would it suddenly get weird in the locker room if everyone knew two people in the room had been fucking?

Well, it probably wouldn't matter anyway. If the players knew, then Dad would know, and Theo and I would both be gone.

The elevator doors opened and I stepped inside. As I rode up to the ninth floor, I reminded myself for the millionth time that I was taking a massive risk.

But also for the millionth time, I didn't heed my own warnings.

Maybe I was playing with fire, but what could I say?

I loved the heat too much to stop.

CHAPTER 17
THEO

The time between when Christian left and when I casually got up from the table was easily the longest ten minutes of my life. I gave the guys some money to cover my portion of the tab and tip, and then I tried not to sprint across the lobby to the elevators.

In the elevator, I pressed the button for the ninth floor, leaned against the wall, and exhaled, willing myself not to get visibly aroused. It would be just my luck someone would get in with me, and then there'd be headlines about the pervy Seattle Rainier wandering a hotel with a prominent boner. Not ideal, especially for someone trying to get a foothold in this league.

And it's so ideal to be banging the hell out of the homophobic general manager's son, who also happens to work for the team?

I grimaced, but I didn't spend too much time worrying about it. I went through that little *"oh fuck, what am I doing?"* spiel every time I was about to meet up with Christian, and it hadn't talked me out of anything yet. I doubted it was going to start now. One look at him—hell, one thought of him—and all logic and reason left the building.

At the ninth floor, I got out and strode down the deserted hallway as the numbered doors counted down to Christian's room. No one had been in the elevator. No one was here in the hallway. No one was going to have a clue where I was going or why.

I bit my lip as I neared his door, but then an uncomfortable sinking feeling followed. One that had been getting more and more noticeable—and familiar—over the past couple of weeks.

Every time Christian and I slipped under the team's radar, I got a little thrill.

Lately, though, another feeling chased that thrill, and it wasn't nearly as fun.

What if what we were doing was only this hot and exciting *because* it was forbidden? If the team found out and Jack decided to let it go, and we could be out and proud as a couple... would it be nearly as fun as sneaking around?

Do we only want each other like this because it's against the rules?

Fuck. That was a thought.

On the other hand, did it have to be anything more than that? The sex was mind-blowing. The secrecy was thrilling. We were just hooking up, so why make it more complicated? If the novelty wore off, we'd move on and go our separate ways. No harm, no foul.

So why did just thinking about moving on make a ball of lead swell in my gut?

Because the sex is awesome and God only knows where you're going to find anyone who can blow your mind like Christian does, so get in there and rock his world, dumbass.

Sounded good to me.

Christian had left the door slightly open, using the swing bar lock to keep it from closing all the way.

Heart thumping and cock thickening, I stepped into the room, flipped the swing bar out of the way, and closed and locked the door behind me.

Oh, fuck.

Christian was waiting for me the same way he had been the night I'd come to his condo—completely naked, fully hard, with his legs spread and his fingers sliding in and out of his hole.

"Jesus fuck," I breathed as I unbuttoned my jacket. "That's a damn good way to make a man come in his pants."

"Don't come in your pants." He gave me a saucy wink. "Come in me."

I snorted, and we both started laughing as I joined him on the bed. He grabbed a handful of my jacket and tie with his free hand and dragged me down into a kiss. Not that I resisted—I met him just as eagerly and hungrily, and I stroked his dick just to make him squirm some more.

"Fuck me," he demanded. "Right now."

"Right—"

"*Now.*" He started undoing the front of my pants.

I shivered with anticipation as I reached for my belt. "You don't even want me to get undressed?"

"Mmm, I love when you're naked," he murmured, "but I also love when you fuck me while you're wearing one of these suits."

I growled softly and claimed his mouth again. Between us, we managed to get my pants and underwear out of the way.

"Lemme get some lube," I murmured.

"Don't need any." He stroked my dick with his slick hand. "Already got plenty."

I closed my eyes and moaned, rutting into his fist. "Fuuuck..."

"C'mon, baby." He nudged the back of my thigh with his heel. "I need your dick. Right now."

Like I was going to say no to that.

He spread his legs wider and I guided myself in, and oh fuck, he wasn't kidding. He took me easily, digging his nails into my shoulder as my dick sank into his well-prepped hole.

"Oh my God," I breathed. "Jesus..."

Beneath me, Christian arched, pressing his head back into the pillow and gripping a handful of my shirt for dear life. "Fuck, yes... God, Theo, that's exactly what I —*fuuuck*..."

I could barely breathe. He looked so sexy, falling apart underneath me, and he was so tight and slick and hot—if I moved any faster I was going to lose it.

He moaned and swore, stroking himself between us with his other hand. His blissed-out expression—eyelids fluttering closed, lips apart, skin flushed—drove me absolutely wild. I'd always loved topping, but there was nothing in the world like topping *him*.

"I have never been with anyone who likes it in the ass as much as you do."

Christian bit his lip. "That a feature or a bug?"

I groaned softly and leaned down to kiss his neck as I pushed back into him. "Have I ever complained about you wanting my dick in your ass?"

The response was a whimper.

"For the record," I mumbled against his throat, "I love fucking you. I love fucking anyway, but when it's you..." I trailed off into some slurred curses as I rocked into him a little faster.

He dug his nails into my shoulder through my jacket as he pumped himself even faster. "Nobody fucks me as good as you do."

I grinned, then rocked into him harder. "Don't you forget it."

He laughed softly, sounding almost drunk, and then moaned as he rolled his hips to drive me on. We fell into sync with each other, moving faster and harder until he was damn near sobbing and I felt so good I thought I might pass out.

"Oh my God," he whined. "Baby, that's so... Ungh, I'm gonna come."

"Good. Make me come too."

The deliciously choked whimper that escaped his throat sent me right over the edge, my orgasm knocking a cry out of me as I fucked into him as deep and hard as I could. Then he was clenching around me, swearing and almost crying as he came between us.

I exhaled and slumped over him. There was cum on my suit now, not to mention sweat, but I just didn't care. I still had two others I could wear on this road trip. Trembling and trying to catch my breath, I buried my face against his neck and let the last few aftershocks roll through me.

"Holy fuck," Christian murmured.

"Uh-huh." I kissed beneath his jaw, reveling in the way that made him shiver. "Something like that."

He laughed softly. "Cocky fucker."

"You better believe it." I pushed myself up on shaking arms and met his gaze. "I can turn you into a crying, coming mess. I've earned the right to be cocky."

"I wasn't crying," he said even as he wiped his eyes.

"Sure you weren't baby." I came down and brushed a soft kiss across his lips. "You sure were coming, though."

"Mmm, you better believe it."

"Think we should grab a shower?" I carefully pulled out, making both of us gasp. "Or do you want me to take off?"

As we both sat up, Christian huffed and rolled his eyes. "Theodore whatever-your-middle-name-is Mathis, do not ask stupid questions." He tugged at my lapel. "Get these clothes off and get in my shower."

I just laughed and started undoing my tie.

CHAPTER 18

CHRISTIAN

After the night Theo fucked me senseless while his teammates were downstairs at the hotel bar, we gave up on staying apart on the road. Whenever we could swing it, we didn't miss an opportunity to discreetly hook up on the road. Sometimes we even got lucky and had a whole evening wide open without a game.

An evening like... tonight. The team had taken a short hop into Vancouver late last night after a home game, and they'd practiced this morning. There'd be a morning skate tomorrow, followed by a game that night, but they had this afternoon and this evening free. A lot of the guys went out to dinner. Or they went golfing and *then* went out to dinner.

Me and Theo? We were staying in tonight. He'd slipped into my room while the rest of the guys took off down to the lobby, and we'd put in an order for room service. The hotel's kitchen was apparently busy as hell, too, because they gave us a solid hour ETA for our dinner. That would've been unfortunate had we been climbing the walls and hangry. Or if we'd been bored.

Neither of us was dying of hunger quite yet, and bored?

We were definitely not bored.

"Ooh, yeah..." Theo carded his fingers through my hair as I licked up and down his shaft. "Fuck, baby, your mouth is incredible."

I hummed around his dick, then teased the head with my tongue, loving the way that made his legs shake. He was sitting up against the headboard with me between his powerful thighs, and every time I looked up at him, my own dick reminded me it needed attention. He was so hot like that, gazing down at me with heavy-lidded eyes, his lips apart as he whispered curses and encouragement. I loved the way his fingers combed through and sometimes tugged at my hair, twitching whenever his hips jerked or his back arched.

"Oh my God," he purred. "I want to come so bad, but I also want you to keep doing that all night."

I ran my tongue down his shaft before teasing his balls with the tip, drawing little light circles on the soft skin because I loved how it made him gasp.

"Jesus fuck..." He was gripping my hair so tight it bordered on painful. "God, Christian..."

I teased his balls some more, then worked my way back up to the head. The salt of precum met my tongue, and I went to town on him, stroking him with one hand while I worked the head with my mouth. I was rewarded with more cursing, more gasping, more of his fingers kneading and pulling and twitching against my scalp.

He exhaled a harsh breath and pushed his dick deeper into my mouth. In his position, he couldn't really fuck my face like he probably wanted to, but he tried his damnedest, and we both moaned as the head slid back and forth on my tongue. I pumped him in time with his erratic half-thrusts, and his shuddering breath and trembling legs said he was close, so close. His dick was rock-hard between my lips, too, his balls pulling up as I licked away more precum.

"Oh God," he breathed. "I'm gonna come. You ready, baby? You want me to come like this?"

My answer was tighter strokes and even more insistent teasing with my tongue, and he shuddered hard as his dick thickened in my hand. Then he gasped and swore. His whole body tensed. His hips jerked, as if he wanted to push even farther into my mouth, and then he was coming, crying out helplessly as I took every drop.

I kept going until he murmured for me to stop. I'd barely lifted myself up off him before he grabbed me, shoved me onto my back, and claimed my mouth, his tongue plunging in as if he desperately needed to taste himself on me. His hand closed around my dick, and his kiss muffled a whimper as he started pumping me. He'd caught me by surprise, but I was so overwhelmed with need—for him, for friction, for my own release—that I just held on and fucked into his hand as he stroked and kissed me mercilessly.

I couldn't have stopped my orgasm if I tried, and I didn't try. It was fast and furious, just a few moments of him kissing me and pumping me, and then I was coming all over both of us, trembling beneath his amazing body as he swallowed all my cries and curses.

When I relaxed under him, he relented, letting his lips skate along my throat while I gulped in air. His hand had slowed to a stop, and he let go. He pulled away just long enough to clean off the cum, then came back and wrapped me up in his arms and started on my neck again.

"I don't know if I've mentioned it," he murmured against my jaw. "But I love making you come."

I shivered beneath him and ran my hands up his back. "I was, uh... I was definitely getting that impression."

He chuckled softly and came up to kiss me on the mouth. It was gentler this time, and I wrapped my arms around his neck as we languidly made out.

He pushed himself up on his arms. He was straddling my hips now, and he gazed down at me with bliss-filled eyes. Combing his fingers through my hair, he said, "Maybe being too sore to fuck isn't such a bad thing after all."

I laughed softly and trailed my hand up his arm. "We don't always have to fuck, you know. I love getting dicked down, but not when you're sore." I studied him. "How sore are you, anyway?"

"Eh, not bad." He shifted a little and winced. "My hip is still salty after last night."

I scowled. "It looked like a pretty hard hit."

Theo made a face. "It was. And no penalty, either." He rolled his eyes.

"Ugh. The officiating last night was trash. The refs let that horseshit slide, but they put Condit in the box for"—I made sarcastic air quotes—"boarding."

Theo huffed with annoyance. He lifted himself off me and eased down onto his side, then flexed and straightened his leg. With a wince, he muttered, "This better be fucking back to normal tomorrow."

I slid closer to him and ran my hand up his chest. "I'm sure it will be. The medical staff checked you out and didn't find anything wrong, right?"

He nodded. "Yeah, they said it would probably be sore for a day or two. I'll see how I feel skating in the morning."

"How was it today?"

He wobbled a hand in the air. "Not great? But I think that was also the flight and lack of sleep."

I grinned. "So, what you're saying is... I should make sure you sleep like the dead tonight?"

He returned the grin. "Exactly. That's why I'm really here—it's physical therapy."

"Uh-huh. I'm sure the trainers wrote you a prescription and everything."

Theo just laughed, and my God, he was so damn cute. More and more, it was moments like this—lying in bed, cuddling and talking—that drew me to him. The sex was off the charts, of course, but *this* was the part I really looked forward to. When we were behind closed doors, naked and comfortable, and we could just... be. Talk about whatever. Kiss. Touch. Be close to each other.

I'm getting in over my head, aren't I?

Yeah. I was. Quite happily, too.

Unaware of my thoughts wandering off, Theo craned his neck to look past me at the nightstand. "Room service will be here in a few. I guess we should..." He gestured at both of our naked, sweaty bodies.

"Good call." I hesitated. "The, um... The staff might recognize you. They know the team is staying here."

His brow pinched. "I mean, they all got a little starstruck over Condit and Sorenson, but I doubt any of them will give me a second look." He paused. "Still, maybe I should duck into the bathroom just to be safe."

I nodded. "Probably not a bad idea."

"Eh, I need a shower anyway." He kissed me lightly, then pushed himself up. "Do you need cash for the tip?"

"I've got it. You can get the next one."

About ten minutes later, our food arrived. Theo had finished showering, but he stayed out of sight in the bathroom. When the coast was clear, he came out, and I swear I felt his mouth start watering when he laid eyes on the steak he'd ordered.

We sat down at the table by the window, and after he

took a bite, he made a happy noise that was almost obscene. "Oh my *God*, that's good."

I scoffed. "So you're more turned on by the steak than by me?"

He met my gaze with an innocent look, then shrugged. "It's a New York strip cooked to a perfect medium rare. What do you want me to say?"

I just laughed and rolled my eyes. "Shut up and eat."

He chuckled, and we continued eating. As we did, we debated what to watch after dinner. There were some hockey games in various cities tonight, and we were both way behind on some TV shows that we could easily stream.

This was perfect in a way it had no business being. We were supposed to be hooking up, but that ship had sailed a long damn time ago. Now... Hell, I didn't know what we were doing, only that it didn't feel like the casual-but-exclusive screwing I'd signed up for in the beginning.

I didn't know what we were doing... but I liked it.

And risks be damned, I still didn't want to stop.

So I didn't.

CHAPTER 19

THEO

My hip was still sore the next morning, but our light practice helped. I spent some time skating before and after practice just to loosen things up, and by the time I headed back into the locker room, I was mostly good. I checked in with Dave, one of the athletic trainers, and he agreed that I'd be fine for tonight.

"If you were on the top line," Dave remarked, "I'd be worried about managing your minutes. But you'll only be playing third or fourth line minutes, so you should be good. Just let me know during the intermissions how you're doing."

I could live with that. Coach seemed relieved, too; after that tsunami of injuries had sidelined so much of the team, the last thing he needed was someone else going down.

Dave did some work to release the tension in my hip and quads, which helped. There wasn't much any of us could do for the places that were bruised; they were going to be tender for a couple of days no matter what. Getting everything moving helped a lot.

After he was done with me, I spent the day carefully

encouraging my hip to unfuck itself the rest of the way. Some light work on the stationary bike helped get things moving without too much pain. Walking like I always did before games also helped. Dave suggested an ice bath after the game, but... no. I'd tried those a few times in major juniors, and all they did was make me cold and—in two super-fun instances—make me puke.

If I was sore after the game, I'd put an icepack on it, but the ice *bath* could go straight to hell.

By puck drop, I was as good as I was going to be, and though there was still an annoying ache in my hip, I played hard like normal.

The game was intense, too. We were neck in neck through the first and second periods, and my line was out now, trying to break the tie so we could start the third with a lead.

Foster sent me the puck, and I tore across the red line toward the offensive zone. A defenseman got on me and was trying to get the puck away. He got me up against the glass, but I still protected the puck, keeping it on my stick and away from his in the narrow space between my body and the boards.

Finally, I managed to slip past him, the puck still on my stick, and—

Someone came out of nowhere and slammed me *hard* into the boards. My pads offered some protection, but they could only do so much, especially for the elbow he shoved into my midsection. Pads or not, it still fucking hurt, and it stunned me bad enough I dropped to the ice while he skated away.

My hip was unimpressed, but it was fine—nothing I couldn't skate off—so I scrambled to get up, but—

Couldn't inhale.

At all.

I dropped onto one hand as panic ripped through me.

Fuck. Fuck, fuck, fuck. I *couldn't breathe.*

Distantly, I was aware of a whistle. Of people banging on the glass. Someone nearby was shouting. There was a hand on my shoulder.

Still couldn't breathe. The air just wouldn't *move.*

Someone suddenly appeared beside me, crouching on the ice. "Hey. Mathis." Dave squeezed my arm through my pads. "Look at me. Look at me, Mathis."

I lifted my gaze.

"You're good." He sounded way, way too calm. "You just got the wind knocked out of you."

Easy for him to fucking say. Did he not realize I couldn't fucking breathe?

"In through your nose," he said. "In through your nose, out through your mouth."

Fuck him. Didn't he understand I couldn't breathe in at all? Christ, my vision was getting dark. I couldn't—

"Come on, kid. In through your nose. Trust me."

It didn't matter how I breathed—none of it was working. Did he not get that—

Some air finally moved.

"That's good," he said. "Out through your mouth. Then in through your nose, as deep as you can."

I closed my eyes and did as I was told. I was still panicky, still freaking the ever-loving hell out, but every breath moved a little more air than the last. The sound of myself wheezing made my skin crawl.

It also made me realize the whole arena had fallen deathly silent.

Yeah, this probably looked scary as hell to anyone watching from the stands or on TV. When someone went down and didn't get back up, it could mean anything, and I'd seen it mean something serious on multiple occasions.

I was good, though. I really had just had the goddamned wind knocked out of me, and as more and more breath flowed freely—as my lungs actually started to fill more and more with each inhalation—that awful feeling of panic subsided. Though I wanted the crowd and the players to know I was all right, I indulged in another few seconds to draw a couple of breaths, just to be sure I really was breathing all right.

"That's it," Dave said. "Think you can get up?"

I nodded. Then I opened my eyes and nodded slowly. "I'm good." My voice still sounded wheezy and taut. "Scared the fuck out of me, but... I'm good."

He clapped my shoulder. "Figured you would be. All right. Let's get you back into the locker room."

I didn't argue. I was probably fine to play on, but he'd want to check me over more thoroughly just to be sure. Besides, the period was almost over. I could come back after intermission.

With the help of Dave and Grekov, who'd been hovering nearby, I slowly got to my feet. As soon as I started to get up, the crowd cheered and all the players from both teams began tapping their sticks on the boards or the ice. I held up a gloved hand to wave at the crowd, and they cheered even louder as I skated toward the bench, still leaning on Grekov as I caught my breath. I knew that relief—seeing someone go down was scary as hell, and seeing them leave the ice more or less on their own power meant they were okay. Banged up, maybe, but okay.

As I passed the bench, I caught Christian's eye. He'd gone white as a sheet, but he flashed a quick smile. Probably as relieved as everyone else in the building.

I gave him a little tap with my glove as I passed, and he patted my shoulder. Nothing incriminating. Nothing that telegraphed we were romantically or sexually involved. Just a staff member offering up some encouragement to a player after a scary moment on the ice.

Dave checked me over in the locker room, and he decided I was fine. I'd be sore tomorrow (what else was new?), but I wasn't showing any signs that I needed to go on concussion protocol. I had full mobility. I could draw a full breath. My chest hurt, but in that way that meant I'd been sandwiched between a large body and Plexiglas, not that I'd broken some ribs or that something was going wrong with my heart or lungs.

By the time the team came clomping in for intermission, I was cleared to return to the game. I got a lot of back slaps and chirps from my teammates.

Christian came over to my locker stall as I downed some sports drink. "How's your gear? Anything I need to fix?"

It was a perfectly valid thing for an equipment manager to check in on after a hit like that, but I still felt conspicuous. As if someone would notice if we held eye contact a little too long.

"Nah, I think I'm good." I smiled up at him, my heart fluttering when he subtly returned it. "Just had to get my lungs working again."

Christian grimaced. "Yeah. That didn't look fun. And everything's good? With your gear and with, um... With you?" His brow pinched with very real concern.

"I'm fine." I tilted my bottle toward Dave, who was talking to Coach about something. "He says I'm good to come back for the third."

"Good. Good." Christian nodded. "Just be careful out there, all right?" His eyes flicked to either side, and he tensed as if he thought Grekov or one of the other guys nearby might read between the lines. He cleared his throat and quickly added, "I don't have an extra chest protector for you, so I'll have to duct tape it together if you break it."

I laughed and rolled my eyes. "Fuck you."

He chuckled, gave me a surreptitious wink, and then left to do his job. There were extras of all of our gear, so I knew he was just talking shit. Knowing him, though, he'd make me wear one wrapped in duct tape just to troll me.

I loved that about him.

When we returned to the ice, the battle continued, but nobody on either side could put a puck into a net. Well, someone from Vancouver managed to, but Coach successfully challenged it for goaltender interference. Then Condit scored, but Vancouver's coach challenged it for offside. For fuck's sake.

Back and forth, back and forth. As I went over the boards or another shift, I glanced up at the screen to check the situation. The game was tied 3-3 with four minutes to go in regulation.

No pressure, or anything.

Vancouver managed to break away and get into our zone. I poke-checked the puck away from one of their forwards just as he got into the zone, but one of their players snagged it before Foster could get to it.

Yanni lunged for the puck, going a couple of feet out of the crease, and he passed it to me.

It landed right on my tape, and I whipped around to send it along the boards to Foster, who was waiting near the blue line.

But I miscalculated my release. Instead of flying toward the boards, the puck zipped straight toward *our fucking goal.*

The instant the puck left my stick, people in the crowd gasped and my heart stopped. The net was still wide open, Yanni still regaining his balance and getting back into the crease.

Grekov came out of nowhere, though. He dashed into the crease, grabbed the puck on his stick, and flew toward the neutral zone.

I wavered on my skates, our fans' collective sigh of relief echoing my own, and then I was chasing Grekov.

As soon as he was in the zone, he slapped it on goal. The goalie stopped it, but we had a faceoff in the offensive zone.

My line returned to the bench while Condit's line came out for their shift. I was relieved, too, and not just because I was tired from an intense minute out there. I was still rattled as I took my seat on the bench.

An own goal was never good. An own goal in the third period of a tied game? Against a division team that was dangerously close to edging us out of the wild card spot? Not. Fucking. Ideal.

I shakily grabbed a water bottle. As I squirted some in my mouth, I tried to will my pulse to come down. We were good. I was good. Grekov had saved our bacon, and we were still alive. Still had a chance to win in regulation if we could score in the next—I looked up—two and a half minutes. I hadn't fucked us over.

Beside me, Abrahamsson clapped my back. "Shake it off, man. Happens to the best of us."

I nodded. "Thanks. I still feel like an idiot."

"Nah." He bumped his shoulder against mine. "Remind me in the locker room and I'll show you the video of Phillips scoring an own goal during the playoffs."

I turned to him, eyebrows up. "Seriously?"

Grimacing, he nodded. "I mean it—happens to the best of us."

Well, that much was encouraging. And, like, I knew it was true. Own goals were rare, and they were embarrassing as all hell, but it wasn't like I would've been the first or the last to score one. Plus, Grekov would now be in every highlight reel imaginable after swooping in and snagging the puck about an inch before it would've crossed the goal line. I didn't even mind people prefacing it with "After dumbass Mathis forgets which goal he's aiming for..." or something.

Okay, I minded. A little. But I tried to hold on to the fact that he'd get some glory out of this, and in the end, it had been a near miss, not a catastrophe. Could've been a whole lot worse.

With ninety seconds left on the clock, one of Vancouver's players went to the box for slashing. Ooh, power play on a tied game. Nice.

Seattle called a timeout. While the power play coach talked with the players on both units, Coach leaned over beside me. "Don't let it mess with your head, kid, all right? You've been holding your own up here. One mistake isn't going to end it all."

I wanted to believe that. I really, really did. Problem was, I knew how easily one mistake or misstep *could* end it all. If Seattle hadn't been mercilessly plagued with injuries this season, I never would've come back to this level at all. With players steadily returning from IR and LTIR, and with some of my Everett teammates shining in the PHL, the Rainiers didn't need a reason to bump me back down. The least I could do was not hand them one.

And it got a whole lot harder to believe Coach and Abrahamsson when I was pulled aside before I even made it back to the locker room.

"You want to tell me what the fuck that was all about?" Jack Hayes shouted in my face once we were relatively alone. "Do you need to go back to major juniors? Huh? Do you not realize you're in the NAPH?"

"No, I-I do," I stammered. "I just misjudged—"

"'I just misjudged,'" he mocked. Then his expression darkened. "I think you need to remember your situation, kid. If your head's not in the game, you let me know." He held up his phone and jiggled it in my face. "One phone call, and I can have you back in Everett with the other kids. Is that what you want?"

I gulped. "No, sir. No. I'm—my head's in the game."

"Is it, though?" Jack narrowed his eyes. "Then what the fuck was that? Huh? Tell me."

"It..." I shifted my weight, my skate blades scraping on the hard floor and giving me away. "I fucked up. It won't happen again."

His lips pulled into a snarl. "Then why the hell did it happen in the first place?"

"It..." I was having a harder time breathing than when I'd been winded on the ice. Air just wouldn't fucking move.

Jack apparently ran out of patience. He stabbed a finger at me. "Get it together, or get ready to go back to the PHL for the rest of your pathetic career."

Then he stalked away, leaving me there with his threats ringing in my ears. I pushed out a ragged breath and slumped against the cold cinder block wall. What the fuck was that all about? Had I really fucked up that bad? Yeah, I'd almost scored an own goal at the worst possible time, but...

Goddamn. Maybe he was right. Maybe I didn't belong here.

Right then, Condit stepped out of the locker room,

jersey off but chest protector still on. "Hey. Kid." The captain's brow pinched as he approached. "You good?"

Well, that answered that—yes, my teammates *had* been able to hear Jack going off on me. Because that made it *way* less embarrassing.

"I, um..." I swallowed hard and ran a hand through my wet hair. "I don't know. I think?"

He glanced in the direction Jack had gone, his lips pulled tight and his eyes narrow. Facing me again, he asked, "What did he say to you?"

Okay, so maybe they hadn't heard everything. The shouting, yes, but not the specifics. And I didn't want to rehash it all. Embarrassment had me wanting to brush past him and head into the locker room. I still needed to shower, and maybe that would help rinse away all the shame that itched on my skin like dried sweat.

Condit sighed. "Listen. Don't take it to heart, okay? Jack's a—" He cut himself off, pressing his lips together as he shook his head. Looking me right in the eyes, he said, "You're killing it out there, okay? Coach sees it. We all do."

"Except I almost cost us the game."

"And Vancouver tied the game after I turned over the puck and basically handed it to one of their forwards."

I blinked.

"Watch the replay." He shrugged. "I guarantee the commentators were apoplectic over it. Especially because the shift before, Wilcox did a drop pass that one of their d-men snatched up and used to score."

"He... oh." I knew that. I'd watched both of those play out from the bench, and I'd nearly had heart failure when I'd realized our guys had given up scoring chances. Especially when those scoring chances paid off.

"You made a mistake," Condit went on, "but it wasn't a costly one. Not at all."

"Thank God Grekov was there," I muttered.

"Uh-huh. And thank God Sorenson was there when I fanned on a shot and they got a breakaway. And Yanni was there for thirty-eight out of forty-one times they were able to put a puck on goal." He chuckled and shook his head. "Man, I know how easy it is to feel like everything is your fault because you made a mistake. But when you step back and look at the whole game, there's always a whole pile of mistakes. Sometimes they cause goals against. Sometimes they don't." He shrugged. "It's just part of the game."

"I guess. Jack sure wasn't happy about it, though."

"Eh. He'll get over it."

"Yeah." I glanced in the direction our GM had gone. "I just hope he doesn't make good on that threat to send me down."

"He won't." Condit sounded sure. Hell, *authoritative*: as if he wasn't just sure—he was going to *make* sure. "There's a reason you've stayed up as long as you have. No one's going to send you back down because you made one mistake that didn't even cause a goal against." He clapped my shoulder again. "Come on. We need to shower and eat before the buses leave."

I nodded and followed him. I felt a tiny bit better after we'd talked, but I was still off-balance and unnerved. I wanted to say I had no idea why Jack had it out for me, but I did. At least... I thought I did. He was still salty about the Pride Tape, right?

But what if he knows he has another reason to be pissed at me?

A chill ran through me.

What if he did? What if he'd somehow picked up the scent, and he knew Christian and I were hooking up?

I wiped a hand over my face. No. He hadn't. We'd been careful, and Jack wasn't subtle enough to let something like that slide if he knew.

I was just getting fucking paranoid, and after getting reamed out like that, I was on edge. That was all it was.

Closing my eyes, I pushed out a breath. Jack was just being a dick. He didn't know anything.

And the longer I stood out here like a dumbass, the less time I'd have to spend curled up with Christian back at the hotel. There wouldn't be any sex tonight, but we could probably squeeze in some cuddling.

With that in mind, I pushed my shoulders back, strode into the locker room, and got the hell out of the arena as quickly as I could.

CHAPTER 20

CHRISTIAN

Sneaking away from the hotel bar was easier than usual.

I'd come back late to the hotel after running all the team's gear to the airport, and after poking my head in to say hi, I went up to my room. No one questioned me when I did that.

The unusual part was that Theo wasn't in the bar with the guys, and apparently no one had questioned that, either.

Gingerly easing himself down on my bed, he said, "They pretty much told me to go upstairs and go to sleep."

"They're smart." I carefully joined him. "How are you feeling?"

He made a face. "Sore as fuck." He met my gaze with apologetic eyes. "There isn't going to be any action tonight." He grimaced. "Everything fucking hurts. I'm sorry."

"Oh my God, don't apologize." I laced our fingers together. "I wouldn't expect anything physical tonight. Hell, I'm amazed you played after that."

"Nah, it wasn't bad enough to keep me from playing." He laughed quietly, wincing a little. "But it's hard to enjoy anything when it hurts like this."

"Then we won't. It's fine. I promise." I brought his hand up and kissed it. "And you're just sore, right? Not actually hurt?"

"I'm fine. I've got some sexy-looking bruises showing up, and my back and ribs hurt like hell. My neck's sore, too." He groaned. "I get hit all the fucking time, but something about the way he got me..."

"I bet." I squeezed his hand. "Not gonna lie—that was terrifying, when you couldn't get up."

Theo drew me in closer. "I'm sorry. I know it scares the hell out of people, seeing us down like that." He pressed a kiss to my forehead. "To tell you the truth, I probably could've gotten up sooner, but I just needed a minute to make sure I wasn't going to pass out."

"I don't blame you at all. And honestly, I could tell from watching Dave that you were okay."

"Yeah?"

I nodded, absently running my thumb along the back of his. "When he sat up and was just kind of holding on to your shoulder, everyone on the bench relaxed a bit."

"Oh, that's good. It makes sense, too, now that you mention it. I always watch the trainers when I'm trying to get a bead on if someone's okay."

"Yeah, it's a dead giveaway sometimes." I kissed his knuckles again. "But I won't lie—I didn't stop freaking out completely until I saw you up and skating toward the bench." I paused. "And... maybe not even after that."

His soft smile melted my heart. He released my hand and caressed my cheek. "I'm okay. I really am."

"I know," I whispered. "And I've seen some catastrophic injuries out there. But..." I swallowed. "This time it was you."

Theo's eyebrows rose, and I had a few panicked seconds

to worry I'd tipped my hand too far. That he might think I was way too deep into this and it was all too much.

But then he gathered me in his arms, pulling me against him even though we both knew his chest and back still hurt, and he kissed the top of my head. "I'm sorry it scared you. I know what it's like, seeing someone out there who might be hurt real bad and there's nothing you can do." He brushed his lips across my forehead. "I'm okay, though. I promise.'

Closing my eyes, I leaned into his warmth. "I know. I've known since you came to the bench. But..." I trailed off, not sure what to say.

It was true, I'd seen far, far worse. Two seasons ago, Condit had been stretchered off the ice after he was boarded so badly that there'd been serious concerns about his neck. The season before that, a puck hit one of Vegas's defensemen in the face, breaking his jaw and costing him four teeth; it had been a solid three minutes before he'd been able to get up and—with a *lot* of help and a bloody towel held to his face—slowly skate off the ice.

And that was to say nothing about the night someone had upended Rusanov and sent him headfirst into the boards. I didn't think I'd ever heard an arena go as silent as it had while he'd been motionless behind the goal, everyone in the building holding our breath as we waited for some sign of life. A pair of his teammates had eventually gotten him to his feet and helped him to the bench, and he'd been weaving badly the whole time. From what I'd heard later, he hadn't even known where he was for a good minute or two after he'd woken up.

Those had all been scary. Especially with Condit and Rusanov, there'd been a real, intense fear that they'd been injured in career-ending, life-altering ways. Both men could've broken their necks. They could've been paralyzed.

The head injuries could've been... Well, that wasn't something I needed to think about. Those men were my friends, and watching them lying that still on the ice while their hits were replayed over and over on the big screen had been some of the worst moments of my career. Of my life, honestly.

As hockey injuries went, someone getting the wind knocked out of him ranked slightly above a hangnail. It was something they could skate off easily enough. Some guys went to the bench and returned for their next shift. Some left until the next period. But much like a stinger when someone blocked a puck with an arm or leg, it resolved pretty quickly and completely.

Still, there'd been a good minute or so where Theo's injury could've been anything. The way he'd crumpled to his knees, then wavered and nearly collapsed all the way had sent my heart into my throat. A million worst-case scenarios had flooded my brain as Dave had hurried across the ice to where Grekov was standing beside Theo and waving for help.

I'd never been able to stomach watching the guys get hurt. It was one of the only things I hated about this job.

But when it was Theo...

I suppressed a shudder. Drawing back a little, I met his gaze. "I'm just glad you're okay."

He stroked my hair. "Me too." Then his expression darkened. "Maybe I should've taken Dave's advice and sat for the rest of the game, though."

"What? Why?"

"You saw what happened in the third period, right? When I almost scored on Yanni?"

"But you didn't. Grekov was on top of things, and you guys ended up winning."

"Yeah, but it was..." Theo chewed his lip, his eyes going unfocused.

Something tightened in my chest. He took it hard whenever he made a mistake, but this seemed... more.

I took his hand again, clasping it between us. "Hey. This isn't just about that mistake, is it?"

From the heavy sigh he released, no, it wasn't.

"What happened?" I asked softly.

Theo swallowed hard, staring down at our hands. "Your dad ripped into me after the game."

Ice prickled down the length of my spine. "He did?"

"Yeah. He let me fucking have it." He exhaled, shaking his head. "I know I fucked up. And I know it was almost costly. But he's like... He's threatening to send me down over it and..."

"He won't," I said.

Theo met my gaze. "He *can*, though. Most of the injured guys are back now, and he's got his pick of forwards to grab from Everett if he doesn't want to keep me up." Theo sighed. "It's only a matter of time before he can justify it by saying the team doesn't need me anymore."

"I doubt it," I said.

Eyes locked on mine, Theo silently begged me to make him believe that.

"Listen, he's being a dick because he's still mad about the Pride Tape." I let go of his hand and stroked his cheek. "He's pissy that you're here and that you're playing so well he can't justify sending you down. That's all it is."

Theo sighed, rubbing his eyes with his thumb and forefinger.

I went on, "I think he knows Coach Baldwin won't stand for sending you back down when you're this damn good. So he's going to harp on any little mistake and make it seem like you're worse than you are. He's just messing with your head, same as before, and he's going to flip shit at you at every opportunity in hopes that you ask to be either sent down or traded."

Theo looked at me through his lashes. "Is that how he does things?"

"He has in the past. There was a player, like... I don't know, two season ago? Anyway, Dad didn't like him. He brought him in because he was supposed to be this big star, but Dad didn't think he was performing up to the hype. Which..." I rolled my eyes. "Give him a chance, you know? It takes a while to adapt to a new team's systems."

"It does," Theo acknowledged.

"Right, so halfway through the season, Dad's just done. He wants him gone." I waved like something flying away. "Whatever it takes—get him out of here. But Coach Baldwin thought he was doing fine and so did the team, and you just don't send someone with two cups down to the minors, you know? Not unless it's a conditioning loan or something."

"Yeah? So what did he do? Your dad?"

"Terrorized him, basically. Any time he stepped out of line or made the smallest mistake, Dad was all over him. Screaming at him. Threatening him. Telling him he wasn't worth the price of an entry-level contract, never mind the seven million he was getting every year. Like, I'm not kidding—there was one night when the whole team was an absolute disaster. You know those games? Where everyone's out of step and it's just mistake after mistake after mistake?"

"Oh, yeah." Theo laughed dryly. "The comedy of errors that isn't funny except to the other team."

"Right. Exactly." I exhaled. "So literally everyone on the team fucked up that night. I think even one of the equipment managers managed to FUBAR something. It was a shitshow. But who does my dad tear into? That guy. And like, all he'd done was a couple of dumb turnovers that led to scoring chances—but not goals—and he took a bullshit penalty for a hand pass when all he did was glove down the puck." I rolled my eyes. "That's not even that bad on a normal night, but that night? He could've been second or third star with that performance."

Theo whistled. "Wow. What happened after that?"

"Guy said he was waiving his no-move and no-trade clauses, and he demanded a trade out of Seattle. He refused to suit up for another game." I made a face. "I still don't know how Dad didn't get fucking fired for that, either. Because he ended up trading a two-time cup winner for a bottom six forward and some fifth-round draft picks."

"He—oh, wait, that was Roberts, wasn't it? I always wondered what happened with that, because it sounded like such a bullshit transaction."

"It was. It's exactly the kind of bullshit transaction that happens when a toxic GM pushes a player to the brink."

"How does he *not* get fired?"

I sighed. "I've wondered that for a long time. I don't know if he's got dirt on the president of hockey operations or what, but he just does whatever the fuck he wants and doesn't care who he screws over."

Theo coughed a bitter laugh. "Yeah, that sounds about right." He rubbed the back of his neck and sighed. "God, it's just... Playing under him, it's so much pressure. Every night when I hit the ice, I have to be playing at my very, very best. Which—I mean, that's what we're all supposed to do, you know? But it feels like I'm on a knife's edge. If I have one off night, your dad's going to jump on that opportunity to send me back down or trade my ass."

I winced. "I know. And it sucks. He's on a power trip, and I wish I could tell you there was any way around it besides just being indispensable to Coach Baldwin."

Theo nodded slowly. "Yeah, I know." He met my gaze. "Do you think it's too much to hope he'll sign me to a one-way contract after this season?"

"You never know."

"Well, I guess all I can do now is get through the season and see what happens." He studied me for a moment. "And I know damn well I shouldn't stack the deck against myself by..." He gestured at each of us. "But I think I'd rather just keep trying not to get caught."

I swallowed. "If you don't want to take the risk, though, I'll understand."

Theo managed a genuine smile, and he lifted his chin to brush his lips across mine. "If I didn't want to take the risk, I wouldn't be here. We've been doing good about not getting caught." He paused. "Which... probably means I should sleep in my room tonight."

He was right. Absolutely right. If he'd been rooming alone, it wouldn't have been an issue, but if his roommate got suspicious or if someone saw him slinking out of my room in the morning...

"Probably a good idea," I whispered. "But hey, we'll be back in Seattle soon. So you'll be able to stay in my condo all night."

God, that smile. No wonder I couldn't pull myself away from him and this amazing thing we had going.

"I'm going to hold you to that." He kissed me again, drawing it out for a moment. "And hey, by the time we get home, I'll probably be up for fooling around again."

"Ooh, I like the sound of that."

He chuckled, and we shared another kiss. "I don't have

to go right now, though. The guys won't be back for another couple of hours."

"Want to watch a movie?"

"Sounds good to me." He sat up, wincing with the movement, and reached for his phone. "Let me just set an alarm so I don't overstay if we fall asleep."

"Good idea. Now let's see what Netflix has on offer..."

It was a good thing Theo had set that alarm. When it went off at around 1:30, we'd both fallen asleep. The movie we'd been watching had long since ended, and I had a stiff neck from leaning into him while we sat against the padded headboard.

"Oh, man." He sat up to twist a crick out of his back before reaching for the phone. "Smartest alarm I ever set."

"I know, right?" I rubbed my neck. "But damn it, I was comfortable."

"Me too. But... I should go." He turned plaintive, sleepy eyes on me. "We'll have an all-nighter when we get home, though, right?"

"Absolutely."

"Deal."

We got up, and after he'd put on his shoes and pocketed his phone, we shared a very enjoyable and protracted goodbye at the door. If he hadn't been so sore, I knew without a doubt we'd have ended up in bed again and *not* sleeping or watching a movie this time. He was still clearly in pain, though, so when we finally pried ourselves apart, he left to head back to his room.

I wasn't sore, and I was seriously turned on, so I took care of that in short order. Not nearly as fun when it was my own hand, but at least it scratched the itch. Once I was in bed with Theo again? Oh, it was on.

I showered and returned to the bed where we'd spent most of the evening, and I found a goodnight text from him. I returned it, then settled in to get some sleep myself. Morning came early, after all, and my crew and I had a busy day ahead of us. After a long, relaxed evening with Theo and a quick and dirty orgasm, getting to sleep would be easy.

In theory.

Staring up at the ceiling, I couldn't stop thinking about our conversation and our situation. Dad was making threats against Theo's career. Coming down on him hard for the kinds of mistakes every player made, and the mistake hadn't even been a costly one tonight. All because he was still pissy over Theo putting some colored tape on his stick last season.

I swore out loud and wiped a hand over my face.

Fuck. Fuck, fuck, fuck.

Rebelling against Dad and his bullshit was fun, but only to a point. The truth was that if Theo and I were caught, the consequences would be real. Theo's career might never recover—for PHL players trying to break into the NAPH, there was a lot of do-or-die and now-or-never, and something like this could keep him down in the minors (at best) until he retired.

I rolled onto my side and gazed at the place where Theo had been lying earlier. I could almost imagine him there now, barely visible in the darkness, his face buried in the pillow and his back rising and falling slowly with his relaxed breathing.

Theo had worked so hard to get where he was. And he was so damn good, too. Even if he wasn't a generational talent or someone with the makings of a superstar, he was absolutely proving himself to be one of those players who had a long, respectable career. Hell, maybe he *would* be a superstar. Not all of the players who made it big were spectacular out of the gate, and he was barely in his prime.

Was it fair of me to ask him to put his career and his future potential on the line just to be with me?

I'd asked myself that question a billion times since he'd first caught my eye, but it was really needling at me tonight. Lying here alone in the dark, I closed my eyes and sighed. The truth—one I'd either been too stupid to notice or too stubborn to acknowledge—slammed into me like a slapshot to the chest.

No, I didn't want to risk Theo's future for our hookups.

But I also didn't want to let him go.

Because... this wasn't just hookups anymore. It probably hadn't been for a long time. Somewhere around the time we'd given up condoms and started spending every possible night together and talking in bed until we couldn't keep our eyes open...

"Fuck," I whispered into the stillness. I was in way over my head, wasn't I?

Every time Theo smiled, it hit me right in the feels. I slept better beside him than I did alone, and not just because he'd usually fucked me into the mattress. I'd been legitimately terrified that he'd been seriously hurt tonight, and even after I'd realized he was okay, I was shaken in ways I wouldn't have been if he'd just been some guy I was screwing around with.

I *cared* about this man. Deeply. I wanted him to be happy. I wanted him to successful. I wanted him to be healthy.

And I couldn't convince myself he could be all three of those things while he was with me.

Yeah, we'd been able to keep it a secret so far, but how much longer that would be true? As long as my dad had all this power over both of us, we couldn't be out. We couldn't do anything without sneaking around and keeping it on the DL.

Was I worth that kind of stress for Theo? That kind of risk? If it was just my own career and stability on the line, it would be one thing. But it was Theo's. And now that we'd been doing this long enough for me to catch the goddamned feels for him, I realized I cared way too much for him to ask him to gamble this hard just to sleep with me. I'd cared about him from the start, cared about his career and his future, but now? Fuck.

I closed my eyes and sighed, wishing he was here so I could cuddle closer to him and feel his warmth. Wondering where along the line this had stopped being about getting dicked down and coming so hard I almost passed out. Sex wasn't a difficult thing to find, and there were probably guys out there who could satisfy me like Theo could.

But I didn't want any of them. I wanted him. I wanted his playful smile, and his quiet laughter, and the ridiculous conversations. I wanted those nights when we needed each other so bad, he fucked me while he was still wearing his suit, and I also wanted him to be the one holding me when we finally drifted off to sleep.

No, I wasn't just in this for sex. I hadn't been for a while, even if I couldn't pinpoint when that had changed.

But that still didn't make it fair for me to ask him to risk everything.

I sighed into the stillness.

Yes, I cared about him way more than I'd thought I would in the beginning.

And that meant I cared way too much to be the reason

he lost everything he'd worked for. But I also didn't want to let him go. I couldn't. Maybe that was selfish—hell, it absolutely *was* selfish—but I just couldn't.

What the hell do we do, Theo?

Because I can't keep doing this to you.

But God help me, I can't let you go.

CHAPTER 21

THEO

Christian was in the hotel's banquet hall when I arrived for breakfast, but he wouldn't even look at me.

At first, I thought it was just part of maintaining our cover. We had to do that sometimes—avoid eye contact, pass in the halls without acknowledging each other—so it wasn't alarming in and of itself.

The moment I realized something was off was when I went to refill my coffee and he was already there. I stepped up next to him, smiled, and said, "Hey. Good morning."

He flicked his eyes toward me, but quickly cut them away as he put the coffeepot down. "It's all yours."

And then he was gone.

I stood there stupidly for a moment, wondering if I was missing something. Was he mad? Had I done something wrong? Shit, was he actually salty that we hadn't been able to fool around last night?

Well, I wasn't going to be able to get it out of him here. I swore under my breath, topped off my coffee, and returned to the table, where Rusanov was regaling Grekov with tales of pranks in the hotel last season. I usually loved hearing those stories, but I just couldn't get into it this morning. I picked at my food. Sipped my coffee without tasting it. Wished I could walk over, ask Christian to step out into the hall with me, and find out what the problem was.

But I couldn't do that, because then someone might notice us. Even texting him ran the risk of someone looking over one of our shoulders. Then they might figure out there was more going on here than a player talking to an equipment manager

Was that the issue? Was he suddenly extra paranoid about us being found out? I had no idea.

"Hey, Mathis." Rusanov kicked me under the table just hard enough to get my attention. "You awake?"

I shook myself, wincing a little as my ribs and neck objected. It wasn't bad this morning—just stiff and sore. "Sorry. What?"

Both my teammates peered at me curiously.

Rusanov tilted his head. "I asked if you remembered what we did to the rookie's room last season."

I searched my foggy brain, then landed on the memory, and I chuckled halfheartedly. "I wasn't there for it, but I saw the videos." I turned to Grekov. "They got into his room when they were in Pittsburgh, and they zip tied his suitcase to the luggage rack." I looked at Rusanov. "Wasn't it like fifty zip ties, too? And the ones that are really hard to break?"

Nodding, Rusanov snickered. "We also told him the bus was leaving an hour earlier than it was, so he was freaking, trying to break all the zip ties and get downstairs." He reached for his coffee. "Then he comes down, and we're all relaxing in the lobby with almost forty-five minutes before we had to be on the buses."

Grekov laughed as he loaded some eggs onto his fork. "You guys are dicks."

"Welcome to the Rainiers," I said.

He grunted and kept eating, and Rusanov kept regaling us with other pranks. At least, I thought he did. I started zoning out again, my ears searching the murmur of conversation in the room for one voice in particular. Most mornings, Christian's voice or his laugh would cut through the generic hum, and though it would distract the hell out of me, I lived for those moments. For that little reminder that he was here. That musical sound of him laughing.

This morning... I didn't hear him at all.

At one point, I got up under the pretense of getting some more bacon, and I stole a glance at the table where the equipment managers had been sitting.

Christian was gone.

Suddenly, so was my appetite, along with any shred of concentration I might've had left.

I left my plate in the bin for dirty dishes, returned to the table, and picked up my paper cup of coffee. "Hey, guys. I'm going to head up and start packing. See you on the buses."

They both looked at me curiously but didn't argue.

On the way to my room, it occurred to me that I knew exactly which room was Christian's. We'd been lying in that bed last night, talking and cuddling; I could find it again without any issue.

But I didn't know if I'd be welcome this time. Not like I was last night. Christian was acting distant and weird, and I wanted to respect his boundaries. We needed to talk, yes, but I needed to feel him out first.

Good thing modern technology had made that easy.

Theo: *Hey, is everything ok?*

I didn't like how many times he started and stopped typing before a response finally came through.

Christian: *We should really do this face to face.*

My heart dropped. Oh, that didn't sound good.

Theo: *Ok. My roommate will be back soon. Can I come to your room?*

Again, he started and stopped a few times, then finally said yes. I was out of my room and halfway down the hall in seconds. Of course, now some of my teammates were coming back from breakfast, milling around between rooms and talking in the hall.

Fortunately, the soda machine was in the direction of Christian's room, so I didn't raise any suspicions by walking this way. As I got closer to his room, I casually glanced back, confirmed no one was looking in my direction, and then tapped on the door.

He opened it, and I slipped inside.

As soon as the door was closed, I exhaled with relief that we were now out of sight, but that relief was short-lived. Christian still wouldn't look at me. Leaning against the door, arms folded loosely across his hoodie, he chewed his lip and stared at the carpet.

"Talk to me," I whispered. "Did I do something wrong?"

Christian winced and let his head fall back against the door, shifting his gaze to the ceiling instead of the carpet. "No. No, you—I mean, I think we both did."

My heart dropped again. "We both did... what?"

His Adam's apple bobbed. "We shouldn't be doing this. Seeing each other. Sleeping together. It's..." He closed his eyes and pushed out a long breath. "This has been the best thing I've had in a long time, but it's such a bad fucking idea."

"Oh." Goddammit. I knew he was right. We'd been

gambling with a lot since the start, and nothing had changed that for the better. But still... "I don't want to stop, though."

"I don't either." He opened his eyes again, and this time he did meet my gaze, his expression full of hurt and pleading. "I want you. I don't want to let you go, and everything we're doing, it's—" He threw up a hand, then let it fall to his thigh as he said, "It's amazing. I don't want to lose that. Or you."

"Then don't." I took a cautious step closer. When he didn't back away, I tugged him into a gentle embrace, and I was relieved when he sighed and leaned into me. Stroking his hair, I whispered, "It's stressful. I get it. But that doesn't mean we have to stop."

"It means we *should* stop," he whispered. "But... I'm too selfish to let you go."

I laughed softly and kissed his temple. "Well, if you are, then so am I."

He drew back and gazed up at me.

"I really do get it," I whispered. "I don't want to put your job at risk either. But I don't want to let you go."

He sighed, shoulders sagging. "I'm just afraid... I mean, the way my dad was threatening you yesterday—that's a shot across the bow. He's letting you know that if you step out of line, you're done. As a Rainier, but probably also in the NAPH." He swallowed hard and shook his head. "I don't want to cost you the career you've worked so hard for."

"We've talked about this, though," I pleaded. "I know the risks. That's why we're keeping it quiet. I don't want to fuck up your career or mine either, but I also don't want to give *you* up."

Christian winced. "I'm worried, though. What if we can't keep it as quiet as we need to? What if someone finds out?" He flailed a hand. "What if my *dad* finds out?"

"He won't." I reeled him back in. "Christian. This isn't just sex for me."

His eyes widened.

Heart absolutely slamming into my ribs, I took a deep breath. "I don't know what it is. I really don't. But I'm not gambling with my career because the sex is hot. It *is* hot, but we can both find good sex anywhere, you know? What I want is *you*. And... whatever the fuck it is we're doing. Yeah, keeping it on the DL is hard and it's stressful. Maybe we don't have to do that forever, though."

"How do you figure?"

"Well, step one—decide if this is something we want to go public with." I let my fingertips brush his cheek, and he closed his eyes and shivered. "When the off season gets here, we can take some time away. Go on a vacation or something, you know? Just the two of us. Disappear for a little while and decide what we're doing. After that, we can come up with a strategy if we want to come out. But between now and then, we just keep it quiet, keep enjoying it, and keep letting it happen, you know?"

Swallowing hard, he nodded. "There will be blowback if we come out, though."

"There will. But we'll know if we've got enough staying power to face that music. Right now, I don't know where we'll land. What we'll do." I shook my head. "The only thing I know is that giving you up isn't an option."

Christian stared at me, his forehead creased. "Really?"

"Yes. Like I said, I don't know what we're doing. I just know I don't want to stop. I didn't want to at the beginning, and now I *really* don't want to."

He held my gaze, silently asking me to connect the last two wires.

Don't make me say it, Christian. I'm too scared to say it. You know what I'm saying. Please don't make me spell it out.

After a painfully long moment, he sighed. Then he wrapped his arms around my neck and pulled me in close. "I don't want to stop, either," he whispered, and before I could respond, his lips were against mine.

I held him tight as we let the kiss go on. The relief... oh God, it was right up there with that moment on the ice when my breath had finally started moving. When I'd been overwhelmed with panic, absolutely sure I'd never be able to inhale again, and then... I did. I could breathe.

Here in this hotel room, holding Christian, kissing him as he held me just as fiercely, I could, once again, finally breathe.

And I realized this hadn't just started at breakfast. The uncertainty had been hanging over us for a while. The "what are doing?" and the "what are we risking?" had been dangling in the back of my mind for a while now, even after we'd talked about it a few times.

Not like this, though. Christian's moment of panic had given us a reason to get that all out on the table and admit that—holy fuck—neither of us was in this for the sex anymore.

We'd figure out the future. We'd figure out how to deal with Jack Hayes and if coming out was on the table.

For right now, though, we were both in this, and not just to get laid.

We'd find a way to iron out the rest during the off season.

I COULDN'T WAIT TO GET SOMEWHERE ALONE WITH Christian. We'd been exchanging smoldering looks ever since we'd ironed things out in his hotel room, and I'd been counting down the minutes until we could finally land in his bed again.

Unfortunately, we still had one more game on the road. At least I made it through that one without getting myself banged up. Though at this point, I could get a concussion and a broken leg and I'd still find a way to ride Christian into his mattress once we got home. I was way too horny—not to mention relieved after his short-lived panic over us—to let something as inconsequential as a serious injury keep me from plowing him.

Or maybe I'd just had a couple too many beers in the hotel bar as my teammates and I celebrated a decisive win over Minneapolis. The powers that be had mercifully scheduled our flight for tomorrow, so we were chilling down here while we wound down from an exciting game. Condit had score his four hundredth goal, Wilcox had notched his five hundredth point, and Easton had his third shutout of the season. Games like that deserved celebrating.

The night was finally starting to wind down, though. We were down to about eight of us in the bar, most of us finishing up our last drinks. Grekov and I were probably going to head to our room in a few; my beer was almost gone, and his was empty. Condit and Rusanov had already paid their tabs and were just hanging out, probably waiting for the rest of us to call it a night.

Christian pushed himself to his feet. "I'm going to go close my tab. Back in a minute."

We all mumbled and nodded in agreement, and he left the table while the conversation continued.

"So we were at the airport in Dallas," Condit was

saying. "And Sorenson gets all the way to the gate and realizes he left his laptop in the lounge. But there's no way he's going to get back in time to—" He suddenly straightened, looking past us as his expression shifted to one of intense concern.

Grekov and I twisted around, and my heart jumped into my throat. A bulky dude in a baseball cap was right in Christian's face, snarling something at him while Christian showed his palms and tried not to make eye contact.

"Oh, fuck that," I muttered, and shoved my chair back to get up.

Before I was even on my feet, Condit, Sorenson, Rusanov, and Abrahamsson had come around the table, and they made it to the bar in seconds.

Condit put an arm between Christian and the guy. "Hey. Hey. Enough."

"Mind your own fucking business," the guy snapped, obviously inebriated.

"He is our business," Sorenson snarled. "Step off."

The guy looked around, suddenly realizing half a dozen of us had gathered around. Most of us were relatively small without our gear and skates—aside from Grekov and Rusanov, who were big motherfuckers—so we weren't the most intimidating bunch on our own. But we had strength in numbers, and even drunk as he was, the idiot seemed to be rethinking his life choices.

Another pair of big dudes appeared behind him, and I cringed inwardly. This was going to become a brawl, wasn't it? Just what we all needed.

But one took the guy's arm. "C'mon. I think it's time for you to sober up a bit."

The guy protested, trying and failing to pull his arm free. "I'm fine. This little queer was just feeling me up."

"Oh, don't fucking flatter yourself," Christian spat. "I bumped you with my elbow."

"Don't lie! You were feeling me up!"

Christian's reply was a sharp bark of laughter. He looked the guy up and down, sneered, and shook his head. "Oh, honey. Honey, no. Just... no."

That pissed the guy off, but his buddies just muttered apologies to us and herded him away from the bar.

As soon as they were gone, Christian exhaled, his bravado vanishing.

Condit turned him. "You okay?"

"Yeah. Yeah. I'm fine." Christian rolled his shoulders. "Thanks for stepping in."

"Any time, man. You know that." Condit gave his shoulder a squeeze, and then he and our teammates returned to the table.

I hung back. "You sure you're good? What was that guy's problem, anyway?"

"Just a drunk homophobe." Christian shook his head, turning his attention to signing his credit card receipt. I pretended not to notice the slight tremor in his hand.

God, it was so hard not to put a reassuring arm around him. "What a dick."

"I know, right?" He pushed the receipt toward the bartender, and as he slid his copy into his wallet, he added, "I'm okay, though." With a smile, he nodded toward our teammates. "They're all like the big brothers I never had. Well, except most of them are younger than me, but still."

I smiled, too. "Yeah, they definitely don't let you take shit."

"There's a reason why I haven't left this team." He pocketed his wallet. "My dad can eat a dick, but I'm sticking with these guys."

"I don't blame you at all."

We headed out of the bar with our teammates sticking close.

I was admittedly rattled myself from watching that whole exchange go down. As much as I was willing to drop gloves on the ice, I wasn't interested in fighting outside of hockey. I didn't want to catch a charge, and I didn't think I could hold my own against a guy that size anyway. But if someone was going to harass or threaten Christian, I'd have been more than happy to throw down.

Fortunately, Condit had noticed the situation before I had, and we'd collectively scared the man off without anyone needing to go hands on.

On the way up to our floor, it occurred to me that I wasn't the only one gambling with my place on this team. Christian had an amazing rapport with all of them, and they were clearly protective of him. He really was the whole team's little brother, age notwithstanding.

If we got caught, Christian would get fired as surely as I'd be sent down to languish in the minors.

I wanted to believe what we had was worth what we were risking. I wanted to believe we could find a way to make this work.

But how would all the men in this elevator feel if they knew Christian and I were together?

And what would it even matter if we were both cut loose from the Rainiers?

Yeah, there was a lot on the line. Way too much to be risking for a man.

Every time I looked at him, though, my resolve intensified.

Christian, I firmly believed, was worth everything I was risking.

CHAPTER 22

CHRISTIAN

I was so exhausted I was on the brink of hallucinating, but if I didn't get naked with Theo soon, I was going to lose my goddamned mind.

I still had to wait, though. Tonight was game two of a back-to-back, and we were leaving for the airport right after the game to head for Calgary. Before that, there'd been some issues with a visiting team's gear; I had no idea how, but one of their travel cases just... hadn't made it onto the plane. My crew and I—and every crew I'd ever worked with—had eleventy billion checks and balances in place to make sure we didn't leave so much as a helmet strap behind, but somehow, one of their cases was still in Buffalo's arena.

So, after we'd picked up the crew and their gear at the airport, we'd all been scrambling to get them everything they needed for the game. That was the thing about equipment managers—we all looked out for each other. We met visiting teams at the airport, helped them load and unload their gear, and helped them get situated in the arena. If something was missing or damaged, we'd help them out. Whenever we were in another arena, the host team's equipment managers did the same for us. There was no competition or backstabbing between any of us; it was our job to make sure both teams had everything they needed to play a proper game.

Sometimes that meant for an incredibly long night. I had planned to meet up with Theo after we got the equipment managers settled into the arena, but once I'd realized something was missing, I'd texted him to cancel. Good thing, too—between their delayed flight and the missing case, I didn't leave the arena until almost four.

That game came and went uneventfully, and then the next crew came in, and after a shorter but still late night, I was running on a handful of hours of sleep. Still, I'd been here in time to set up for the morning skate, and thanks to a few gallons of coffee, I was still on my feet.

When I got home tonight, all I was going to want to do was faceplant in my pillow and pass out for a few short hours. I was so tired I could barely stand, goddammit.

But that didn't stop me from wishing I could have a moment alone with the man wearing number sixty-one.

For the last few days, Theo and I had barely had time to look at each other, never mind touch, and I was losing it.

Now we had a lull in between the morning skate and warmups. My crew and I had finished everything we needed to finish. Steel was sharpened. Sticks were taped. Jerseys were hung. Skates were drying. One of Rusanov's socks had needed patching and Condit's jersey had a tear in the sleeve from last night. I'd fixed the tear enough to finish the game, and then I'd reinforced it today.

Everything was done, and we had about two hours before warmups. Most of the players were in the building. They'd had a team meeting after the morning skate, and now they were trickling in to start their pregame routines.

A few of them were playing two-on-two soccer in the hallway as they always did. Rusanov and Grekov were taking their usual walks around the upper, lower, and ice levels.

Theo also took walks before warmups, but he always went alone. He'd put in his AirPods, disappear into his own thoughts, and make a few laps around the ice level before he did a light workout.

I was restless when he came in to put on his workout gear before his walk. I desperately wanted to go sleep for a bit—Marty had already stepped out to take a nap in his car—but I knew myself. I couldn't relax. No matter how exhausted I was, I was too wound up, and that had everything to do with Theo.

I missed him. I wanted him. Even if I was too exhausted to get it up, I just wanted to *touch* him, for God's sake.

When Theo left for his walk, my heart started pounding.

Should I?

Absolutely not, but is that going to stop me?

Also absolutely not.

He always went counterclockwise, so I went the other way, running through my mental map of the arena to figure out the best place to pull him aside. Someplace that would be empty. Hidden from view.

As I came around a curve, a familiar alcove caught my attention, and I grinned.

Oh, yes. This would work just fine.

I made sure no one was around, then dipped into the alcove and took out my phone. Theo usually listened to music while he was walking, so I was confident he'd have his phone with him.

Christian: *Meet me by the Zambonis.*

My heart went wild as the message sent. Even wilder when "read" appeared beneath the message.

He didn't reply.

I waited, shifting my weight and trying to will my pulse to come back down. We wouldn't be able to do much—assuming he actually took me up on this—but I didn't care. I just wanted a moment alone with him. That would tide me over until we got through this game and the next road trip. Even a stolen kiss would be enough to keep me sane until—

Footsteps approached out in the main thoroughfare, and I closed my eyes, silently begging for them to turn into this alcove.

Please be Theo, please be Theo, please be Theo.

They turned.

I opened my eyes.

And oh, God, yeah, it was him.

He didn't say a word, though. He walked right up, pushed me against the Zamboni, and kissed me deep and hard. It was like the first time we were in here, but also different. There was no hesitation this time. No uncertainty. His kiss was anything but tentative, his hands sure as they slid all over my body.

My knees shook under me, but Theo and the Zamboni kept me upright. I wrapped my arms around his neck and indulged in the kiss I'd been craving for the past few days.

It occurred to me then that this might not actually help me stay sane. His thickening hard-on rubbed mine through our workout pants, and it was going to be *how long* before he could fuck me again? Damn it!

Eh. I could hate myself for this later. For right now, I surrendered completely, loving the way his body felt against mine and how he explored my mouth like it was the first time all over again.

"We have to stop meeting like this," he murmured against my lips.

"Fuck that." I slid a hand up into his hair. "We can't go out like a normal couple. We can at least sneak off and make out between the Zambonis."

Theo laughed, and then he reclaimed my mouth. I hummed into his kiss, melting all over again between him and the Zamboni. God, he was such a good kisser. So good in bed, too. And just...

So *good*.

I liked being close to him. Even when we were hanging out in a bar with his teammates, carefully keeping some space between us so no one caught on, I liked it. Catching his eye and seeing that smile—whether it was shy or devilish or somewhere in between—could have my heart fluttering for hours.

In over my head? Abso-fucking-lutely.

Theo broke the kiss again, breathing hard as he met my gaze. "You know, we *could* actually go out like a normal couple."

I stared at him. "We—How?"

"Meet somewhere. A movie." He slid his hands up my sides. "We don't go in or out together, but we have, what? Two, three hours to watch a movie?"

I thought about it. Movies had never been my ideal dates because... I mean, what was the point of going on a date and *not* talking for a couple of hours? But sneaking around behind closed doors had left me a little stir crazy, and the thought of sitting in a movie theater with Theo—in the dark but in *public*—had some serious appeal.

Who was I kidding? Just being with him under any circumstances had a ton of appeal.

"A movie could be fun." I lifted my chin for another kiss. "Maybe when we get back in town after the road trip?"

Theo's lips curved against mine. "Sounds perfect."

Yeah, it did.

And I couldn't fucking wait.

CHAPTER 23

THEO

"I have a question." Grekov peered at me across the small table in the café where we'd stopped for lunch.

"Okay, sure." I dragged a fry through some ketchup. "What's on your mind?"

He stared at his plate for a moment, and I studied him waiting for him to ask. He seemed vaguely uncomfortable, which had me worried.

All morning, he'd been fine. We'd had practice, and then he and I had gone for a light run around Green Lake. Now we were chilling and having a late lunch. He'd been joking and talking hockey, but now he was suddenly... off.

After a moment, he finally spoke. "So, Jack..." Grekov jabbed his straw at the ice in his Coke. "He is not... He doesn't like gay men."

I scowled. "No, he does not." Rolling my eyes, I added, "So of course he has a gay son."

Grekov raised an eyebrow. "He's a dick to his son about it?"

"Yep. He's a dick to all of us, but especially to his own

son." I took a drink, not that it did much to rinse the bitterness out of my mouth. "Christian deserves so much better."

Grekov eyed me, and my stomach knotted. Shit. Had I tipped my hand too far? Let it show that I gave more of a damn about Christian than I should?

Then he lowered his gaze to his barely touched lunch. "I was worried, coming to Seattle. The rumors..." He thumbed the edge of the table and gnawed his lip. "Doesn't seem safe to come out here."

I studied him. Then the piece clicked, and I sat up straighter. "No, it is. The guys—everyone is great about it." I half-shrugged. "No one in a Rainiers sweater has ever given me grief about it, and they've known since day one that I'm gay."

His brow pinched. "But the GM..."

"Yeah. I know." I sighed. "It's... I don't want to tell anyone to stay in the closet. But I get why someone wouldn't want to be out." I studied him, then cautiously asked, "Are you...?"

The way he dropped his gaze and blushed, squirming uncomfortably in his seat, screamed *yes*.

"Hey." I gave his forearm a quick squeeze before withdrawing my hand. "I won't say a word to anyone. Promise."

He looked at me through his lashes, blue eyes full of fear that I wasn't used to seeing in a ballsy defenseman like him. "You'll tell no one?"

"No one. It's not my secret to tell." I paused. "And if you want to know where all the good clubs are within a hundred miles of here..."

His blush deepened, but he laughed, shaking his head. "No, no. I don't think—I don't like clubs."

"Eh, I don't blame you." I reached for my drink. "They fucking suck. The apps, too."

Grekov laughed with a little more feeling. "I don't need the apps. Or the clubs. I would just..." He half-shrugged. "I'm not ready to come out. It... I can't. Not yet. But I want to be *able* to when I'm ready, you know?"

I nodded. "Oh, yeah. I totally get it. And trust me, man —the team will have your back. I'm not the first queer guy on the team. And like, you've seen them go to bat for Christian."

"True." He sipped his drink. "I was... That was a surprise, you know?"

"The longer you're around these guys, the less surprising it'll be. Trust me." I picked up another fry. "But don't feel like you have to come out, either. If you're not comfortable with Jack knowing, or you're just not ready to be out..." I half-shrugged. "It's your prerogative, you know? It's all good."

He studied me, then managed a faint smile. "I'll remember that. Thanks."

AFTER WE'D FINISHED LUNCH, WE LEFT AND WENT back to our cars. Grekov seemed to be in a better headspace now, so that was a relief. I'd had my suspicions that he was queer, mostly because he was *so* secretive about his personal life, and I was glad he'd felt safe enough to tell me. Whether he'd come out to the team or not was up to him, but at least he knew he wasn't alone.

Man, that had to be rough, too. The language barrier was already a struggle for him. Then on top of that, he was gay and not sure about coming out. Thank God he hadn't ended up on a team with no Russian players (though most teams had at least one, if not more) and he'd landed someplace with openly queer players and staff members.

Shame there wasn't much any of us could do about our homophobic GM. Ugh.

But at least for today, Grekov seemed to be feeling better about things as we got into our respective cars. He was going out to Snohomish to play golf with Rusanov this afternoon, which would be good for him too.

As for me, I drove away from Green Lake, but I didn't head home. I didn't go to Christian's condo, either.

Instead, I followed my GPS's instructions to a movie theater up on Capitol Hill. I'd bought a ticket online earlier today, which I showed to the usher on my phone, and then I headed inside.

This was one of those small indie theaters with about fifty seats in each auditorium where obscure, usually foreign films played. I wasn't even sure what this movie was about. It was in French, that much I knew, and it had a run time of like three hours, but beyond that... nada.

I didn't care either, because I hadn't come here to pay much attention to what was on the screen.

The auditorium was mostly empty. A few college kids occupied the middle rows, munching on popcorn as their phones bathed their faces in bright light.

And there in the center seat of the back row was the reason I'd come here in the first place.

"Hey." Christian grinned up at me as I took the seat beside him. "How was your run?"

"Not bad." I slung my arm around his shoulders. The armrest was up, so he leaned against me without anything jabbing into either of our ribs. Trailing my fingers up and down his arm, I said, "There were a lot of people out, though. Jesus H."

He chuckled, sliding a hand over my thigh. "It's Saturday, baby. People come out on Saturdays."

I tsked. "But then the jogging path is crowded. Rude."

Christian laughed and lifted his chin for a light kiss. "So sorry, sweetheart. I'm sure if you wait until it's nasty and raining, you'll have the path all to yourselves."

"But then I'll get cold and wet."

"But it won't be crowded."

I grunted unhappily.

He nudged me with his elbow and leaned against me.

I kissed the top of his head. "What did you do this morning?"

He groaned. "Paperwork. *So much* paperwork."

"Really? For what?"

"Ordering parts. Inventorying parts. Getting bids from a new supplier on some parts and tools that another manufacturer is discontinuing." He sighed theatrically. "Such bullshit."

Laughing, I pressed my lips to the top of his head again. "So much hard work. I don't know how you manage it."

"Keep it up and I'll start delegating it to the players."

"Pretty sure there's a rookie and a couple of PHL guys who are lower in the hierarchy than me."

"Ooh, this isn't about seniority, darling." He patted my thigh. "It's about who I decide is the right person for the job."

"I don't think that's allowed under the CBA."

"Ugh. You assholes and your *union*."

I cackled triumphantly, which earned me an elbow to the ribs. "Oof. Fuck you."

He looked up at me and grinned. "Promise?"

"Of course." I drew him in and kissed him. God, I could not get enough of kissing him. Even when it was neither the time nor the place for sex, I loved the way he kissed. Yeah, it turned me on, but that could wait until later. Right now, in this moment, his soft, insistent lips against mine were more than enough.

Some music started, and when I opened my eyes, I realized the auditorium had gone dark. On the screen, the previews began.

"Oh, I guess it's starting." Christian shifted around again, leaning against me with my arm still around his shoulders. "Do you need me to read the subtitles out loud?"

I snorted. "Shut up."

He vibrated with laughter beside me, and I chuckled as I kissed his temple.

All through the previews and into the beginning of the movie, I barely noticed what was happening on the screen. The subtitles weren't a problem; I was just way too caught up in how nice it was to hang out like this in public. We'd watched plenty of movies in bed, but there was something amazing about going out together. Even if it was in the dark where no one was liable to stumble across us, we were together. In public. On an actual date.

I wish we could do this all the time.

Maybe after this season, we'll find a way.

CHAPTER 24

CHRISTIAN

These dinners with my parents were getting exhausting. They had been for years, but these days, I couldn't look at my father without getting filled with rage over how he treated Theo and how secretive our relationship had to be. Every time we were in the same room, I found myself fuming over how Dad had taken the slight on his ego and fucked Theo over professionally. What if the Rainiers hadn't been plagued with injuries this year? What if the club *hadn't* been forced to call him up? He'd have languished in the minors, possibly for the rest of his career, all because he'd defied my dad.

You are such a vindictive, egotistical dick, I thought as I chewed a piece of steak. *I can't believe we're* family. *Ugh.*

Conversation went on around me as I ate and pretended to be in a good mood. I kept my participation to a minimum and just counted down the minutes until I could politely get the fuck out of here.

Don't provoke, I told myself over and over. *Don't engage.*

I hadn't realized there was a lull in the conversation

until, without preamble, Dad said, "Christian, were you aware that there's been a problem with theft at the arena?"

There was something oddly pointed about the question —some subtext I was probably supposed to pick up—but it wouldn't click in my brain.

I shrugged as I picked up a forkful of rice pilaf. "Uh. No?"

"So your inventories have all been correct."

They were, but nothing made me second-guess myself more than being in Dad's crosshairs, so I paused to consider it as I chewed my food. After a moment, I shook my head. "Yes? I thought I was missing some visor screws, but they'd just rolled under a travel case. Otherwise..." I shrugged again.

"I see." Dad took a sip of wine, letting the silence hang in the air while my mom, sister, brother-in-law, and I exchanged puzzled, uneasy looks. When he set the glass down, he said, "Well. I'm looking at the security footage from every camera in the arena over the last few months. I've been checking some of them *personally*."

My neck prickled. Again, there was something there I was supposed to catch—something that made me nervous—but I just couldn't figure out what he was getting at.

"That must be time-consuming," Aiden remarked flatly. "Especially for a GM."

"Aiden," Chelsea said quietly.

Aiden focused on his food, but he was grinning to himself. Under any other circumstances, I'd have been biting back a laugh as well; it was always satisfying when someone managed to get in a swipe at my dad.

But I wasn't laughing this time. I was still edgy from my dad's comments. I just couldn't shake the feeling that I was missing the lines I needed to read between. I didn't want to take his bait if he was just fucking with me, but I also didn't want to miss a warning or a veiled threat. Dad was absolutely the type to get right in someone's face and threaten them, telling them in no uncertain terms exactly where the lines were and what would happen if they were crossed. But he could also play these games where he'd drop vague hints that made no sense in the moment but were, in hindsight, ominous warnings. I'd never been able to beat him at this game, but that hadn't stopped me from trying.

I sipped my own wine. "What exactly has been going missing? I haven't heard a thing."

"No one *reports* to you," he replied tersely.

I had to fight so hard not to roll my eyes. Yeah, yeah, I was nowhere near as far up in the hierarchy as he was, blah, blah, blah. "If it's related to the team's equipment, they usually at least give me a heads up."

"Well." He offered a thin smile, narrowing his eyes just slightly. "They probably wanted to wait until they had a solution before they bothered you with it."

I tongued the back of my teeth and tried not to let my irritation show. I knew that whole thing with the jerseys would come back and bite me eventually. Everything always fucking did. Keeping my voice as even as I could, I asked, "So what's missing?"

"Tools, mostly." Dad swirled his wine and locked eyes with me. "For maintaining the Zambonis."

Something icy slid down the center of my spine. A memory flickered through my mind of being pressed up against one of the Zambonis, but I quickly shut that down before I blushed or got flustered. Keeping my voice casual, I said, "Too bad there aren't any cameras over there."

Dad's grin made my heart slam to a stop. "There are."

"There—" My mouth went dry. "Since when?" I

managed a laugh, hoping it sounded genuine. "I thought they gave up fighting you on it."

"They did." He shrugged. "But after there were some... concerns about people going in there who didn't need to be there, I suggested they put in some cameras. So they did."

Oh. Fuck. Yeah, that matched him—shut down what someone else wanted, then pitch it like it was his idea.

My brother-in-law broke in. "Why is the team's general manager even involved in that? Seems like that's the arena's domain, not the club's."

My mother and sister both stared at their food and shifted nervously as Dad turned to my brother-in-law. I just tried to will my heart to keep beating and my face not to betray my sudden panic.

"It's in the club's best interest to be on top of the situation," Dad growled at Aiden. "If someone's willing to steal from the arena, then what's to stop them from stealing from the Rainiers? So we put in cameras to catch them."

The two of them sparred back and forth, Aiden picking away at Dad's logic while Chelsea probably wished he would just *shut up, shut up, shut up*. Dad fired back with increasing irritation, but I didn't hear much of what either man said.

My tongue stuck to the roof of my mouth as I studied the food I suddenly no longer wanted to eat.

There *was* no theft. Deep in my bones, I could feel it.

If someone had been stealing tools from the Zamboni crew, everyone who worked in that building would've known about it. There would've been tighter security. The crew would've come to ask the equipment managers if we'd borrowed something or if we'd seen a random tool lying around somewhere.

And Aiden was right—even if there was a theft problem, investigating it was hardly the team GM's domain.

No, Dad wanted me to know he was scrutinizing security footage from the arena.

He wanted me to know it had something to do with the Zambonis. And that he'd finally won the battle with facilities over a camera in the Zamboni bay... by being the one to suggest they install one.

I didn't dare ask when the cameras had been installed. I didn't dare ask anything, because I could feel it all the way to my core that this was Dad letting me know that he knew about me and Theo.

Had he seen the footage? Was he just bluffing because one of the drivers had told him they'd seen Theo and me leaving that alcove? Shit, had they told him, and that was why he'd installed cameras and cooked up this whole "thief" story?

I had no idea, and I was too freaked out to push the issue.

I SPENT THE REST OF DINNER FORCIBLY MAINTAINING my poker face. I didn't want Dad to think—to *know*—he'd gotten under my skin. If he was bluffing, I needed to call his bluff by not reacting. If he *wasn't* bluffing—if he'd somehow figured out I'd been in the Zamboni bay when I shouldn't have been—well, the best I could think to do was try to convince him he was threatening me with a giant nothing burger. That had always been the best play—don't let him know he was under my skin. Don't let him know I had anything to hide. Don't let him think he'd busted me.

It was one of those games we'd played when I was a kid.

When he'd make ominous comments like, "I told you I'd ground you if you cut class again, didn't I?" And I'd immediately break down and apologize and say it wouldn't happen again. Only after the fact would I realize he hadn't actually known I was cutting class—he'd just thrown it out there to see how I'd react.

So tonight, I was pretending like there was no reason anyone would ever suspect me of cutting class. Or, well, in this case, of "stealing Zamboni parts," which he and I both knew translated to, "fraternizing with one of the Rainiers."

Mercifully, he didn't bring up the subject again during dinner. It was Chelsea and Aiden's turn to stay behind and help Mom with the kitchen, so as soon as the meal was over, I said my goodbyes and got the hell out of there.

Tried to, anyway.

I was putting on my shoes in the foyer when Dad appeared.

"You haven't had too much to drink, have you?" he asked.

"I only had one glass and it was over an hour ago." I took my jacket off the hook. "I'm fine to drive."

"Good." He smiled thinly. "Well, I'll see you at the arena tomorrow. And hopefully the problem will resolve itself." He locked eyes with me. "So often, it's really a misunderstanding. A tool left where it doesn't belong. Someone accidentally walking away with it." He half-shrugged as he slid his hands into his pockets. "If the culprit puts things back the way they are, then there's no reason for things to get messy."

My mouth went dry again. Ooh, I could read between *those* lines.

If the "thief" knows what's good for him, he's going to

unfuck the situation, go back to the status quo, and not provoke me any further.

"Okay." I nodded. "If, um... If I hear anything, I'll let you know."

"You do that." Dad's smile was impossible to parse. "Have a good night, Christian."

"Yeah. Will do."

I booked it out of the house and down to my car, and I found myself sitting there for a long time, engine idling and mind racing.

Dad knew something. How much he knew, I had no idea. If he had actually seen what Theo and I had done back there, I doubted he'd just be giving me rope to hang myself. He'd have fired me by now and would probably be making Theo's life hell too.

So I didn't think he knew everything. But he knew something. Enough to be suspicious and probably watch me like a goddamned hawk going forward.

Likely Theo, too, if my hunch was correct and it was the Zamboni drivers who'd seen him and then told Dad. They must've seen me, too, since I'd only left a moment or so before Theo had. And maybe someone—the drivers, the facilities managers, or Dad—had seen us in there recently when we'd stolen a few minutes together.

Whatever the case, this was bad.

I swore as I took out my phone and started writing out a text.

I needed to tell Theo, and it couldn't wait.

CHAPTER 25

THEO

Christian: *We need to talk. Tonight.*

I stared at the text. Well, that sounded ominous. I'd been winding down, ready to go to bed, but I was wide awake now.

Theo: *I just had a beer, can't drive. Come by the hotel?*

He'd never been here before—too risky—but if this was urgent, then we might have to take the chance.

He responded that he was on his way, so I sent my room number.

About twenty nerve-racking minutes later, there was a knock at my door. When I opened it, a very uneasy Christian looked back at me.

"Hey." I stood aside to let him in. "What's going on?"

He stepped into the room, pushing a hand through his hair. "My dad knows about us."

I froze, still holding the door open "He... *How?*"

"I'm not sure. And I'm not even sure how much he knows. But he was telling me how there is a theft problem at the arena, and how he's helping them out by checking the security footage." Christian met my gaze. "And he was really emphatic about how it was mostly happening around the Zambonis."

My heart dropped into my feet. "Oh. Fuck. But... there's no cameras there."

"There are now," he said grimly. "And I don't know how long they've been there."

"Ooh, shiiiit."

"Yeah." He shook his head. "Jesus..."

"So... What now? I mean, he knows about us. Is he..." I gulped. "Is he firing you? Sending me back down?"

Christian shook his head again. "Not... Not yet." He wiped a hand over his face and leaned back against the couch. "And I'm not even sure how much he actually knows. Like if he saw the tapes, or if he's just guessing because of the Zamboni drivers who saw you. Maybe they saw both of us. I don't know. Anyway, Dad made some cryptic comments about how he hopes the situation resolves it self. You know, like the thief returns the tools and everything goes back to normal."

My throat tightened. "So... he's giving us a chance to call this off."

Without looking at me, Christian nodded slowly. "I think so. That's... That's the best I could get from what he said."

I watched him, and my heart sank even deeper. "So that's..." I moistened my lips. "That's what we're doing, isn't it? Ending it?"

Christian swallowed. Then he looked me in the eyes. "No."

I blinked. "It isn't?"

"No. It... I won't lie—on the way here, I seriously thought about it. I don't want either of us getting fucked over because of this, you know? You're coming into your prime, and you've got an amazing career ahead of you." He sighed. "I don't want to be selfish. But... I am selfish. And just like before, whenever I think about ending this..." He dropped his gaze and shook his head. "I just *can't* do it."

There weren't enough words in the English language to describe all the feelings tumbling through me right then. I was relieved he wasn't calling this off, but I also thought I should be the smart one and call it off, but I *also* realized just how much it would hurt if we ended this. Weren't we just fooling around? Wasn't this kind of a friends with benefits thing? Yeah, we'd agreed to be exclusive, and we'd even managed to sneak out for one discreet date, but were we...

Oh, fuck. Yeah, we were. We really had segued into an actual relationship when I wasn't paying attention. It had been so effortless and natural, I hadn't noticed until I was in this far over my head.

"I can't do it either," I whispered, squeezing his hand. "I know it's a huge risk for both of us. But... I don't want to let us go. Not even if it gets me a one-way ticket back to the minors."

"But your career..."

"I can get my career back on the rails," I said softly. "No, it's not ideal, and yes, I'm going to try like hell to break into the NAPH for real this time. But if that doesn't happen, I'll be a free agent eventually, and I—the point is, there's still options, you know? I won't be stuck playing for the Everett Orcas for the rest of my life." I brought his hand up and pressed my lips to the inside of his wrist. "But there's only one you."

Christian released a stuttering breath. "There's only one you, too. I'm just scared I'll be the reason you—"

My kiss stifled his protests, and he whimpered as he melted against me.

When I was sure he had well and truly shut up, I touched my forehead to his. "If there's any blowback because of this," I murmured, "it's not your fault. You didn't do this. *We* went into this with our eyes open. *We* knew the risks."

"We did." Then he laughed softly. "And the fact that I've thought about ending this twice and can't fucking do it... That should tell us something, you know?"

"It should, yeah." I kissed him again, relieved he hadn't been able to follow through with that either time. I wasn't mad about it, either; I totally understood why he'd wanted to pull back. It wasn't about us. It was about all the shit that would hit the fan if someone found out about us.

Yes, it was still a risk.

And yes—God, yes—I was still willing to take that risk.

Anything for you, baby.

THE INJURY FAIRY HAD RELENTED RECENTLY, AND apart from the two Rainiers still on LTIR, everyone had either come back or would shortly. One by one, players who'd come up from the PHL were being sent back down.

I had mixed feelings. It was always a relief to see an injured player getting reactivated. Even if they were on a rival team, no one ever wanted to see someone seriously hurt.

But sooner or later, as the roster leveled out again, it was going to be my turn to go down. At the very least, I'd be healthy-scratched like Larsson, who'd been filling in for an injured defenseman. He'd been benched for four games while the other guy had played again, and yesterday, he'd gone back to Everett.

Now more than ever, I *had* to shine. I had to stand out and make myself noticed so that when I did go down, Coach would have me at the top of his list of call-ups next time someone was injured. I had to hope that I'd made enough of a name for myself here that it would override Jack's disgust for me. Coach had made a case for keeping me on the roster all this time, even after Mackenzie came back last week. That meant something, didn't it?

I wasn't holding my breath. Coach had managed to keep me here, but I doubted Jack would be willing to bring me back unless the Rainiers were desperate like they had been this season.

There were two PHL players left on the roster right now—me and Brody. The last injured forward who'd be back this season, Stevens, had just gone to Everett on a conditioning loan, so he'd probably be back on the Rainiers within the next week or two. That meant either me or Brody would be on the bench soon, and likely headed back up north.

There *was* room on the roster for one of us to stay. Jack had made some trades in recent weeks, including a fourth line winger in exchange for a handful of draft picks and future considerations. That left room for one of us to stay here even after Stevens was fully reactivated.

No pressure or anything.

Great time to shoot yourself in the foot by continuing to date the GM's son, huh?

I grimaced. How well would I have to play to stay on this roster with *that* black mark?

Well, all I could do was play my hardest and hope Coach demanded that I stay here. At the end of the day, the club wanted a winning team above all else, and there was only so much they were going to let the GM compromise things based on his own ego or personal issues. So the only way I was going to hold on to this spot was to make myself too valuable for him to send down without raising eyebrows.

Yeah.

No pressure.

Fuuuck.

It didn't help that when I got to the arena for the morning skate, I was immediately summoned into Jack's office.

Ooh, that didn't bode well...

I was being sent down, wasn't I? This was it. This was the *"pack your things, check out of the hotel, and get your ass back to Everett"* conversation. At least I didn't have much to pack. I could be out of that room in under twenty minutes.

Still have to go get all the stuff I've left at Christian's place, though...

I shoved that thought away. The last thing I needed on my mind when I faced off with Jack was how many clothes and toiletries I'd left in his son's condo.

I went upstairs to where the team's staff had offices. They were smaller here than the ones at the practice facility, which was where they conducted most of their business. But sometimes there were trades in the works on game night, especially in the run-up to the trade deadline, so they needed some office space.

I thought Jack's enormous office at the practice facility was over-the-top, especially with some of the staff cramped into shared offices and cubicles. Walking into the tiny one he had here, though, I'd have given my right nut to have this meeting in the bigger office.

I did *not* like being in close quarters with Jack Hayes. As I stepped into the suffocating office, the walls were seriously closing in, and sweat beaded on the back of my neck. "You, um... You wanted to see me?"

"Yes. Sit down."

I did, staying ramrod straight because I didn't dare relax.

Jack folded his hands on the desk and stared at me for an uncomfortably long moment. "I'm sure you're aware that Stevens is conditioning in Everett right now."

I nodded slowly, my heart sinking because I knew what was coming.

"Right." Jack sat back in his chair. "You and Brody will both dress for tonight's game, but as soon as Stevens is ready to come back to the lineup, Brody is going back to Everett."

Wait. What?

I shifted in the chair. "Oh. He is?"

"Yes. I was absolutely ready to send you back down. You've been playing well, but I've never been a fan of rewarding defiance." He narrowed his eyes. "I haven't forgotten about the tape incident."

I had no idea how to respond. I was afraid to move. To even breathe.

Jack went on, "If Coach Baldwin wasn't so emphatic about keeping you over Brody, you'd be the one going back to the PHL. Make no mistake of that." His expression shifted to a sour one. "But he wants you on the bottom six, and he's not interested in any of your Everett teammates. So for the time being, you're still here."

He sounded *exceptionally* irritated by this.

I gulped. "Okay. Um." What was I even supposed to say?

"I would suggest," he continued ominously, "that you live up to the expectations of a NAPH player. No fucking up like you did in Vancouver. And no thumbing your nose at authority figures. Am I clear?"

I nodded. "Yeah. Absolutely."

"Good. Get out of my office."

I didn't hesitate. I got the hell out of there, and I speed-walked down the hall until I reached one of the stairwells. There, I stopped and leaned against a cold wall. I tilted my head back, closed my eyes, and took some slow, deep breaths. My heart was going a million miles a minute, and my stomach was somersaulting around the breakfast I was trying hard to keep down.

I'd known from the moment I'd been called up that this was my last chance with the Rainiers. Quite possibly my last chance in the NAPH unless I managed to sign with another team when I hit free agency after next season.

But now the pressure was on. Not only did I have to shine like I never had before, I also couldn't fuck up. I couldn't so much as lose an edge or turn over the puck. I may have been playing on the third line but I had to play as if I was one of the stars on the first.

I had to play like my career depended on it... because it *did*.

I was on precariously thin ice with Jack Hayes.

There was a chance he knew about the red line I'd crossed. The one I kept crossing and couldn't make myself uncross.

I had to shine tonight and every night going forward. I had to keep impressing Baldwin enough that he stood firm with Jack and refused to have me sent down.

I'd played under pressure before. I could do it again.

Right?

Fuck my life.

CHAPTER 26

CHRISTIAN

Something was off. Theo had been distant and distracted all day. During the morning skate, he was just... somewhere else. After his pre-warmup walk, he'd been wound up and twitchy, not relaxed and ready to skate like he usually was.

And then during warmups? Christ, he was on another planet. He managed to not lose an edge or anything, but he kept losing his place in the flow of the team's routine. During line rushes, he couldn't control the puck, which he usually did like it was the most effortless thing in the world.

Normally, I didn't interact with him or the other players once warmups started. Not unless they needed me to fix or swap out some gear. They had to be in the zone and focused on the game, and they were usually getting distracted enough by reporters. My crew and I just stayed out of their way.

This time, though, I stopped Theo on his way back to the locker room. "Hey, let me take a look at your helmet." I gestured at it. "The visor screw looks loose."

He blinked. Then he stepped out of the line of players

coming off the ice, took off his helmet, and handed it over. "It feels fine."

"Well, just to be sure..." I tugged a screwdriver out of my tool belt. As I "checked" the screws on his visor, I glanced up at him. "You okay tonight?"

Theo's shoulders dipped, his pads creaking with the movement. He glanced around, probably making sure we were alone. Then he quietly said, "Your dad called me into his office earlier."

I almost dropped the screwdriver. "For what?"

"To let me know he's not sending me down," Theo gritted out. "Yet. He *wants* to. Now that Stevens is coming back, he really wants to send me down. But I guess Coach made a case to keep me, and your dad agreed to it. So he just wanted me to know that if I fuck up—if I do anything to give him a reason to send me down—I'm gone."

"Jesus fuck," I breathed, and handed back his helmet. "Look, Coach Baldwin respects you enough to go toe-to-toe with my dad over keeping you. Because I guarantee that was not a pleasant conversation."

He swallowed, staring down at his helmet.

"You've got this, okay, baby?" I squeezed his arm, though he might not have felt it much through his pads. "Don't let him get into your head."

Theo chewed his lip uncertainly.

"I mean it. Don't let him fuck with your confidence." I gave his pads a firm pat that I knew he'd feel. "Listen to me—I've been watching this game my whole life. I've seen good players, mediocre ones, generational talents, and people who clearly only got to this level out of nepotism. I can see talent and skill, okay?"

He studied me but still didn't speak.

"You've got hockey IQ to burn," I went on. "I love

watching you play because I can see your mind working. I can see you working out plays and being three steps ahead of the guys around you."

His eyebrows rose. "Really?"

"Mmhmm. And I know Coach Baldwin sees it, too. That's why he's fought so hard to keep you even as the injured Rainiers have come back to the roster."

Theo dropped his gaze. "Oh."

"Dad's gonna talk a big game, but remember, the owners expect a winning team. If he's making decisions that are detrimental to the team, that's going to reflect badly on him and he knows it. I mean, right now, the press is raving about how smart he was, bringing you up and keeping you up after you showed so much talent." I smiled. "That's going to massage his ego enough that he's not going to risk the humiliation of sending you down while you and the team are on a hot streak."

"So you think he's just trying to trip me up?"

"Pretty much." I rolled my eyes. "Right now, he's probably super pissed that you're exceeding expectations and he has to just live with it. Just keep doing what you've been doing, and you'll be fine." I paused. "And don't sweat over the small mistakes. You *all* make them during *every* game. Coach Baldwin will lose his shit if Dad tries to send you down over a turnover or something."

Theo laughed. "Okay, true."

"Exactly. And even with Dad maybe knowing about us, it isn't like we're doing anything out in the open. We know the Zamboni bay is off limits now, so we'll stick to the safe places." I smiled. "Don't sweat about it. We'll be fine."

He exhaled, which made me think I'd read him right—he was sweating about it. "Okay. Okay, you're right. We'll just keep it behind closed doors." He started for the locker room but paused. "And, um... thanks for the pep talk." He offered up a grin that raised goose bumps along my arms and spine. I didn't expect anything in return for helping him rally, but the gleam in his eyes said he'd be rocking my world later as a thank-you.

"Any time," I said, returning the grin. "Now get in there before someone comes looking for you."

"All right. See you after the game." Then he winked, and he was gone.

I shivered. He'd see me plenty between now and then, but I knew what he meant—he was looking forward to hooking up at the end of the night.

Me too, baby. Me too.

Alone in the hallway, I paused for a few slow breaths. It wasn't fair, the way Dad kept fucking with Theo's head. It was like he wanted to sabotage him and his career. And why? Because he put some rainbow tape on his stick? Jesus fucking Christ.

You know that's not all it is.

I shivered, rolling my shoulders under my hoodie.

No, that wasn't all it was. Dad had been pissed about the tape, and he'd been irritated he'd had no choice but to bring Theo up from the minors. But if he knew what I thought he knew, then he had to be incandescent with fury.

I closed my eyes and rubbed my forehead.

Sooner or later, something had to give.

I just hoped the fallout didn't fuck over Theo or his career.

And for the millionth time, I hoped I didn't lose him.

I HAD JUST COME BACK FROM THROWING JERSEYS INTO the washing machine after the game when Dad went storming out of the locker room. He didn't even give me a second look, thank God. When he was pissed off about something, he tended to get tunnel vision, and I'd learned as a kid how to be very quiet and unnoticeable when he was angry. That way I didn't end up the target of his fury.

It worked this time, and once he'd disappeared down the hall, I continued into the locker room.

Marty was the only one left, and he was red in the face and slamming sweaty towels into a laundry cart.

"Uh," I ventured cautiously. "What was that all about?"

"Your dad being the dickhole to end all dickholes." Marty threw a handful of towels into the cart. "He had a hair up his ass about the fans." He nodded to the large fans we set up to dry out gear overnight.

"What?" I cocked my head. "We've been using those for years. What's his problem?"

Marty made an irritated sound and waved a hand. Yeah, I could read between those lines. Dad didn't like anything that made noise, and he'd probably been incensed that we had the audacity to be running fans when he came into the locker room. Didn't matter that it was part of our normal routine, that it helped everything dry out in time for the next game, and that the equipment managers before us had done the same damn thing.

That was Dad's M.O., too. If he was bitchy about something, he'd find the nearest annoyance to blow up over. Like when he was still coaching, and he came home from a five-game road trip that his team had managed to completely blow. He'd noticed our bicycles in their usual spot in the garage, and suddenly he was furious that they were leaning the wrong way. After that, my sister and I always made sure the bikes were pointing in the opposite direction and leaning against the wall, rather than tilted slightly into the flow of traffic because of their kickstands. I was pretty sure that had pissed him off at some point, too, but whatever.

Marty tossed another handful of towels into the cart, then gestured at the door Dad had stormed out of. "Dude, what is your dad's damage, anyway?"

I gave a caustic laugh. "You think I have a clue?"

"Okay, no, but like... He's been *extra* douchey lately."

I pressed my lips together.

Marty studied me. Then he inclined his head. "What?"

Shifting my weight, I avoided his gaze.

"Christian. Come on. Level with me." He gestured at the door Dad had gone through. "Do you know what's up his ass right now? Because I'm about this close to having a chat with some of the fuckers on high about it."

I swallowed. Then I glanced around the room and gestured for him to follow me out into the hallway. We found one of the small conference rooms, and after he'd gone inside, I shut the door behind us.

"Okay, you *have* to promise me that this stays between us." I looked pointedly in his eyes. "No one else knows, so if it gets out, I'm gonna *know* it came from—"

"Whoa, whoa." Marty showed his palms. "Slow your roll, man. I'm not gonna repeat your business. You know that."

Guilt added to the apprehension in my chest. Yeah, I knew that. I trusted Marty implicitly. But I was paranoid and really couldn't apologize for that.

"Okay. I..." I glanced toward the door as I moistened my lips. Meeting my friend's eyes again, I quietly said, "I think he might've caught on that, um... that I've been seeing one of the players."

Marty's eyes went huge as his jaw slowly went slack. In a hoarse whisper, he asked, "Are you *shitting me?*" He flailed a hand toward the door. "If he finds out for sure, he will end you. Both of you!"

"I know! I know." And there was a distinct possibility Dad had already confirmed it, but I wasn't going to show *that* card to Marty. "That's why I need to keep it..." I gestured between us.

He nodded. "Yeah. Smart. But still—what are you *thinking?*"

"That I fucking love the guy, that's what."

My teeth snapped shut.

For a heartbeat, I wondered if I'd actually said that out loud, but one look at Marty's face said I absolutely had.

He opened and closed his mouth a couple of times like a fish. Then he sighed, his shoulders dropping. "Christian. Are you insane?"

I leaned against the wall and raked a hand through my hair. "Probably, yeah. And you don't have to tell me I'm playing with fire or that my dad'll be pissed. I've known that from the start and so has—" I bit my lip. "So has... the other guy."

Marty rolled his eyes. "Just admit it's Mathis."

It was my turn to stare at him in disbelief. "It... How the fuck did you know?"

He laughed and clapped my shoulder. "C'mon. I've known you had a crush on him since forever. I just... uh... Didn't realize..."

My face was on fire. "Yeah, no one was supposed to know." With a grimace, I added, "Especially not my dad."

Marty sobered. "I mean, you guys have been pretty subtle. I knew you had a thing for Mathis, but I had no idea you were hooking up with him. Or, uh... Doing more with him."

The heat in my face intensified. Yeah, I was definitely doing more with Theo. Now that I'd said it out loud, I was itching to tell Theo the truth. That when I said this went beyond sex, I meant it went *way* beyond sex.

I do love him, don't I? Man, I am so fucked.

Marty cleared his throat, drawing me out of my thoughts. "So, you think that's what your dad's pissy about? Or is he just being extra dickish today?"

"Could be a little of both," I admitted. "I'm not really sure." I glared at the doorway and grumbled, "I'm so tired of his shit, though."

"Yeah, me too. And he's even worse to you. I don't know how you put up with it."

"Do I have a choice?" I was suddenly exhausted. "I mean, yeah, I could try to find a job with another team, or—"

"Try?" Marty snorted. "We have to practically threaten every other team not to poach you. All you'd have to do is make a vague comment on social media that you're thinking of changing teams, and you'll have every GM in the league blowing up your phone."

I laughed. Honestly, he wasn't wrong; I'd had more than a few head equipment managers and general managers approach me about coming to their clubs. They usually backed off, saying they understood I wanted to work for my dad, but I suspected that was more that they didn't want to provoke Dad by poaching me. If I said I was looking for a job, though...

Sighing, I shrugged. "I don't know. Maybe? But then I'll end up someplace else while Theo stays here. Or while he plays in Everett. Either way, we wouldn't be able to be together."

Marty frowned. "Man. That sucks." He quirked his lips, then shook his head. "I guess all you can do is keep it on the DL and hope for the best."

"Pretty much, yeah," I murmured.

Though I still had the worst inkling that that particular ship had sailed.

It should've been a relief that Marty had noticed my crush on Theo but hadn't figured out we were together. Still, Dad's cryptic threats needled at me.

It occurred to me then that Dad bluffed about a lot of things. It wouldn't be beneath him at all to tell me there were now cameras in the Zamboni bay just to make me squirm, while at the same time, he still told the facilities workers that they couldn't have the cameras they'd been asking for.

Which... huh. Now I was curious.

I slipped out of the locker room and down the hall. I walked casually aside from glancing around to make sure no one else was around. Then I ducked into the Zamboni bay.

I stayed close to the wall so I'd hopefully be out of view. Inching closer, I scanned any place a camera would make sense.

Nothing.

Laughing to myself, I rolled mye yes and exhaled. Yep. Bluffing. Called it. I fucking called—

A tiny green LED caught my eye. I squinted.

And... there it was. Right above the Zambonis. With a bird's eye view of the gap between them.

A fucking camera.

My blood turned colder than the ice my boyfriend would be skating on.

I slipped back out into the main hallway and walked fast, trying to will myself to stop shaking. So there *was* a camera. It was entirely possible my father did know, at least that we'd made out in there.

But what I'd told Theo was still true. Even if Dad had busted us in there, he had no proof we were *still* seeing each other. Aside from our brief interludes between the Zambonis, we'd stayed out of sight. We were good at keeping it on the DL.

All we really had to do was keep doing what we'd been doing. Stay behind closed doors. Stay off Dad's radar.

And holy shit, Theo had to do everything he could to avoid getting sent back down, because God knew Dad would be *looking* for a reason now.

We had to stay out of sight, and Theo had to keep playing at an elite enough level to stay on the Rainiers.

No pressure, baby...

CHAPTER 27

THEO

As we often did before practice, we sat down as a team to review film. The training facility had a small theater where we'd all sit and watch clips of other teams as well as ourselves on the big screen. Today, we were prepping to play against Dallas, and they were killing it this season. Some teams were mediocre but backstopped by spectacular goalies, so we'd focus mostly on how to get around the netminder. Others had killer defense in front of so-so goalies; get far enough past the blueliners to get a shot on goal, and there was a good chance the puck would go in. Going up against those teams, we strategized every imaginable way to get around the D. And of course there were the teams with top-scoring offensive players who could probably find the back of the net from the damn locker room. Seriously, some of those guys were magic with the puck.

Sometimes a team came along that shouldn't have been as good as they were. Somehow, the roster of players no one would bother picking for a fantasy team came together as a force to be reckoned with. The goalie made just enough stops to keep the score in their team's favor. The defense kept just enough players away to lessen the opportunities to get past the goalie. The offense generated just enough scoring chances to put a few goals on the board. Combined, they put up a winning record and steadily mowed through the league, plodding past future hall-of-famers and Cup contenders on their way to a wild card spot.

That was Dallas this season. Reasonably good goalies, pretty solid defensemen, and middle-tier offense. Looking at all the players' individual stats, they really shouldn't have been a difficult team to beat, but they were coming into Seattle on a nine-game point streak.

So, we pored over footage of their power play, their penalty kill, their starting and backup goalies, faceoffs—everything. We wouldn't need to dial anything up dramatically to beat them, just exploit their many weaknesses and keep them from capitalizing on ours. My line in particular did a lot of stretch passes, and Dallas was very good at intercepting those, so we'd need to be cautious about that. Protect the puck as much as possible and be extra mindful of where opposing players were when we passed.

"They love takeaways," Coach said. "Let's not make it easy for them."

Easy enough. Their starting goalie was weak on his blocker side and was especially vulnerable to top shelf shots. He was smaller than a lot of netminders, and if he thought a shot was coming in low, he'd drop down to make the stop... but then he couldn't always get up fast enough to block the puck coming in high.

"Fake him low," Nelson, the offensive coach, told us. "Then go right over his shoulder. Ideally on the blocker side —he's *fast* with his glove."

Easy enough. In the front row, Condit and Sorenson shared a fist bump and a quiet laugh; if I had to guess, they were plotting to send dozens of shots over this goalie's shoulders, or they were making a bet to see if someone could five-hole him. Either way, the result would be goals from our top offensive line.

We were just finishing up discussing the weaknesses of Dallas's forwards when the door side opened, which wasn't unusual. Some of the coaches came and went while we were doing this, and sometimes the brass would sit in.

It *was* unusual for the equipment managers to join us, though.

I got my typical little thrill at the sight of Christian walking into the room, but it quickly died away when I saw his expression. All four of the equipment managers wore confusion on their faces, exchanging glances and shrugging. Was Dallas notorious for damaging our equipment somehow? Weird.

Coach didn't seem to understand either. He eyed the equipment staff, but only missed a beat or two in what he was saying to the centers about faceoffs.

Just as Coach was wrapping up that little spiel, Jack strode in, and my hackles went up.

Christian also fidgeted, eyeing his father uneasily. He very pointedly didn't look at me, so I tried to avoid looking his way despite my curiosity. And my rising panic.

Oh, fuck. No. Please tell me he isn't about to...

Jack stood in front of the room by the now-darkened screen. "I'm going to let everyone get to practice, but first, we have an issue that has been brought to my attention, and that we need to address as a team." He scanned the gathered players and equipment managers. "The Seattle Rainiers expect a lot out of those who wear our logo, whether on the ice or behind the bench. And no team of mine is going to tolerate those who disrespect all of us by behaving inappropriately."

Confused murmurs rippled through the group.

I caught Christian's eye, and the uneasiness in his expression had shifted to fear, which sent a rock into the pit of my stomach. Was this about...

No. No way. It *couldn't* be about us. We were just being paranoid because that was a byproduct of sneaking around under his asshole dad's nose. Especially after he'd caught on to us recently.

So what *was* going on?

"I'm going to show you boys a video." He plugged a flash drive into the projector and took the remote from Coach. "Then we're going to have a conversation as a team about how this kind of behavior should be dealt with, and why it needs to be prevented going forward."

Before I could ponder what in the ever-loving hell that meant, he clicked the remote. The projector lit up again.

A video started of sharp, black-and-white CCTV footage. I instantly recognized it as the bay where the Zambonis were parked when they weren't in use.

My blood turned cold. There *were* cameras in there now. Fuuuck.

And then Christian walked into the frame. He paced a little. Rubbed the back of his neck. Leaned against the Zamboni.

In the auditorium, Christian said, "Dad. I don't think this is   "

"Quiet," Jack snapped.

They exchanged a few hissed words, but the video kept going behind them. On the screen, Christian stood straighter, looking at something off-camera, and I covered my face and exhaled, but I still *felt it* when I appeared on-camera. Probably because of the confused murmur rippling through my teammates.

Though I really, really didn't want to, I lowered my hand and looked at the screen, and the whole team and I—along with the equipment managers and coaching staff—watched myself stride right up to Christian, push him up against the Zamboni, and kiss him.

Fuck me, but that had been one of the hottest moments of my life. Even as acid burned in my stomach and shame burned on my face, I could still feel that rush of much more pleasant heat as we'd given in after too damn long.

Here in the room, Christian opened his mouth to speak, probably to try to explain what happened, but he wasn't fast enough.

"Are you *kidding* me?" Condit roared to his feet. "Are you fucking *serious* right now?"

I gulped. Christian cringed and avoided everyone's eyes. I tried to melt lower in my seat, hoping it would open up and swallow me whole.

Jack paused the video, freezing that image of Christian and me locking lips against the Zamboni. "As you can see, we have—"

"That's messed up," Sorenson said, disgust dripping off every word.

"No shit," Abrahamsson agreed.

"What in the hell?" Yanni chimed in. "If this is the shit the Seattle Rainiers do, then I'm out of here. Fuck this club. Jesus." Other voices agreed, talking one over the other about how this was not what they signed up for, it wasn't cool, and either something changed *immediately* or they were demanding trades.

Oh, God. I covered my face as the shame burned hotter. We knew we'd been caught. And I'd kind of known the team would hate us for it. Still, it hurt that they were *this* pissed about it. They'd skipped right over wanting me sent back to the minors or having Christian fired, and they went straight to getting themselves traded out of here. Fuck. I'd known we were playing with fire, but was it really *that* bad, the two of us being together? Had we really ruined the whole fucking team?

"We let this guy in the locker room with us," Wilcox said, "and *this* is the shit he does?"

I squeezed my eyes shut. I couldn't even look at Christian, never mind my coaches or teammates. This was a *disaster*.

"Coach, I am not joking." Condit's voice boomed over everyone else's. "Tell the owners they can either find a new GM, or they can find a new captain."

More loud agreement.

Wait. Did he say...

A new...

What?

I cautiously lifted my gaze. Across the room, Christian looked as mystified as I felt, and the stunned expression on his father's face was almost funny.

"This is an invasion of privacy," Sorenson declared furiously. "What the actual fuck?"

"You just outed *your own son?*" Abrahamsson scoffed.

"What... I..." Jack shook his head, then squared his shoulders. "I didn't out him. You all know they're both gay."

"Yeah, we do," Condit growled. "And we also know you have a problem with that because you're worse at hiding it than they are at hiding that they're together." He narrowed his eyes. "What gives you the right to out them as—"

"This is inappropriate behavior for two men working for—"

"Inappropriate behavior is you filming them and showing it to all of us," Condit threw back with more fury than I'd ever heard from him. "What the fuck is wrong with you?"

Instantly, Jack was shouting at him, probably threatening him, but I couldn't hear it over the roar of our teammates backing up our captain, who was *right* in Jack's face. They had Condit's back, and they...

They had ours? Christian's and mine?

As I scanned the room, everyone was visibly livid—either glaring in anger and horror at our GM or joining Condit in reading him the riot act. They were angry... on our behalf. Defending us. Threatening to leave Seattle over this.

My throat tightened and my eyes stung. I was humiliated and terrified, but also... God, the only time I could remember feeling anything like this was at a youth tourney when I was fourteen. A kid had caught on that I was queer, and he'd been giving me all kinds of shit for it... right up until the U16 and U18 kids stepped in and shut him the hell down. People had told me a gay kid wouldn't go far in sports, that the other boys wouldn't put up with it, but there were those high school boys stepping in and telling that asshole his homophobia wasn't acceptable. They'd even gone to the organizers and ended up getting him booted from the tournament. That was the safest I'd ever felt in this sport. The most protected and accepted.

Right up until today. Until this moment in the practice rink's theater—the PHL call-up in this room full of NAPH players who were miles above me—listening to the entire team not just rallying around me and Christian, but threatening to mutiny over it.

The room had reached a deafening level when Coach blew his whistle.

Everyone instantly fell silent. A few of my teammates dropped back into their seats. The tension thrumming in the air? Ooh, shit.

Slowly, Coach turned to one of the other coaches. "Text Bruce. We need a sit-down immediately." Then he pointed sharply at the door and growled to Jack, "You too. Wait for me in conference room four."

Jack blinked. Then he straightened. "I don't think you quite understand the chain of command here, *Coach* Baldwin."

"And I don't think you quite understand how far out of line you've just stepped, Jack," Coach gritted out. "Because if *one* of these players walks, you won't have to worry about firing me. I'll be walking right out the door behind them."

All around me, my teammates broke into cheers and applause that rivaled the hometown crowd after a goal. Jack stared at Coach. At us. At the room full of people he'd clearly expected to be on his side.

My heart was thundering with more emotions than I could name. I was still in shock over the video. I'd also been bracing for the team to turn on me and Christian. This? I had not expected this. Definitely not from the whole fucking team.

Through the chaos, I found Christian. He stared back at me, wide-eyed with *"is this really happening?"* written all over his face. I suspected I was telegraphing the same thing because... holy hell, *was* this really happening?

Jack apparently caught on that he was woefully outnumbered and no one was taking his side, because he stormed out of the room. Coach said something I didn't catch to Condit, and then he strode out, the rest of the coaching staff on his heels.

The doors shut behind them. For long seconds, silence hung in the air, everyone exchanging glances and every pair of eyes noticeably flicking toward me and Christian.

Condit looked at each of us. "Uh. So… how long has this been going on?"

My throat was too tight and my stomach too volatile to even try to speak.

Christian glanced at me, then muffled a cough as he shifted his weight. His voice came out more timid than I'd ever heard it. "Since… um…" He nodded toward me. "A little while after he got here."

Condit exhaled sharply and cuffed Sorenson upside the head. "See? I fucking told you."

"Oh, whatever." Sorenson smacked his arm. "You were just guessing."

I couldn't help laughing, which made the tension in me snap. Good thing I was sitting down, or I'd have probably melted to the floor in a relieved heap. From the way Christian wavered, and the way Marty steadied him, I wasn't the only one.

When he'd recovered a little, Christian ran a shaky hand through his hair and exhaled. "Why am I not surprised you guys figured it out?" He gestured at Marty. "Even he didn't know."

"Pfft." Condit crossed the room and clapped Christian's shoulder. "You should know by now—you can't hide *anything* from us."

Christian smirked up at him. "I didn't realize you guys were that observant."

"We're not," Sorenson said. "You're just not subtle."

Christian's smirk fell as color rose in his cheeks. I groaned and covered my face.

Beside me, Rusanov howled with laughter, and he slapped my back. To my other side, Grekov was chuckling, but he sounded more relieved than anything. I wondered if anyone besides him and me knew why.

After a moment, Christian cleared his throat. "Look, I appreciate all this. Honestly. I'm sure Theo does too."

Some heads turned toward me, and I nodded. "Yeah. Absolutely."

He went on, "But you don't have to ask for trades or—"

"Yeah, we do," Sorenson said firmly. "It's fucked up that he did that to you." He glanced at me. "*Both* of you. But the fact that he'd do it to anyone?" He shook his head emphatically. "Absolutely the fuck not. I'm not playing for someone who would invade anyone's privacy and out them like that. Straight or gay. I don't give a shit. You just don't do that."

Nods and murmurs of agreement all around.

I cleared my throat and timidly said, "But are you guys okay with, uh..." I gestured at myself and Christian.

"Of course." Condit shrugged. "Man, if we had an issue with it, we'd have pulled you guys aside privately and said something. But everyone knows about it and I haven't heard anyone say anything negative."

My face burned as my teammates nodded their agreement.

"This isn't about just you two," the captain said. "What you guys are doing isn't affecting us. That shit?" He pointed at the door. "I'm not putting up with it. No way."

"No kidding." Wilcox nodded sharply. "I've got a gay nephew who's almost old enough for the draft, and over my dead body is he playing in a league where that bullshit's acceptable. No fucking way."

"My little brother is gay and playing in the PHL," Yanni said. "Like *hell* am I staying on a team that treats people like him this way."

Other players agreed with them. Loudly. In no uncertain terms, this team was way more incensed about Jack outing us than they were over me and Christian being together. They didn't ask if we were serious or if this was just a fuck buddy situation; they quite clearly didn't care.

After a few minutes of the team vocally letting us know where they stood, Condit cleared his throat. "All right, look. The people in suits will deal with Jack, but we're still a team, and we've still got a game to win. So how about we go over some of these clips again and get our focus back so we can practice?"

Everyone groaned with theatrical exasperation and sat back down.

Christian laughed. "Do you boys need us for this part?"

"Nah, man." Condit waved toward the door. "Go iron our jockstraps or whatever."

Laughter rippled through the room. Christian flipped him off. "So, starch your jockstrap? Got it!" Then he darted out of the room.

Wilcox barked a laugh. "He's gonna do it, Condit. You know he will!"

Condit stared ruefully at the door, then sighed as if to say, *oh, fuck my life*. "Can we just look at this film so I can go hide my jock from him?"

We did go over the clips again, but it probably wasn't the most professional film review we'd ever done. Still, it pulled everyone's focus back to the task at hand, and it reminded us all of the things we'd need to concentrate on during practice and at the game. When we were finished,

Condit dismissed us, and everyone headed to the locker room to gear up.

On the way, Sorenson fell into step beside me. "You gonna be all right today, kid?"

"I think so, yeah." I slid my hands into the front pocket of my hoodie. "I, uh... I didn't expect you guys to all go to bat for us like that, though."

"Nah." He put an arm around my shoulders. "We're a team. Don't matter if you're a one-game call-up or a regular part of the roster. You're a Rainier, and we've got you."

I had to work to swallow. "I appreciate it." Right then and there, I vowed to work as hard as humanly possible to make this roster for good next season. The men in that room —the men who'd been furious for me and Christian—were the men I wanted to play beside. I glanced up at Sorenson. "Out of curiosity, when did you think this started?"

Sorenson chuckled. "Last season, when the two of you were eye-fucking at the bar."

My jaw dropped. "You... You knew about that?"

He laughed, rolling his eyes, and he clapped my shoulder. "My dude, I'm as dumb as they come and not observant at all unless there's a puck involved. You two were *not* subtle."

My cheeks were on *fire*.

He just laughed some more and shoved me ahead into the locker room.

God, I loved this team.

CHAPTER 28

CHRISTIAN

The only thing more nerve-racking than being called into that theater was being called into one of the conference rooms.

I'd been confused and uneasy earlier, wondering why in the world anyone needed the equipment staff to join the team to review film. I'd guessed once my father had walked in, but I couldn't stop him.

Now I was terrified of what was going to happen next. Yes, the team had rallied around me and Theo, but the powers that be probably weren't happy that an employee had been banging a player. Least of all when that relationship had resulted in the whole team and staff turning on the GM. Causing waves that size was not going to go unanswered.

Which meant that, more than likely, one or both of us was fucked. Most likely me, since I was a lot more replaceable than a player who was notching points like mad for this team. Even with the support of Theo's teammates, the suits didn't have a lot of tolerance for people who rocked the boat.

So, my days—hell, my hours—with the Seattle Rainiers were likely numbered.

At least I'd managed a moment alone with Theo. I'd pulled him aside after he'd geared up for practice, as he was heading for the ice.

"Are you okay?" I'd asked.

"I'm good. Just... kind of trying to process."

"Same." I'd squeezed his hand. "I'm sure the fallout isn't over, but I'm glad the team has our back."

"Me too."

Then he'd had to join his teammates for practice, and it wasn't long at all before I was summoned upstairs.

When I stepped into the room, Bruce, the team's president of hockey operations, sat at the table beside Jerry Vincent, who I'd met briefly in the past. Jerry was part of the group that had majority ownership of the team, and he usually came in as a representative when an owner's presence was needed.

His presence in *this* meeting... did not bode well.

"Have a seat, Christian," Bruce said. "Thank you for joining us."

I took a seat in the single chair across from them, and I pretended I wasn't about to throw up all over the giant table. Today had been a disaster, and I doubted it was going to improve before I left this room.

"So, in light of what's happened," Bruce said, "we've consulted with our legal team, who has agreed that while your father was ostensibly enforcing a rule, the way he went about it was *highly* inappropriate and unacceptable. As a result, he has been asked to resign as general manager of the Rainiers."

I closed my eyes and exhaled. I didn't even want to imagine how this was going to affect my family. Dad would be insufferable when he got home. Should I text Mom and Chelsea to give them a heads up? Maybe suggest they pick today to be anywhere but home?

Before I could make a decision in that regard, Bruce continued. "On behalf of the Seattle Rainiers and the entire organization, I want to apologize for what you and Mr. Mathis have been subjected to. It's not behavior that we condone or allow."

I nodded and murmured, "I appreciate that," but my guard was still firmly up. There was a "but..." coming. I could feel it.

He didn't keep me waiting.

"The problem is that we reviewed the rules and bylaws that players and employees are expected to abide by." Bruce grimaced, and my heart was sinking even before he went on. "And there *is* a clause in there that explicitly states that fraternization of a romantic or platonic nature between employees and/or contractors is grounds for termination. Specifically, about employees and/or contractors fraternizing with players."

My heart hit the floor. "Oh. I..." I sagged back against my chair. "I probably knew that. I just..." What? Forgot? Never committed it to memory because I never thought it would affect me? And I wasn't sorry. Maybe sorry I broke the rule and had undoubtedly just gotten myself fired, but I wasn't sorry for what I'd done. Finally, I went with a quiet, "I don't have any excuse."

"We don't expect you to." Jerry sat up a little and folded his hands on his notes. "But after talking with the staff—including the coaches and some of the players—we can't deny that you're an invaluable member of the Rainiers. Arguably more so than your father has ever been."

I blinked. "Seriously?"

"Yes." Bruce nodded. "It's been said that equipment managers are the unsung heroes of this sport, and you've made it very clear that's more than just lip service." He gave a quiet laugh. "Quite frankly, we would be stupid to let you go."

I wanted to be relieved by that, but the other side of the coin was plainly obvious, and I swallowed hard. "You're going to send Theo back down, then." I winced. "Please don't punish him. You've seen how he's played since he's been here. He deserves a shot on—"

"We know," Bruce said quietly. "Mathis has put up impressive stats since he's been up. Condit and Coach Baldwin have both raved about him and told your father repeatedly that we need to keep Mathis up even as injured players have been reactivated."

Pride swelled in my chest. God, I was so happy for Theo. Every minor league player knew they had to shine when they came up, and he'd done that in spades.

My smile fell before it really came to life. "So Theo is valuable on the roster. I'm... you don't want to let me go." I shrugged tightly. "What happens next, then?"

The two men exchanged looks.

"Well," Bruce said. "We discussed it, and we realized that even if Theo wasn't an up and coming star, and even if you weren't a very popular and competent equipment manager, the rule is... unfair. It's an overstep of the organization."

"It... It is?"

"Yes," Jerry said. "So to answer your question, what happens next is that we change the rule."

My lips parted. "Really?"

"Yes," Jerry said. "It was written with the intent of avoiding interpersonal conflict and conflicts of interest, but we realize now that it is perhaps more draconian than necessary. After all, everyone—staff, players, and what have you—fraternize on a regular basis. It helps to promote a good atmosphere in the locker room. So if we were to enforce this rule for you and Mr. Mathis, then we would also have to crack down on the friendships forged between others employed by the organization. Quite frankly, that would be detrimental to the team, and it would diminish the camaraderie that we believe is necessary."

"Oh" was all I could think to say.

"It'll take some time," Bruce warned. "It needs approval by all the majority owners, not just Jerry, and we'll discuss it with the team. The league and the players' association will also need to review and approve the change. All we ask during that interim is that you and Mr. Mathis keep your relationship out of the public eye. Once everything has been approved by all the necessary parties, then you'll be free to be open and public without consequence."

I swallowed. "That's... Yeah, we can do that." I huffed a relieved laugh. "We've been doing it all along, so..."

"All right. Well." Bruce nodded sharply. "We'll keep you apprised of everything that happens. Hopefully it won't take long."

"Hopefully," Jerry confirmed. "And on behalf of the Seattle Rainiers organization, I again want to sincerely apologize to you and to Mr. Mathis for what happened today. This is not who we are as an organization, and going forward, I assure you, there will be zero tolerance for that kind of behavior."

"Thank you, sir," I said quietly.

There wasn't much left to discuss after that, so they adjourned the meeting. Before I left, they came around the table, each offering me a handshake.

"Thank you for this," I said. "I know twenty years ago, things would have played out very differently, but—"

"Fortunately," Jerry said, "that was twenty years ago. Times have changed, and the Seattle Rainiers are determined to keep up with them."

"I appreciate that." I paused. "And, um... if it's not pushing my luck to ask... Is there any chance we can reinstate Pride Nights?"

The other men exchange glances, and there were some shrugs.

Jerry looked up at me. "We'll certainly discuss it with the team for next season."

I smiled. "Thank you, sir. It means a lot to the community. I know there's backlash and people who complain about it, but our community—we really appreciate it."

"That's good to know, kid. Thank you."

I gave him a quick smile and a nod, and then I stepped out into the hall. I paused outside the door just to let the relief and adrenaline crash over me. I'd been so certain that Theo and I were both epically fucked, but the team—including the higher ups—had rallied around us in ways I'd never anticipated. Sure, I knew the guys would intervene if someone tried to gay bash me in a bar, and I knew the higher ups would do lip service in favor of Pride, but this? Players openly demanding trades if my father wasn't fired? The brass changing rules so that Theo and I could still be together? We could be *out* together? *Publicly?*

Fuck. I was dizzy from all these emotions rushing through me. I'd known I was stressed over all of this, but I hadn't known just *how* stressed until all that weight was suddenly off my shoulders.

No more walking on eggshells.

No more working for my father.

No more keeping my relationship with Theo a secret.

Once the league and players' association had approved the rule change, we could be completely out and open about being together. The men we worked with—the players, the staff, the executives on high—didn't object.

Holy shit. We made it. All we have to do now is—

"I hope you're happy." My dad's voice cut through my thoughts, and my eyes flew open as he stalked toward me. "This is your fault, you know. Entirely on you. You flaunting your lifestyle all over the place cost me my job. Do you realize—"

"You're the one who showed that video," I threw back, and I said it fearlessly because goddammit, this man couldn't do anything to me anymore. "You aren't getting fired because you have a gay son. You're getting fired for—"

"Don't you talk to me that way!"

"Or what?" I glared at up at him, gritting my teeth just to keep them from chattering because oh, fuck, I really was standing up to my dad. "You gonna fire me? Ground me? Disinherit me? You can't do shit to me anymore, Dad."

He gaped at me. His face was beet red, his lips pulled back across his gritted teeth. "You ungrateful—"

"Fuck off," I snapped. "You brought this on yourself, and I'm not—"

"Mr. Hayes." Bruce's voice was sharp and hard.

I spun around to face him, apologies at the tip of my tongue, but before I could speak, I realized he wasn't looking at me.

He meant the *other* Mr. Hayes.

Striding closer with Jerry behind him, he growled, "I will not have you harassing Seattle Rainier employees."

"This is a conversation with my son," Dad said. "It's none of—"

"He is an employee of this organization," Bruce pushed back. "You, on the other hand, are not. I would suggest you clean out your office and leave the premises without harassing any more of our staff, or else I will be happy to have Seattle P.D. join security in escorting you out."

The shocked expression on my dad's face was a sight to behold, and I didn't care if it made me a bad person—seeing him like that was so fucking satisfying. He'd bullied everyone in his vicinity his whole life, and now he'd been stripped of the one and only thing he actually cared about: power.

In silence, and without giving me another look, he turned and walked back to his office with his proverbial tail between his legs.

God, I wished I'd filmed that for posterity.

Bruce put a hand on my shoulder. "I apologize for this, Christian. Again, behavior like his will not be tolerated in this organization any further."

I swallowed against an unexpected lump in my throat. "Thanks."

It really was over. Dad had no power here anymore. He couldn't touch my career or Theo's. He couldn't do a damn thing to stop us from being together and living our lives.

It felt like I'd been holding my breath not only since I'd started dating Theo, but ever since I'd started working here, terrified to make a move or even a noise because Dad might shout at me or fire me.

Today, right now, I could breathe. Fully and freely.

And I needed to go find my boyfriend.

CHAPTER 29

THEO

"You okay, Mathis?" Condit put a heavy hand on my shoulder. "After all that shit?"

I swallowed and managed a nod. "Yeah. Kinda rattled, but... yeah."

He studied me. Then he glanced around the locker room as he withdrew his hand. "Where'd Christian go?"

I pointed at the ceiling. "Upstairs. The brass wanted a meeting with him."

Condit lost a shade of color. "Oh. Shit. Do you... Do you think anything will happen to him?"

"I have no idea." I pushed an unsteady hand through my hair. "I don't know what's going to happen to me, either."

He was already shaking his head. "You're not going anywhere. And we'll fight to keep him, too."

I blinked.

"You've got a shitload of potential," he explained. "You're not going to be a bottom six forward forever, and the Rainiers would be stupid to cut loose someone with your hockey IQ over..." He flailed a hand in the general direction of the auditorium. "And Christian, I mean, I've worked with a lot of equipment managers in my career, but he's—let's put it this way, if there's an equipment manager equivalent to a generational talent, Christian is it."

I laughed. "Yeah, he kind of is, isn't he?"

"He is. I was here when they onboarded him, and it was like night and day. He fixes things seamlessly. He got the crew to pack things way more efficiently." Condit shook his head. "They'd be stupid to let him go. Especially over something like this."

I knew it wasn't that simple. Rules were rules, and the people in charge of things could very easily act like their hands were tied. It was entirely possible I'd get traded over or released this, or Christian might get fired.

I was restless to the point of queasy as I waited for him to come back from that meeting. Some of the other guys offered the same encouragement Condit had, which I appreciated. Though I'd known they were fine with gay players and they adored Christian, it was always a relief to see that support continue—and even intensify—when the rubber met the road.

Grekov appeared beside me as I was thumbing through social media on my phone. In Russian, he said, "You were right—they really do support players like us."

I met his gaze and smiled. "Told you."

He laughed, but his relief was almost as palpable as my own. There was no telling if it would be enough for him to come out any time soon. At least he knew that if and when he did, he wouldn't be rejected or ostracized. For someone already feeling as isolated as he sometimes was, that must've been a huge weight off his shoulders.

I hoped he came out. On his own time, of course, and I would never push him, but I quietly hoped he found that courage and told our teammates. I knew what it was like to be scared to show that card, and I wanted him to feel how liberating it was when he didn't have to hide it anymore. When the guys all said, "Cool, just let us know if you're bringing your boyfriend to Thanksgiving" or something.

He'd get there in his own time.

A few minutes later, Coach stepped into the room, his expression unreadable. "I just want to let you gentlemen know that, effective immediately, Jack Hayes is no longer the general manager of this team."

Despite the earlier rebellion, the cheer that went up caught me by surprise.

"Thank fuck!" someone said.

"It's about damn time," came from somewhere else.

"Does this mean they'll hire us a GM who isn't a raging asshole?" Condit asked. "And maybe not a homophobe either?"

"Well, I intend to be very involved in that process," Coach said. "And we'll definitely be looking for... improvements."

More cheers, which made me smile. Grekov, too.

"What about Christian?" Marty asked. "He's still MIA."

Coach sobered, which sent my heart into my feet. "He was still meeting with Bruce and Jerry when I came downstairs. I couldn't tell you what's going on there."

"They'd better not be firing him," Rusanov said. "Or we'll fucking riot."

Nods and murmurs of agreement all around.

Coach made a placating gesture. "Whatever's happening, it's out of my hands. But I hope he's sticking around, too." His gaze landed on me. "And Mathis, I'm sorry for all this. I had no idea what was going on, or that Jack was going to out you like that."

I nodded. "It's okay, Coach. It didn't seem like something you'd have been involved in."

"Not a chance." He paused, then smirked. "I suppose this means you want to stay up here rather than going back down to the minors."

My face heated as I laughed. "I mean, I want to stay anyway, but..."

"Who said anything about sending Mathis down?" Wilcox said. "He's been killing it up here." He smacked Sorenson with his glove. "Send *him* down instead."

"Hey!" Sorenson smacked him back.

"What?" Wilcox shrugged. "You could stand to spend some time in Everett."

Sorenson rolled his eyes and flipped him off, which had everyone in the locker room laughing.

We all went back to changing and getting ready. Despite everything going on, we still had to stick to our schedule, which had already been disrupted. With film review and practice out of the way, we were all heading to the gym for a light off-ice workout. Sounded good to me—I needed to blow off some steam, and lifting weights was always great for that.

But damn it, I still wanted to get eyes on Christian and find out what was going on with him.

My teammates were starting to leave for the gym when Christian finally came back. I didn't know what expression I expected to see on his face when he returned from that meeting, but one thing was for sure: I did not expect to see him grinning from ear to ear.

I rose off the bench, heart pounding as he crossed the room.

I didn't even have to ask how it went, both because of the look on his face and because he went right to telling me: "The higher ups found a thing that says fraternization isn't allowed," he said, his voice full of excitement and relief, "but instead of holding us to it, they're gong to change the rule."

I blinked. "They—seriously?"

Glee radiated off him as he nodded. "They said we need to keep things on the DL for a little while, until they have a chance to get it all squared away with the league and the players' union, but... yes!"

"Holy..." I shook myself. "Holy shit. So we can... We're both still with the team *and* we can be together?"

The way he smiled almost made me swoon. "And we don't have to put up with my dad's shit anymore."

I laughed with sheer joy and relief as I gathered him in my arms. "We can be out, we still work for the Rainiers, and your dad is gone. It's like a hat trick!"

Christian laughed too. "Best hat trick ever."

I chuckled, but then I just pulled him in tight and closed my eyes as I held him. Out in the open. Right here in the locker room. Both of us still on the Rainiers' payroll. "Holy shit."

"I know, right?" He stroked my hair. "I thought for sure they were going to can my ass, but..." He trailed off and just held on.

"I won't say I'm happy he outed us," I murmured. "But I'd say everything worked out okay."

"Yeah, it did." He kissed my cheek. "And now we don't even have to put up with my dad at all."

"I heard. Thank *fuck*."

"Right?" he laughed.

Behind me, Coach cleared his throat. When Christian

and I separated and turned to him, he said, "Gentlemen, if you don't mind—since you *are* both still employed by the Rainiers..."

Oh. Right. We still had work to do, didn't we?

I felt myself blushing as I released Christian. "I, um..." I glanced down at my sneakers, which were still on the bench. "I'm almost ready."

He nodded. Glancing back and forth between us, he cracked a little smile. "You've got five minutes."

"Got it, Coach. I'll be right up."

Then he left.

Christian smiled. "Well, don't work too hard in there, okay?" He tugged at one of the strings on my hoodie. "Save some for me?"

I bit my lip. "You gonna wait for me in bed?"

He winked. "Guess you'll find out, won't you?"

Oh, fuck. I couldn't wait.

I'd give Jack Hayes this much—at least he didn't blow up his own world on game day. For one thing, it would fuck up the team's chemistry and concentration. He probably knew that, which was why he'd waited until an off day.

One benefit he probably hadn't foreseen? No game meant that as soon as Coach cut us loose for the day, we could take off and not come back until tomorrow's morning skate. Which meant that as soon as I'd finished showering and putting some food in my face, I burned rubber out of that parking garage and headed straight for Christian's place.

He'd been gone before I even came back from my workout. From the wink Marty had given me, he knew exactly why Christian was ducking out early. I probably blushed bright red, but whatever—I was on my way to be with the man who I could finally openly date.

And just like the night I'd walked into his condo earlier this season, Christian was waiting for me—naked, hard, and fingering himself.

Oh, but I wasn't doing this with my clothes on. Not this time.

"Come on, baby," he whined as I stripped off my T-shirt. "I don't care about your clothes."

"Patience." I tossed my shirt on the floor and started on my jeans. "Fucking you while I'm dressed is fun. But I want to feel *everything* this time."

The way he squirmed and bit his lip—I almost said to hell with getting naked after all. Holy hell, I wanted him.

I did manage to kick off my clothes, though, and when I climbed into his bed and on top of him, it was well worth it. His hot skin pressed against mine. My hard dick slid beside his. His nails burned their way up my bare back.

And his kiss... God. I could never, ever get enough of Christian's kiss, and right now, he was especially needy and demanding.

"Would you just fuck me already?" he asked between deep, hungry kisses.

"I will." I nipped his bottom lip hard enough to make him shiver. "Patience."

"Fuck no." He clawed at my back again. "I want your dick."

"And I want you." Then I kissed him again, drawing a whimper out of him as he arched under me. I wanted to be balls deep in him right then, but I could wait a little while, if only so this wouldn't be over too quickly.

I'd been afraid that too much of the appeal of this relationship was how forbidden it was. When we no longer had to sneak around, would it be nearly as fun? What if we could finally come out, and then it wasn't as exciting anymore?

As I held Christian in his bed, kissing him and winding him up and losing my mind with anticipation, all those worries and fears evaporated.

The secrecy had been fun, but it had also been stressful and frustrating. With all of that off my shoulders, I completely lost myself in how much I wanted this man. In how amazing his body felt against mine. In how his kiss could make my entire world stop or start it spinning again.

I had never wanted or needed anyone like I did Christian, and that had nothing to do with all the reasons I shouldn't have been with him all this time. I wanted *him*. Full stop.

"Jesus, Theo." Christian grabbed my hair and growled, "Get the lube, damn it."

I laughed. "I love it when you're like this. Kind of want to tease you until—" I gasped as he closed his other hand around my dick.

"You were saying?"

I thrust into his hand, overwhelmed for a moment by... hell, by everything. "Lemme get the lube."

He gave a triumphant little laugh and let me go.

I sat up and grabbed the lube off the nightstand. As I poured some in my hand, I said, "Turn over."

Christian bit his lip and arched off the bed, but he nodded. He turned onto his stomach, and I molded myself to him as I guided my dick to his ass. I eased in carefully, and in no time, I was moving fluidly and perfectly, driving little whimpers and moans out of him as he trembled beneath me.

"Oh my God..." He sounded on the verge of tears. "Baby, you feel so good."

I slid my arms under him and hooked my hands over his shoulders, both of for contact and for leverage. "You feel amazing. You always do." I thrust in a little harder, and I didn't even know whose moans were whose anymore. I buried my face in his neck, inhaling his scent and loving the vibration of his voice against my lips. He gasped, clenching tighter around me, and I damn near came.

Somehow, though, I stayed in control. Maybe it was a good thing I'd done a light workout before we did this. I wasn't sore or tired, but there was just enough fatigue to keep me from going off too soon.

I didn't want to go off too soon. I wanted to savor every stroke and every sound. I wasn't ready for this to be over.

It isn't over. It won't *be over.*

I closed my eyes and exhaled against his shoulder. We'd run headlong into the worst-case scenario, and we'd landed here anyway. I wasn't going to lose him, and I was more grateful for that than I'd ever been for anything in my life.

It was no longer just sex, either. In those panicked moments where I'd been sure this was all slipping through my fingers, it hadn't been the loss of my career that scared me the most. It had been the end of all those nights lying in bed with him. Bantering. Talking. Watching movies and hockey and stupid sitcoms. I'd been certain in that theater today that I was never going to wear a professional hockey jersey again, but what had almost driven me to tears was believing I'd never wake up next to Christian again. I'd never hold him close to me again.

But here we were.

He still had his job. I still had mine. Above all else, we still had each other.

And moving inside him like this, holding his naked body to mine as we rocked together, felt better than it had since day one. The sex had always been amazing, but this time, it was...

Liberating. Liberat*ed*?

Whatever the word—we weren't weighed down by risk and secrecy anymore. It was just us and all the heat and desire we could stand. After we came, after we caught our breath, we'd both still be here. Nothing was over.

I gripped his shoulders tighter and thrust harder. "I want to come in you. Holy fuck, I'm so..." The rest came out as a shuddering breath.

Sometimes Christian would respond with something dirty, or with some encouragement to help me over that edge.

This time, all he did was whimper and shiver, and oh, God, that meant he was on the edge, too. So close he couldn't form words.

I grabbed on and rode him for all I was worth, driving myself in as deep and hard as this position allowed. At this angle, he'd get all the friction he needed against the sheet while I pounded away at his ass, and from the breathless, helpless sounds he was making, I was right on target.

"Come for me," I panted. "Take me with you."

A strangled sound escaped his throat, and then he bucked under me, clenching impossibly tighter around my cock, and the whole world went white. I thrust a few more times, trying to get as deep as I could, and then we both relaxed.

I pressed my forehead to the back of his shoulder, but pushed myself up on my forearms so he could breathe.

And for a minute or so, that was all we did:

Breathe.

After we'd showered, we ended up dozing in Christian's bed for a little while. The day had finally caught up with us, and between everything from earlier and the sex, we both just ran out of steam.

The sun was going down when my eyelids fluttered open. In the warm light, Christian was still asleep on my chest, my arm around his shoulders and his draped across my stomach.

Smiling to myself, I closed my eyes. For all I'd been afraid the thrill of the secrecy was the only thing keeping us going, it was plainly obvious now that that wasn't the case. We were out. Soon, we'd be out publicly. And I still wanted him even more than I had in the beginning. From the way he'd kissed me and begged for me, the feeling was mutual.

Beside me, Christian stirred, and I opened my eyes as he pushed himself up. He was adorably rumpled, his hair having dried going in every which direction. "Did I fall asleep?"

"We both did." I stroked his cheek. "I think we needed it."

He met my gaze, and though his eyes were still sleepy, his focus sharpened a little, and he smiled. "Yeah, we did. What a day, right?"

"No kidding." I stroked his hair, sort of managing to tame it. "I won't say it was fun, but... I'm glad it happened."

"Me too. And I'm glad we ended up here." His cheeks colored as he cut his eyes away. "I wasn't sure how things would shake out with us. After... I mean..."

"I get it," I whispered. "Getting involuntarily outed sucks. But I'm not going anywhere. Not unless you want me to."

"Absolutely not," he said quickly, snapping his gaze back to mine. "I definitely don't want you to go anywhere."

"Then I won't." I grinned. "Especially not if you feel like getting drilled again."

That broke through the sudden tension, and he laughed. "I'm always game for that." He sobered a little and studied me. "I'm, uh... The sex really isn't the only reason I want you here, you know. Hasn't been for a while."

"Same," I said softly. "It was hookups in the beginning, but now..." I didn't know how to finish that.

"Exactly." Christian touched my face. "I didn't take all these risks to be with you because the sex was hot. That part was great, obviously, but..." He chewed his lip, the blush returning to his cheeks. "I stuck around because I love you."

My heart did things it had never done before. Sliding my hand up his back, I said, "I love you, too. I wouldn't have gambled with my career if I didn't."

Disbelief registered across his features, but then he smiled and leaned in to kiss me. "Same. Though the hot sex didn't *hurt* anything."

I laughed. "No, it didn't. So, you know, if you want to keep doing that part, I'm totally—"

"Oh, shut up," he chuckled, and claimed my mouth.

I grinned into his kiss and wrapped my arms around him.

I still couldn't believe we'd landed here, but at the same time, it felt almost inevitable. As if nothing—not a homophobic GM, not a club's fraternization rules—could stop this thing we had.

And for the millionth time...

I was so damn glad I'd asked Christian for a roll of rainbow tape.

EPILOGUE

Christian

Next season

LIFE AFTER DAD ON THE SEATTLE RAINIERS WAS amazing.

Theo and I were very openly dating now. We'd attended Sorenson's wedding over the summer as a couple, and we'd even been featured in a post the team did about players' partners and families.

It wasn't just us finally releasing our breath, either. Nobody on the team felt like they were skating on eggshells anymore. Our new GM had an open-door policy and was completely chill about everything. Business was still business and she still sometimes had to make tough decisions—like when she traded Foster in mid-October for someone who could shore up our defense—but that was just hockey.

She also didn't have a single objection to certain special theme nights, and I had been looking forward to tonight since the season started.

There was something deeply satisfying—even triumphant—about seeing all the Pride Night banners and T-shirts in the crowd tonight. With every rainbow jersey I'd hung beneath the rainbow nameplates in the locker stalls, I felt like we'd *won*. Pride Night was back, and there wasn't a goddamned thing my father could do about it.

I even imagined he was somewhere watching the game on TV and grumbling to himself about how awful it was.

I hoped he hated every last second.

Shortly before warmups, as I made the rounds to check everyone's gear for last-minute issues, Condit called out, "Hey, Christian—we've got something for you."

I straightened. "You do?"

He grinned and held up a hoodie. It was black like the ones I usually wore during games, but instead of *Rainiers* in white font, it was the same logo they had on the front of their jerseys.

Printed in rainbow colors.

"Holy shit, guys." I took the hoodie from him and stared at the logo. "Is this—you really did this for me?"

"Absolutely."

"So are you gonna put it on?" Sorenson asked. "Wilcox worked really hard, trying to color inside the lines!"

"Fuck off," Wilcox said, and threw a balled-up sock at him.

"Hey!" I wagged a finger at Wilcox. "Don't you be throwing gear that I have to fix."

He offered an exaggeratedly sheepish look. "Sorry."

I chuckled and looked at the hoodie again. "Anyway, hell yeah, I'm wearing this." I tugged off my own hoodie and pulled on the new one. I glanced down at the rainbow logo, and I damn near got choked up. God, I loved these guys. Before my emotions could get the best of me, though, I struck a dramatic pose. "Well? Do I look fabulous or what?"

The guys all laughed and applauded.

I turned to Theo, who was sitting on the bench, and he smiled up at me. "You look amazing."

"Yeah?" I grinned and stepped closer, then sat on one of his powerful thighs. In his ear, I murmured, "Do I look fuckable?"

He patted my leg. "Baby, you always look fuckable."

"Jesus Christ, you two." A sock flew past our heads. "Get a room!"

"Hey!" I twisted around in Theo's lap. "What did I *just* say about throwing gear?"

"Sorry, Christian."

Theo chuckled. I got up so he could finish getting ready, and we exchanged smiles.

That was a relief, actually. He'd been a little quiet all day today. Not withdrawn or frosty, just up in his own head a bit. That wasn't unusual before a game, and he was still being affectionate now, so I didn't worry about it. He was probably just focused on hockey. This was a match-up between divisional rivals, after all.

I started to walk away to get back to work, but he called after me. "Hey, Christian?"

I turned around. "Hmm?"

His smile was the most beautiful thing ever. "Do you have any rainbow tape?"

I smiled back. God, the first time he'd asked me that question, he'd been so full of both courage and fear, and my heart had melted.

Today, there was no fear, but my heart still melted.

"Your stick is already taped," I pointed out.

He glanced at the blade and handle, then shrugged, a mischievous little grin on his lips. "Yeah, but it's good luck to ask you for rainbow tape on Pride Night." He winked.

"So, you think you're going to get lucky just because you asked for some tape?"

Theo batted his eyelashes. "Well, I was hoping I'd get lucky anyway, but—"

"Jesus Christ." Grekov threw a glove at Theo's chest. "You two are disgusting."

Theo cackled as he tossed the glove back. "Your jealousy is *so* transparent."

Grekov rolled his eyes and muttered something in Russian. Theo fired something back, and they both laughed. I didn't ask them to translate; there were, after all, some cameras and hot mics in here, and we really didn't need them to get recorded translating their Russian swearing. *Again.*

Grekov's English was getting better and better as time went on. He could mostly carry on conversations with the other guys, even if he didn't always understand the jokes and idioms. We still kept him and Theo next to each other in the locker room. They were great friends now, and they'd spent a good chunk of the off season training together along with Rusanov, whose stall was on Grekov's other side. If Grekov had had any worries about finding his place in this locker room when he'd come here, those worries seemed to be long gone.

He was planning to stay here a while, too. Days after the season had ended, he'd signed a five-year deal with the Rainiers with a no-move clause. Six weeks later, Theo, Rusanov, Marty, and I had helped him move into a condo not far from where Theo and I were living now. Then

Grekov went on vacation for a couple of months, and he returned… with a ring on his hand and a husband in tow.

Turned out, he'd secretly been with Mikhail since their youth days in Russia. They'd talked about getting married once Grekov was situated in North America, though they'd both been hesitant because they weren't sure how a team would really accept an out gay hockey player. Grekov hadn't been sure about his previous team, largely because the language barrier made it too difficult to really get a bead on his teammates.

In Seattle, he'd made two Russian-speaking friends, and he'd witnessed for himself just how vehemently and unapologetically the Rainiers would have the backs of their queer teammates.

"After I heard Condit say that either Jack Hayes went or he'd demand a trade," Grekov told us over dinner a few weeks ago, "I called Misha. I told him we could be home here."

On the way home that night, I'd asked Theo, "Did you know he was gay?"

He'd nodded. "He begged me not to say a word to anyone. I told him it was fine—I was out and proud and everybody knew it—but he was still scared."

"Right up until he saw how everyone stood up for us."

"Exactly." Theo'd shaken his head. "He kept the Mikhail card close to his vest, though—I had no idea he had somebody."

Of all the reasons I was glad everything had blown up last season, it hadn't occurred to me that we'd had a closeted queer player just waiting for a sign that this team was safe. They'd been living thousands of miles apart, keeping their relationship a guarded secret, until they could be sure it was safe to step into the light.

The relief was plain to see in Grekov, too. He was less reserved off the ice, and on it, he played like he no longer had the weight of the world on his shoulders.

I would be forever grateful that the Seattle Rainiers had had our backs when Dad outed us, but that gratitude ran *miles* deeper for what they had unknowingly done for Grekov and his husband.

I made my rounds in the locker room, making sure everyone's gear was in working order, and then it was time for them to start warmups. One by one, the guys headed out, rainbow-taped sticks in hand. The coaches, trainers, and equipment managers brought up the rear, finding our places by the bench while the players hit the ice.

Gazing around at warmups, the thrill of Pride Night sank in all over again. People had signs, flags, banners, shirts, hats. The Rainiers had started selling Ally shirts—rainbow hoodies with *ALLY* printed down the sleeves, and I could see at least a dozen of them from here. From what the PR director had told me, the bids were already flying on the auctions for the signed Pride jerseys and sticks. It was too soon to tell how much the team would be donating to the homeless LGBTQ+ youth initiative, but it would be... a lot.

I hope you're watching this, Dad. I hope you're absolutely miserable knowing what we're doing without you.

My gaze landed on Theo, and I couldn't help smiling. The night he'd taped his stick in rainbow colors had been amazing. I just hadn't fathomed what wheels it had put into motion. That when I'd handed over the roll of stick tape to the bright-eyed forward from the minor team, I was making my first ever connection with the man I'd eventually live with.

We hadn't had to move into my condo, either. Theo had signed a three-year one-way contract with the Rainiers during the off season. Coach had told him that as long as training camp went well, Theo had a virtually guaranteed spot on the third line when the season started. His time on the Everett Orcas was, most likely, in the rearview.

So, we dropped the hammer and moved into a beautiful, sunny condo near Elliott Bay.

Training camp came and went, but it turned out Theo wouldn't be on the third line after all. He'd shined during camp, and he'd found some incredible on-ice chemistry with Maxwell, a dynamite center who'd signed with Seattle a few weeks earlier. Now Theo was firmly on the second line, playing alongside a former nineteenth overall draft pick, and they'd been tearing it up ever since the season started.

That wasn't to say the last several months had been perfect. For us, yes. Everything with Theo was amazing, even the little squabbles and annoyances that came with living together. Those never lasted long, and I mean—you couldn't have makeup sex if you didn't argue once in a while, so whatever.

But other aspects of my life had been... bumpier.

Despite his absolutely toxic bullshit, there were rumors that Dad might get picked up as a GM or a head coach elsewhere in the league. None of that had come to fruition yet, but given some of the utter asshats I'd seen at the helms of various clubs and teams, it wouldn't surprise me if someone finally signed him.

Wherever he went, he'd be going there alone. For all my dad had treated my mom like crap for their entire marriage, it was what he tried to do to me that finally drove her out the door. The surprise silver lining there was when Mom's lawyer used Dad outing me to leverage some flexibility with their prenup. Apparently some thinly veiled threats—mostly threats of tell-alls and interviews relating to how

Dad had treated his gay son all his life—had persuaded my father to part with some assets in the name of keeping Mom quiet.

So, Mom was now living in a condo he'd bought her just north of Seattle. After they sold the house, she planned to put her portion in savings, and she'd live off that as well as her paycheck from the Rainiers. Alongside my brother-in-law—who'd gotten his job back—she was working in the team's public relations department. It wasn't the high life she'd had as the wife of Jack Hayes, but she had freedom she hadn't known since she was twenty. I had never seen her as happy and relaxed as she was these days.

It was a relief, being away from my dad and seeing my mom find life after him, too. I was glad my brother-in-law was back in the job he loved without Dad breathing down his neck.

But the process hadn't been fun. Mom and Dad's divorce was still in progress and would be for a while, and Dad still hadn't accepted that my sister and I were no-contact with him. He sent emails, he called—he even sent letters via snail mail. We blocked him everywhere we could and ripped up the letters that came.

The relief was huge, even if the process hadn't been fun. Now I had a better relationship with my mom, I was watching her and Aiden come back to life, and I still had both my job and the man I loved. Everything had worked out, even if getting here had been a little rough.

"Hey! Christian!"

I shook myself and turned toward the sound of my name. Over by one of the faceoff dots, I found Grekov waving me over. In front of him Theo was kneeling on the ice, trying and failing to stand.

A jolt of panic straightened my spine, but then my brain

caught up. They were calling me over, not one of the trainers, so he wasn't hurt.

Grekov gestured at his own skate, then at Theo.

I nodded sharply, gave a *just a minute* gesture, and stepped back into the tunnel. I didn't know if Theo had lost his blade, broken it, or it had just come loose, so I grabbed an extra blade out of the case and hurried out onto the ice where he was waiting. During a game, he'd have to drag himself back to the bench—hopefully with a teammate to help him—and get it fixed while the game went on. During warmups? Eh. I could come to him.

"I'm coming, I'm coming," I said as I carefully made my way across the ice. When I was almost to him, I asked, "Did you lose it or break it?"

"Neither." Theo looked up at me. "My skate's fine."

I halted. "It's—then what—"

But then I realized he was smiling.

And he wasn't just kneeling—he was down on one knee.

And when he turned his glove over, there was a velvet box I'd have recognized from clear back on the bench.

"Theo..."

"I couldn't think of any better time to do this than Pride Night." He shook off his other glove, then opened the box, and as the stadium lights caught on the gold band, he asked, "Will you marry me?"

For a few seconds, my heart was pounding so hard, I couldn't hear anything except my pulse and his words. We were surrounded by his teammates and the fans, and I was distantly aware of them all cheering, but it may as well have just been him and me.

I managed a laugh just to get my breath moving, and I nodded. "Are you kidding? I'd be dragging you to Vegas right now if you didn't have game to play."

Theo laughed too, and he pushed himself to his feet—onto his perfectly intact skates—and collected me into a hug. "I love you," he murmured, and then he kissed me. Right there on the ice. In front of his teammates, the fans, the cameras, with my ring still in his hand, he kissed me.

All around us, sticks tapped on the ice and cheers went up from his teammates and the crowd.

"I've been thinking about this for a while," he said just loud enough for me to hear. "Tonight seemed like the perfect time."

"It was. It's... Have I told you lately how amazing you are?"

"Hmm, you have, but I'm always game to hear it."

I laughed and rolled my eyes. "All right, you dork. You need to get back to warming up."

"Okay. But let me make sure you get back to the bench safely."

I rolled my eyes again. I was perfectly capable of crossing the ice without skates on. Who was I kidding, though? I wasn't going to say no to my gorgeous hockey player boyfriend—gorgeous hockey player *fiancé*—escorting me off the ice.

As we neared the bench, the crowd still roaring all around us, Coach Baldwin shook his head and said to Theo, "Is that why you wanted to be miked up tonight?"

I eyed Theo. "Wait, you were miked up?"

Theo tried for an innocent smile but failed miserably. "Um. Yes?"

I laughed. "You dork."

"Always."

I just chuckled.

"Congrats, boys," Coach Baldwin said. "Beers are on me after the game." He inclined his head. "*After* the game.

But we've sixty minutes of hockey to play between now and then, all right?"

"You got it, Coach." Theo kissed me lightly. "I gotta go warm up before I get in trouble."

"Yes, you do." I winked. "I'll see you after the game."

He bit his lip. Then he skated off to continue with warmups.

I leaned my hip against the bench, utterly dazed by what had just gone down.

Two years ago, after my dad had cancelled Pride Night just to be a dick, a kid from the PHL had defiantly put rainbow tape on his stick.

Tonight, with rainbows and love and support all around us, that same kid—now firmly ensconced in the NAPH—had put a ring on my finger right there on the ice.

This team, this league, these fans, this sport—this was my world. It was my family and my life.

And that gorgeous man wearing number sixty-one?

He was my future.

ESTD 2024
THE GAMES WE PLAY

JUST ADD ICE

L.C. CHASE

THE GAMES WE PLAY, BOOK 2: JUST ADD ICE

Sparks fly when ice meets fire.

After eight years in the minors, Rayne "the Pain" Hamilton has realized two things: One, his chances of getting called up to the Big Show are rapidly dwindling with each passing season; and two, he needs a plan for life after hockey. What he doesn't bargain for is the gorgeous instructor at the fire training center who ignites his heart with burning desire.

Nick Seavers had a great life until his husband died suddenly, and his sun blinked out. A demanding career fire-fighting and teaching the next generation of firefighters are the only things keeping him sane. The last thing he wants is one of the new trainees, a larger-than-life hockey player with mischievous eyes, taking up space in his head and making him feel things he never thought he'd feel again.

As the heat rises between Rayne and Nick, trade rumors begin circulating and Rayne has to decide: Move to yet another city and start all over again or step off the ice and into the fire with Nick.

The Games We Play is a multi-author minor league hockey romance series. All titles run concurrently through the same hockey season, and the books can be read in any order, so jump in anywhere!

Just Add Ice is available June 19th.

EVEN STRENGTH

CARI Z & ANN GALLAGHER

THE GAMES WE PLAY, BOOK 3: EVEN STRENGTH

Marek Stetina is so close to getting called up to majors, he can taste it. Maybe he wasn't a number one draft pick like his brother, and maybe he'll never be a Hall of Famer like his father, but he's *almost* made it.

Right up until a serious injury puts his hockey dreams—major league or otherwise—on ice.

Up-and-coming MMA star Carson Wrede's career—hell, his entire life—has been off the rails ever since a mishap during a fight put him in the hospital. Now he's trying to find his balance again, both literally and figuratively. With each passing day, his chances of returning to the cage grow slimmer… as do his chances of paying that growing pile of medical bills.

Maybe a TBI support group isn't the most romantic place to meet someone, but Marek and Carson can't complain. While their worlds seem to be crumbling around them, they lean on each other through endless setbacks and frustration.

But is this just two guys helping each other through a

tough time? Or is the connection between them real, honest love?

And is that love enough to see them through some unavoidable decisions about the careers they once lived for?

The Games We Play is a multi-author minor league hockey romance series! All titles run concurrently through the same hockey season, and the books can be read in any order, so jump in anywhere!

Even Strength is available June 26, 2024.

For more books by L.A. Witt, or to subscribe to my newsletter, please visit

http://www.gallagherwitt.com

Newsletter perks:

- Exclusive discounts & giveaways
- Access to ARCs
- All the latest news about pre-orders, collaborations, and more!

Romance * Suspense

Contemporary * Historical * Sports * Military

Titles Include

Rookie Mistake (written with Anna Zabo)

Scoreless Game (written with Anna Zabo)

The Hitman vs. Hitman Series (written with Cari Z)

The Bad Behavior Series (written with Cari Z)

The Gentlemen of the Emerald City Series

The Anchor Point Series

The Husband Gambit

Name From a Hat Trick

After December

Brick Walls

The Venetian and the Rum Runner

If The Seas Catch Fire

...and many, many more!

ABOUT THE AUTHOR

L.A. Witt is a romance and suspense author who has at last given up the exciting nomadic lifestyle of the military spouse (read: her husband finally retired). She now resides in Pittsburgh, where the potholes are determined to eat her car and her cats are endlessly taunted by a disrespectful squirrel named Moose. In her spare time, she can be found painting in her art room or destroying her voice at a Pittsburgh Penguins game.

Website: www.gallagherwitt.com
Email: gallagherwitt@gmail.com
Twitter: @GallagherWitt

Made in the USA
Middletown, DE
24 June 2024

56099245R00184